CANVAS FOR LOVE

By the Author

A Palette for Love

Love in Disaster

Canvas for Love

Visit us at www.boldstrokesbooks.com

CANVAS FOR LOVE

by
Charlotte Greene

2017

ISBN 13: 978-1-62639-944-0

This Trade Paperback Original Is Published By
Bold Strokes Books, Inc.
P.O. Box 249
Valley Falls, NY 12185

First Edition: July 2017

CREDITS
EDITOR: SHELLEY THRASHER
PRODUCTION DESIGN: STACIA SEAMAN
COVER DESIGN BY SHERI (GRAPHICARTIST2020@HOTMAIL.COM)

Acknowledgments

Thanks to Becky for helping me choose the title and to Ula, my first reader.

Special thanks to Shelley, without whom my characters would be muddled in a quagmire of overdramatic gestures and dialogue tags.

For you, always.

CHAPTER ONE

When I opened the door, Emma looked frozen solid. Her lips were a little blue around the edges, and she was visibly shivering despite a light jacket, a thin, gossamer scarf, and bright-red mittens.

"Christ, Emma, get inside!" I said, pulling her in by one arm.

She was too cold to do much except nod, and I closed the door quickly behind her.

"Let me get you some tea," I said.

"It's okay. I'm fine. I hate tea."

"Coffee?"

She shook her head.

"Well, at least let me get you a hot-water bottle. You need something to warm up. Sit down. I'll be right back."

She followed my directions wordlessly, still shuddering from the cold.

After I put the kettle on, I came back into the room, and she sat huddled under my afghan. She looked so much like a lost little orphan I had to smile. Her color looked a little better now, but she was still shivering.

"Did you walk over here?"

She nodded. "Stupidest idea I've ever had. I was at Brennan's for lunch, and it didn't seem like it would be a big deal—it's less than a mile. I got about halfway here before I realized it was a mistake, but by then it seemed stupid to call a cab."

"I could have come to get you."

She shrugged. "I made it, and now I know better than to step outside for more than a minute or two."

New Orleans was in the middle of a cold snap. We have them occasionally, but they're rare enough that most locals have no idea what to do with themselves. I've known New Orleanians who don't even own a heavy coat, and Emma appeared to be one of them. Usually our cold snaps pass in a day or two, but we'd all been stuck in a freezing fog and sleet storm for days. I'd kept my heat cranked up all morning, but because of the high ceilings in my apartment, it took a while to warm up. I heard the kettle start to whistle and left the room to make myself some tea and fill up the hot-water bottle.

When I came back, Emma had taken off her scarf and mittens. I gave her the water bottle and sat down, clutching my tea. Something about seeing her so cold had given me the shivers, and I held my mug in both hands, the warm vapors tickling my face.

Emma is the sister of my girlfriend, Amelia. Amelia was on a business trip in Montreal this week and last, buying and selling art for her company. It was turning out to be the longest two weeks of my life. We hadn't spent more than a couple of consecutive nights apart since we'd started dating, and now it had been twelve. I was originally supposed to go with her, but I'd gotten a terrible case of the flu just before we were set to leave. Amelia had been loath to leave me behind in my condition, but I'd insisted. I'd regretted it almost the minute the limo left for the airport, but I also knew it was for the best. Amelia put a lot of planning into her trips, and if we delayed this one, all of her work would go to waste. Also, I was only now just beginning to feel like a human being again, so it wasn't like she'd missed much besides seeing me sleep and look like hell.

Today was the first day I'd been back to work since she left. I'd made myself get up and go to the office this morning because I'd scheduled the first meeting with a new major client today, a restaurant called Teddy's in the Marigny. Teddy's is a local institution. While it had opened only a little over ten years ago—making it a baby by New Orleans fine-dining standards—it was already world-renowned. The waitlist for a reservation was so long, I'd never actually eaten there. Despite the fact that Amelia raved about how much she loved the food there, we hadn't managed to get a reservation even once since I'd moved back to the city. Even money couldn't buy a reservation there—and Amelia had tried. The restaurant was so successful, they'd opened another branch in the Quarter last year. When I'd scheduled the meeting with them earlier this month, I hadn't realized Amelia would still be gone, or I would have postponed. I'd been too sick to think about anything the last two weeks, and now I was locked in to going. My friend Meghan was out of town, so I'd asked Emma along for moral support.

Emma's face had regained the rest of her color, and she was looking around the room with curiosity. I'd been living in my new apartment for a little over two months now, and it finally felt like home. Amelia and my friends and family had gotten it ready for me to move in as a surprise last Thanksgiving, but it had taken a while to get things set up where I wanted them and make it my own. I'd moved some artwork around on the walls, put up framed photographs, and rearranged the furniture several times. Now everything was exactly the way I wanted it to be, and I was proud of the way it had turned out.

"Your place looks great," Emma said, smiling. "I'm sorry I haven't been to visit in so long. When was the last time? Christmas Eve?"

"That sounds right." Amelia and I had hosted an informal family gathering with my aunt, her boyfriend Jim, and most of Amelia's family on Christmas Eve. Amelia decided it was best to spend Christmas Day apart with our separate families, at least this year, so the Christmas Eve party had not only been our personal holiday celebration, but a way for our families to meet. Everyone but my friend Meghan—whom I consider family—and Amelia's sister-in-law, Ingrid, had been able come, so it was a big success. I didn't think my Aunt Kate and Amelia's mom got along very well, but that was to be expected. Aunt Kate is gregarious and kind, and Amelia's mom is cold and reserved. Everyone else made nice with each other, however, so Amelia and I were pleased overall.

"Warmed up?" I asked her. "Ready to go?"

"Only if we drive," Emma said, shivering. "It's like hell out there."

I laughed. "It's literally two blocks away."

She seemed reluctant, but she finally nodded. "Okay. But you owe me a cocktail for all of this."

"Done."

I regretted walking almost the moment we were out the door. The air was the kind of bitter cold that happens only in humid places. It gets under your skin, inside you. No coats or clothes exist that can do much for you when you're in that kind of cold. Emma looked miserable despite the warmer jacket I'd lent her, and about a block from my apartment, the wind picked up, sending little ice crystals flying into our faces. My eyes stung and my nose was running by the time we made it to Teddy's.

We were at the restaurant long before the dinner hour, so there was no line to get in. Even on a cold night, one would likely form later. After we stepped inside, stomping our feet to bring feeling back to our numb legs, Teddy herself appeared from the kitchen, clearly waiting for us. I'd seen pictures of her in various local magazines and newspapers, but seeing her in person was something else. For one thing, she's gorgeous. She has the dark olive skin of the Spanish Creoles and the accompanying black, curly hair, which was short and stylishly cut in a faux-hawk. She was trim and muscular. She wore a black chef's uniform, and because her sleeves were rolled up, I spotted several dark tattoos on her lower arms. Even from a distance I could see that her eyes were a warm, dark-chocolate brown, and when she smiled at us, my stomach dropped. She looked like a dangerous but alluring predator.

"Yikes," Emma whispered next to me. "She's hot."

"Shhhh!" I said, widening my eyes at her.

When Teddy came closer, I could see that she was a little older than I'd first thought—maybe her early or mid-forties. It made sense. After all, she'd opened her own restaurant over a decade ago and had likely been working and training before that. That made her about fifteen to twenty years older than me. Her dark hair was flecked with gray, and she had little laugh lines around her eyes. It didn't matter—she was still one of the most gorgeous women I'd ever seen.

Her handshake was firm, her skin actually a little hot when we shook, and I noticed Emma's eyelids flutter involuntarily when their hands touched.

"I'm so glad to meet you after all this time," Teddy said. "I feel like we've been on the phone back and forth for weeks."

"I hope you don't mind that my friend Emma came along," I said, gesturing at her.

Teddy shook her head. "Of course not." She looked at Emma. "You're welcome to wait at the bar, Emma, while we talk. My bartender likes to experiment when we're closed, and she rarely gets the opportunity to have a guinea pig."

"You just said the magic words," Emma said and walked over to the long bar on the far side of the room.

"So how does this work?" Teddy asked, meeting my eyes again. Her gaze was unnerving. She was looking at my face, but something about her seemed to suggest that her eyes were elsewhere, wandering up and down my body. I had to suppress a thrill of nervous energy.

I broke eye contact. It was hard to concentrate with those eyes on me.

"Uh," I said, realizing she'd asked me a question. "Sorry. Lost my train of thought." I shook my head to clear it. "We'll do a few things today. I want you to show me the space as much as possible. I'll make notes on the size and the lighting, and then we can discuss some options."

"Do you have everything you need? Can I offer you some wine?"

"Maybe after we finish our business," I said. "Let's look at the space first."

The restaurant was spare and warmly lit. Some of the walls were made of exposed red brick, and the rest were a bright-white clapboard, resembling the inside of a farmhouse. The tables were mainly constructed of a heavy, dark wood in the center of the room, but the sides of the room had little elevated alcoves with tables for two, tucked away for romantic dinners. Everything was bathed in a soft yellow glow from the lights.

The current artwork consisted mainly of landscapes—seascapes, to be more precise. All of them were somewhat lonely-looking, empty of people and with minimal distraction. They went well with the overall look of the place: somewhat stark and minimalist, as if to keep attention focused on the food.

I measured one of the walls in an alcove with my little tape measure, and then we stopped in front of a large back wall that currently had nothing hanging on it. My tape wasn't long enough to measure it, which sent my mind spinning at the possibilities. This large space should hold the showcase piece. I made a few more notes and then turned to Teddy, smiling.

"This is excellent," I said. "We'll be able to do a lot here. Do you want to get started now? I brought a portfolio of local artwork with me."

"Absolutely. But if you don't mind, let me go get my wife. She wanted to be here for this part."

I smiled and nodded, and she left for the kitchen. I was more pleased that she was a lesbian than the fact probably merited. In truth, besides my friend Lana and her partner Jess in New York, I didn't really know any other lesbians beside myself and Amelia. Amelia was a very private person and had no close friends. All of my friends in New Orleans were straight. As Amelia and I didn't go out to bars and clubs, I'd felt somewhat isolated lately. It was nice to finally meet some other women like us.

When Teddy returned a few minutes later, a pretty, slight woman with bright-red hair and pale skin accompanied her. The woman was wearing a white baker's uniform, and when she came closer, I caught a distinct whiff of vanilla.

"Hi, I'm Kit," the woman said, shaking my hand. "Sorry I wasn't here earlier—I was in the middle of making beignets."

"Mmm," I said, grinning. "My favorite."

"Have you had the beignets here before?" Kit asked. "I'm not bragging when I say they're the best in town."

I shook my head. "I'm embarrassed to admit this, but I've actually never had the chance to eat here." They both looked shocked, and I had to laugh. I held up my hands. "Not by choice. I've never managed to get a reservation. And I only moved back to town last September."

"Well, we'll have to rectify that," Teddy said, one eyebrow raised.

"We will. My girlfriend has been raving about it for months." I put a slight emphasis on the word "girlfriend."

"Ah," Teddy said, smiling. "Do you mean the famous Amelia Winters?"

I blushed. Of course Teddy knew about Amelia. Everyone did. Amelia could hardly go out in public without someone taking a picture of her, and the local media had long ago cottoned on to the fact that she was gay. That was yet another reason she and I stayed at home most of the time. It was tiring to see speculations about us and about me in the society columns every time we went out to eat.

"I'm sorry," Teddy said, holding up her hands. "I didn't mean to offend you."

"You didn't," I said.

Kit swatted Teddy's arm. "That's what you get for being so nosy, hon. You're always putting your foot in it."

After an awkward pause, I changed the subject.

"Are you ready for my suggestions?" I gestured around me.

Teddy nodded and indicated a nearby table. The three of us sat down, and I opened my notes.

"First of all, I wanted to ask you about the lighting in here."

Teddy frowned. "What about it?"

Kit swatted her again. "Don't be so defensive."

"I didn't mean to sound like I was criticizing it, Ms. Rose," I said.

"Teddy," she said absently.

"I just wanted to know if you would be willing to brighten it a little bit for the exhibit. A lot of the artwork I plan to show you is much more…colorful than what you have now. It wouldn't look quite right in the light you have in here. Brighter light will make the colors in the paintings and drawings stand out more vividly."

"What do you suggest?" Teddy asked.

"For one thing, we'll need to replace the golden bulbs you have now with a standard white. We might be able to keep the wattage low like it is now as long as the light was white, or we might need to bring up the wattage just a little. We can experiment with a single alcove and go from there."

Teddy and Kit shared a glance and then both turned back to me, nodding. "That seems easy enough."

I made a note in my notebook.

"As to the art itself, I have several photographs with me in my portfolio. I hope you'll keep an open mind about what I'm going to show you. All of it is very different from what you have in here now."

"She means it's not boring," Kit said, grinning at Teddy.

"Hey!" Teddy said in mock outrage.

Kit looked back at me. "When we redecorated a couple of years ago, Teddy insisted on these paintings." She turned to Teddy. "Don't get me wrong, honey—they're lovely. They're just a little…well, depressing. Especially when there are so many of them."

Teddy rolled her eyes and didn't engage with what was clearly an ongoing disagreement. She turned back to me.

"Please," Teddy said, indicating the portfolio. "Show us what you've brought."

Although there are exceptions, many local artists in New Orleans are known for using bright, bold colors. Many local artists are also famous for painting New Orleans-specific scenery and subjects, and much of the portfolio was filled with pictures depicting sights from town. Music, on the whole, is a major part of life in New Orleans, and paintings of musicians, instruments, and even some symbolic depictions of music itself abound. Other artists focus on famous landmarks and renditions of local streets, the river, and the famous live oaks, and some produce bold, abstract art.

Kit and Teddy stayed bent over the portfolio for a long time, flipping back and forth between different pages, making satisfied sounds and chattering between themselves over what they saw.

"I'm not sure how we would ever choose," Teddy said, sighing. "I like everything in here."

"That's the beauty of it: you don't need to choose. Amelia and I plan to showcase everything in the portfolio on a rotating schedule."

Teddy and Kit grinned widely, and I smiled in response, pleased that they were pleased.

"I especially like this one," Kit said, opening and then tapping one page.

Teddy looked down and nodded. "That's my favorite, too."

I leaned forward to see the piece, and my stomach dropped. Somehow a photograph of my most recent painting had ended up in the portfolio. I'd asked Janet, the administrative assistant at the office, to make a print portfolio of all of the local artists we had on file at our office and didn't have any idea this photograph had been included. My expression must have seemed off, as both women suddenly looked confused.

"Is something wrong?" Teddy asked.

"Was it already sold?" Kit suggested.

I shook my head. Not wanting to explain, I continued my spiel. I talked on autopilot about sales and commissions and installation, my mind far away. I knew exactly who'd put the photograph in the file at the office, because I knew exactly who'd taken it: Amelia. She was playing with her new camera the day I finished the painting and insisted on photographing it. I hadn't thought anything of it, then, but now I knew her ulterior motive. Ever since she'd first seen my artwork, she'd been trying to get me to showcase it somewhere in town and sell it. I never thought she'd go behind my back like this, though. I'd have to talk to her later.

"So when can we get started?" Teddy asked when I finished.

"I can schedule the lighting experiment for this week, if you like. Same time?"

"Perfect," Teddy said. "Let's do it Thursday, if that's okay."

"Yes," I said. "Once we take care of the lights, we can start the installation at any time." I glanced around the room. "It's a large space, but we have a lot of employees. After the lights are in, it shouldn't take more than a single afternoon for them to set up."

"That sounds wonderful," Teddy said, her eyes warm with pleasure. "I never thought it would happen so quickly."

"We aim to please," I said with a smile.

The three of us shook hands and then stood up.

"Would you like that glass of wine before you leave?" Teddy asked. "Or a cocktail? It looks like your friend is enjoying herself. We have one of the best bars in town, if I do say so myself."

I looked over at the bar and grinned. Even from across the room I could tell that Emma was listing a little on her barstool. I heard her laugh a little too loudly, and the bartender laughed in response.

"I'd love some wine," I said.

"Good," Teddy said, clearly satisfied. "I always like to seal a deal with a drink."

We walked across the room and Emma grinned at me, crookedly, as we approached.

"Candy here," Emma said, waving vaguely at the bartender.

The woman corrected her. "Katy."

"*Katy* here," Emma said, "has been the perfect hostess. I've tried all three of her newest creations." Her words were slurred slightly, and I had to laugh.

"It sounds like it," I said.

Emma frowned deeply. "What's that supposed to mean?"

"Nothing," I said, laughing again. "Just that you might want to call a cab when we get out of here."

"I'm sure as shit not walking home." She shook her head in disgust. "It's like hell out there."

"I'll drink to that," Teddy said, waving at the bartender. "Katy, would you please pour the three of us—"

"Four," Emma said.

Teddy laughed. "Okay, the *four* of us a glass of the Toulouse Anderson Pinot? The 2006 if we have it."

Katy nodded and disappeared into the back for the wine, then returned a few moments later and poured us each a glass. Emma almost sloshed hers completely out of the glass, causing me a stab of deep embarrassment. Teddy and Kit didn't seem to mind, however, as they both grinned at me. Teddy winked.

"To the beginning of a beautiful friendship," she said, holding up her glass.

"Hear, hear!" Emma said, then drank her entire glass in one long gulp.

I closed my eyes, too embarrassed to watch Teddy's reaction. When I opened them again a moment later, however, everyone was smiling, and Emma had her arm around Teddy's shoulders.

"I can tell we're all going to be great friends." Emma slurred her words.

I picked up my purse, my notes, and the portfolio. "And with that, I think I should call that cab for my friend here."

"That might be for the best," Teddy said. Her eyes were sparkling with merriment.

CHAPTER TWO

Right next to Louis Armstrong International Airport is a smaller airfield for private use. Unlike the regular airport, this airfield has few amenities, as if making up for the luxury of the private jets. The last time I'd been here, I'd barely noticed it, as I'd gotten out of the car and directly onto the Winters Corporation jet. But, in my nervous excitement for Amelia's return, I'd gotten here too early and had to wait inside the tiny terminal.

The little waiting room was poorly appointed, with one smelly little bathroom, an uncomfortable bench, and a coffee table littered with old aviation magazines and overflowing ashtrays. I was also alone except for the pimply young man behind the front desk. He was clearly annoyed that he had to pretend to work while I was here. I poured myself a cup of bad coffee simply to hold something warm. It was still dreadfully cold outside, and this little room seemed to have no heater. It was marginally better than being outside, but only just. For the fifth time since I'd been sitting here, I cursed myself for not waiting in the car with the heater on, environment be damned.

I heard the plane before I saw it. It was about an hour behind schedule. Amelia had told me that might happen and that I should simply wait at home for her, but I'd wanted to surprise her. I stood up and looked out the window to watch the plane come in, but with the rain and mist in the air, I didn't see anything until it was almost landing. The plane taxied for a long time, driving in circles around the airfield despite having the run of the place. It finally came to a stop and then just sat there on the runway.

Too impatient to wait any longer, I ran outside to meet it and stood there shivering in the cold until the plane door finally opened. The little stairs unfolded, and then, finally, Amelia was there at the top of them. I ran up them to greet her, and she was finally back in my arms.

We kissed several times, both of us laughing, before she led me back down to the ground. As the rest of the crew bustled around us, we stared at each other, both sets of hands linked.

"My God, it's good to see you," she said. "I didn't know if I was going to make it that long."

I shook my head. "Me either. I hated every minute of it."

"What are you doing here?" she asked. "I thought I told you to wait at home. You shouldn't be out here in the cold."

I shrugged. "I couldn't wait that long. I needed to see you."

She lifted one eyebrow. "Needed?"

"Yes, needed. Do me a favor, Amelia, would you? Please don't leave me alone like that again. It was awful."

She nodded. "Agreed. I've never been more eager to come home." She looked around. "Where's your car?"

"Parked over there." I gestured.

"Let me tell the luggage handler, and we can wait in the car. I can't believe how cold it is here. It might actually be chillier here than in Montreal."

We linked elbows and slowly walked back to my vehicle. Now that she was here, I was in no hurry to do anything but stand next to her.

Her face suddenly scrunched up and she sneezed, loudly, and then again. We stopped as she fished around in her handbag and dug out a tissue. She blew her nose—a honking, wet-sounding trumpet—then folded up her tissue in disgust before putting it in a pocket.

"On top of everything, I caught a cold this week. I'm getting better, but I'm still dripping like a faucet."

I nudged her slightly. "And here I was worried you'd get the flu, too."

"How are you feeling?" she asked as we walked. She looked concerned.

I laughed. "I'm fine. I told you that. Just a little weak, but better every day."

She stopped and turned me to face her, looking at me for a long time. Finally, she nodded. "You look better, but you're still very pale. You've lost some weight, too."

"Of course I have. I had the stomach flu. I could barely keep anything down. Even Aunt Kate's soup wouldn't settle there for a few days."

"I'm so glad you had her to take care of you while I was gone. I don't know if I could have left if you hadn't."

We'd made it to my car and climbed in. I turned it on, and blissful heat was soon streaming out of the vents. Having a new car, I'd found out recently, meant never having to wait for the heater or the air conditioner. Amelia had given me the car two months ago, and while initially I'd been reluctant to accept it, I'd almost gotten used to owning it. It still bothered me that she'd bought me this ridiculously expensive car, but I'd made peace with the idea. She could certainly afford it, and she was free to spend her own money as she liked.

Amelia was sitting in the passenger's seat with her eyes closed, and, now that I was looking at her more closely, I could see lines of fatigue on her face. We'd done a business trip to New York together a while back, and I knew what a trip like that could mean in terms of work and stress. A trip meant running around town all day long, staying up all hours with dinners and parties, and having long phone conversations with shipping experts and the office. And we'd gone to New York for only a week. Amelia had been in Canada for almost two. Her nose was red-rimmed from her cold, and her lips were chapped. All in all, she looked less like herself than I'd ever seen her.

I waited a while longer as they loaded Amelia's luggage into my trunk. Amelia dozed off in the meantime, and I realized then that no matter how tired she looked, she was actually far worse. Amelia gets by on five hours of sleep most of the time, and she had never, as far as I could recall, taken a nap in my presence. I'd rarely even seen her sleep. I was grateful once again for my new car, as the excellent shocks absorbed the roughness of the road, letting her sleep in peace as I drove.

She didn't wake up until we pulled into my driveway, and even then, she still seemed confused and sleepy.

She blinked a few times and frowned. "Why are we here? I wanted to go back to my place."

I hadn't thought of that. Of course she would want to go home.

She'd been away for more than two weeks now. I stared at her blankly for a long moment, and her face clouded over with confusion.

"I'm sorry," I finally said. "I was being selfish. I wanted you to stay over tonight. I can drive you home now, if you want."

It was the right thing to say, as her face brightened happily. "Of course I'll stay over, Chloé. I can't promise you much more than a snotty, sleepy idiot, but I'd love to." Her face clouded slightly. "Though I do wish you didn't mind coming to my place so much."

This was an ongoing tiff between us—not a major one, but certainly something we'd discussed frequently. In general, we spent four or five nights together every week, and when we were together, we were almost always at my apartment. I was incredibly uncomfortable at Amelia's stately home. While her house was beautiful, it was also cold and impersonal. It looked more like a museum than a place where anyone actually lived. It didn't help that she had several staff members working for her—a cook, several gardeners, and two maids. None of them were live-in, and no one but the cook was there more than a few days a week, but I was always afraid I would run into one of them in the hallways of her house. I also had no idea how to act around them. It was, at best, like being in a hotel with no lock on the doors, but in general much worse. Not wanting to get into this argument with her right now, I nodded vaguely, and she sighed, also clearly in no mood to talk about it.

"Let's get inside, and I can draw you a nice, hot bath," I suggested. "Then you can sleep for a while."

She chuckled a little. "Really, Chloé. I could have done all of this at home. It sounds boring for you."

I shrugged. "Not at all. I want you around even when you're not exciting." She grinned slyly at this comment, and I blushed. "I mean, you're *always* exciting—"

She held her hands. "It's fine. Let's get inside before we freeze to death out here."

We left her luggage in the car and went inside. I'd left the heat in my apartment blasting, but it was still a little chilly. At some point I would need to ask my landlord—Amelia's dad—to look at the heater to see if it could be fixed to make my place a little warmer, but not right now.

A while later, both of us warmed from a hot bath, I was standing in my bathrobe at the foot of the bed looking down at Amelia. She'd crawled under the covers a few minutes ago and was limp and boneless in sleep.

I'd been looking forward to seeing her with a kind of crazy desperation since she left. Even at my sickest, I still craved her touch, waking up in a feverish desire several times during her absence. Looking at her now, I grinned wryly at my fantasies about our reunion. All of that would have to wait.

CHAPTER THREE

Despite her illness and my remaining weakness, we both got up early the next morning to pick up our gowns. In a couple of days, it would be Amelia's birthday. Her three brothers also had birthdays this past week and next, and Amelia's mother was having her annual Winters Family Birthday Gala and charity dinner for them later today.

An invitation to Hilda Winters's annual party was a mark of distinction. Every year, Hilda pulled out all the stops for the elite of the city. It was her way of showing off the family wealth without being ostentatious. Like any good society lady, Hilda Winters knew that you shouldn't throw a huge, lavish party without an associated charitable cause. It was unseemly to spend money without a reason. Hilda and Ted's ruby wedding anniversary last fall was one thing—a party attended only by close family and friends. Over three hundred people were coming to the gala tonight. It would be irresponsible to let the opportunity to bleed all of these socialites go to waste. I'd struggled with this concept when Amelia first told me about it. It seemed like asking for money to attend what was ostensibly a social gathering, even if it was a large one. Moreover, it took attention away from what was supposed to be the point of the evening: the birthdays of four members of the Winters family.

While I was looking forward to it out of a kind of horrified curiosity, the whole thing sounded cold and impersonal. It basically disgusted me until Amelia told me that last year they'd raised over a million dollars for the Louisiana Wetlands. Put that way, it did seem like it would be a wasted opportunity to raise money. Nearly everyone coming tonight could clearly afford to give some of their money away.

Further, this year's cause was Amelia's choice. She and her brothers took turns choosing the charity. She'd chosen a local art coalition that brought artists and art workshops into local public schools and daycares that would otherwise be unable to fund them. A million dollars would go a long way toward making sure that a local budding artist would have a chance to find his or her passion.

Hilda required the whole family to greet the guests when they arrived, which meant that I would arrive separately from Amelia later. Amelia chose my gown to complement hers, but she had to leave early that afternoon to join her family for some last-minute arrangements. In the meantime, I painted for a few hours and then drove over to Amelia's house to finish getting ready. After I was dressed and styled, I sat in the front parlor, trying not to wrinkle my gown. I was waiting for my escort, Billy, Emma's boyfriend, to take me to the party. Amelia's oldest brother, Dean, was allowed to have his wife with him, but only because she was legally part of the family now. Billy and I would be upgraded to honorary Winterses only if we married our respective partners—not before then. Amelia had taken her mother's edict with better grace than I would have, but then again, she was used to her.

Billy finally arrived about five minutes before we needed to leave. As he approached Amelia's house on the small stone walkway, I was once again struck by how incredibly huge he was. With a massive red beard and matching fiery hair, he looked like a lumberjack stuffed in a tuxedo. I opened the door and had to crane my neck to meet his eyes, and when he offered me his arm, I had to reach up to take his elbow.

"Are you ready for this?" he asked as we walked down the front stairs.

"As ready as I'll ever be," I told him. "I'm not really sure what to expect."

As it was only a couple of blocks between Amelia's house and her parents', we were walking to the party. I was relieved to notice that it was marginally warmer than it had been for over a week now, but I was still cold in my dress and light wrap.

He grinned down at me. "This is the third one of these things I've been to, so I can give you the scoop if you want."

This comment surprised me. I knew Emma and Billy had been dating for a while but would never have expected it to be quite so long.

He was looking down at me and must have read something in my face. "I know, I know—I should propose one of these days, right?"

I blushed, embarrassed to be so transparent. "It's not my business. I'm sorry."

He stopped and I looked up at him. His face was red beneath his beard, but his anxiety looked more like nervousness than embarrassment. "The truth is, I've been carrying a ring around for a long time now. I bought it last summer, actually."

"Oh!" I said, pleased and surprised. I knew Emma was head over heels for him.

"I feel like I can tell you, because you're not part of that family yet either, and I know you won't leak it—even to Amelia."

I shook my head. "Of course not."

He still looked nervous and I patted his giant arm. "Don't worry about it, Billy. I can only imagine how hard it would be to propose. You'll know the right time."

He nodded, but he was clearly troubled. I grabbed his arm again, and we continued to walk. Neither of us was in a rush to get there, so we moved slowly.

"Anyway, about tonight," he finally said. "You can expect to be shuffled around like a piece of meat, and you'll be incredibly lucky if you manage to talk to Amelia at all. That mother of theirs is ruthless about decorum. She probably has you seated as far away from the family table as possible—at least that's what she does with me."

I was surprised and dismayed. I'd assumed that after the formal lineup, the family would join the rest of the guests, and Amelia and I would get to spend the evening together. Apparently I'd assumed incorrectly. It bothered me that Amelia hadn't told me about this arrangement. I wouldn't have been any happier about the situation, but at least I would have been prepared.

We could hear the party long before we reached the right block, and when we could see it, I was stunned. Thousands of twinkling lights covered the outside of the house and the trees and yard. The house itself is a stark white in the Greek Revival style, with large columns at the front. It takes up an entire city block in the Garden District and has been in the Winters family since it was built in the early nineteenth century. Listed on New Orleans "Must See" lists for tourists, it's gorgeous but impersonal and cold, especially on the first, tourist-accessible floor, which is kept roped off with period-appropriate antiques. The twinkling lights helped make it seem friendlier, but the crowds I could see were already intimidating.

A long line of cars wrapped around the block, and several valet attendants were taking keys and moving vehicles to a nearby lot. As we approached, I saw a flash of cameras as a rich-looking couple climbed out of a limo, and I suddenly realized that the press was here in force. Suddenly feeling a little stupid for walking, I motioned Billy toward the side of the red carpet, where it appeared we could sneak around the press and in through a different door. Unfortunately, the reporters saw us anyway, and I'm sure we looked guilty once we were spotted. Billy helped me endure the gauntlet of cameras and microphones, shielding me from the pushiest of the press. We finally made it past the media crowd and were climbing the little steps up to the front door when someone called my name from the crowd of cameras and people in the press pit. I couldn't help but spin around, and what seemed like a thousand flashes greeted my eyes. I tried to shield myself from the light, but it still dazzled me and left me half blind. I squinted, trying to see if someone I knew was in the crowd, but a moment later Billy's arm was around my waist, gently leading me toward the front door.

Once inside, we joined the line waiting to greet the family. I could just see Amelia's parents from our spot inside the door, but the rest of the family was hidden by the crowd talking to them and shaking their hands. It resembled a receiving line at a wedding, and I had to swallow a little flame of annoyance at how ridiculous and tiring this all was—for me and for them. It was no secret that Hilda Winters insisted on this party every year, and while her children seemed inured to this bizarre tradition, I couldn't help but wonder what it would have been like for Amelia to grow up with a mother who valued her as an individual rather than an accessory to her vanity. The whole family was Hilda's showpiece for the public tonight.

The antechamber we waited in was lined with easels full of artwork made by local children and teens. Each piece had an artist's write-up, very much as if it were being displayed in a museum. The write-ups were amusing and cute, and the works displayed were, at times, impressive. I knew without asking that Amelia had created this little art showcase all on her own, and my heart grew two sizes thinking about how hard she'd clearly worked on it. I didn't mind that she hadn't brought me in on this project, as it was clearly a personal endeavor. She always managed to have the best surprises.

Long before we reached the receiving line, Billy was shifting impatiently from one foot to the next. He'd been to this party twice before, I remembered. He was clearly uncomfortable in this setting— even more than I was—but he was willing to put up with it, even if he only got to see his girlfriend in passing. I smiled at what this suggested about him. He was clearly a loyal and good man. I asked him a few times what was happening at the front of the line, and he gave short, impatient answers, his eyes clearly fixed on Emma. His love for her was moving and adorable.

After what seemed like an eternity, the two of us made it to the front of the line. The Winterses were arranged in birth order, from eldest to youngest, including the parents. Ted Winters, Amelia's father, was first. He is a tall, fit man in his late sixties, with a full head of beautiful wavy, gray hair and a nicely trimmed, steel-colored beard. He has sparkling, kind green eyes and a brilliant smile.

"Billy!" he said when he saw him. They clasped hands and did that awkward man hug, one arm tapping the other's back before quickly moving apart. Ted spotted me and he grinned. "And you're here with Chloé!" He pulled me into a real hug and then held me at arm's length, looking me up and down. "I probably shouldn't say this to you, Billy, but I think you might have the prettiest escort in the whole place."

I couldn't help but color at his compliment, and both men laughed.

"I count myself lucky," Billy said. "Last year I brought Aunt Trudie."

Ted's laugh was a bark of merriment, and I saw Hilda Winters give him a dirty look. Billy and I moved a couple of paces over to her, and she shook our hands. She is without argument a stunning woman, with gorgeous, porcelain skin, beautiful silver hair, and impeccable clothes. She is a little too thin, if anything, but very attractive in a cold, remote way. She had a phony, plastic smile for us and some empty platitudes, but she was already looking back toward the line, anticipating the next group of people before either of us had a chance to say hello. Billy and I shared an amused glance, neither of us surprised by her behavior. I'm fairly certain she hates anyone who steals her children's attention away from her.

Dean and Ingrid were next, standing so close to each other we didn't have to greet them separately. Dean was moderately warmer than his mother—or at least faked it better—but his wife barely met my eyes. She was nicer to Billy, but I couldn't tell if this was because she was more familiar with him or because of her dislike for me, personally. At the few family gatherings I'd attended so far, she and Hilda had regarded me with poorly veiled disdain, but I didn't want to write off Ingrid quite yet. It was just possible that she simply took a while to warm up.

Bobby was next in line, and only then did I realize that his children were missing. Dean and Ingrid's were also not in attendance, but it seemed less natural for Bobby to be here without his three daughters. They were all so close, he seemed incomplete without them. He brightened perceptibly when he saw us, and we went through a similar process with him as we had with Ted a few minutes ago.

"You look fantastic, Chloé. I'm so very glad you came. I know Amelia's been waiting for you all night."

I glanced over past her brother Michael at Amelia and saw her chatting with an older couple. She regarded them with fully focused interest, but something in the set of her shoulders suggested that she knew I was here a few feet away. My heart gave a spasm of yearning and happiness. She was easily the most attractive woman in the room, and she was mine.

I looked back at Bobby and Billy, and they were both watching me, clearly amused.

"You've got it bad," Bobby said, chuckling. "Did you even hear anything I just said?"

"What? No. I'm sorry," I stammered.

He shook his head. "No problem."

"Happy birthday, by the way," I added.

Bobby smiled. "Do you know that you're the first person to say that to me all evening?"

My jaw dropped involuntarily, and he laughed at my expression. He held up his hands, "Don't worry about it. Everyone knows what this party is really about—and it's certainly not any of us kids."

The line of people finally moved forward, and we were greeted by Michael and Jenna. Michael is the youngest son in the Winters family, and Jenna is his girlfriend. Both Michael and Jenna play in my friend Meghan's band, and they had flown back from tour to be here tonight. We all embraced, and Jenna and I complimented each other's dresses.

"How's Meghan?" I asked.

Michael laughed. "Crazy, as usual. We left her in some little divey hotel in Florida when we flew out this morning. It was five in the morning, and she was up from the night before. We're flying back there tomorrow."

Billy leaned close to him conspiratorially. "How did you get Jenna in line with you?"

Michael and Jenna laughed.

"Well, as you know," Michael said, "I'm not much of a rule follower. My mother barely acknowledges my existence, let alone Jenna's. I decided yesterday that I've gone along with her silly rules long enough, so I just brought Jenna with me today when I got here. Even Hilda Winters wasn't rude enough to send her away, though she did give us some really lovely glares this afternoon."

"Damn," Billy said, rubbing his chin. "I wish I'd thought of that."

I did too, but then again, Amelia had been the one so adamant that we follow her mother's strictures—not me. I didn't like it, but I knew she was trying to get me on her mother's good side. For now, I would follow her lead.

When the line finally moved again, Amelia dropped all decorum and came to me, folding me into her arms and kissing me soundly in front of everyone. She was sagging with fatigue, and her face was still drawn with jet lag, stress, and her cold. She and Billy greeted each other briefly, but his eyes remained on the last person in line—Emma—who was speaking to the older couple just in front of us with clear impatience.

"You look good enough to eat," Amelia whispered, her breath warm on my ear.

"Later," I whispered back. I was amused to see her eyes flare in shock.

"When will I get to see you again?" I asked.

She shrugged with defeat. "I don't know. This line always takes forever, and then it's time for the speeches and dinner. Then I have to walk around schmoozing people for money. We might get a chance to dance once or twice in a couple of hours." She paused and appeared apologetic. "I'm sorry, Chloé. I should have told you it would be like this—I just sort of forgot about it."

She looked so sad and downtrodden, I didn't want to make her feel any worse, so I lifted my shoulders and smiled. "It's okay. At least I have Billy here with me."

She looked troubled and then sighed. "You're actually not sitting with him tonight. My mother does the table arrangements, and she put you in different parts of the room."

I had to laugh. Something about this seemed so typically Hilda, it wasn't actually a surprise. But, before we could talk about it anymore, the space in front of us finally cleared, and Billy was literally picking Emma off the ground in a bear hug. Amelia and I shared an amused glance and a quick kiss, and I moved aside to make room for the people behind me. Amelia refocused immediately, chatting with them, and, as Billy and Emma continued their PDA, I stood awkwardly to the side, trying not to stare at their antics.

Emma finally spotted me and stepped out of Billy's arms to give me a quick hug. "I'm sorry I got so drunk the other day. I'm still hung over, if you can believe it. I blame that bartender. She was flirting with me, I think."

Billy's eyebrows shot up in surprise, and Emma and I laughed.

Emma patted his arm. "Don't worry, honey—she wasn't my type. That Teddy, on the other hand…" She looked at me and waved a hand in front of her face as if she were overheated.

"Wait, who's Teddy?" Billy asked, looking even more confused.

Emma and I laughed again, and then I stepped aside to give them a moment alone for their good-byes.

Finally free of the line, Billy and I fought the crowd over to another shorter line in order to receive our table assignments. When we compared our cards, I saw that we were seated almost as far away from each other as possible. We both grinned, amused that Hilda could be so—at best—utterly clueless or, at worst, cruelly manipulative.

"We don't have to sit down right away," Billy said, trying to sound reassuring. "Do you want to get a drink first?"

"That sounds like a good plan."

We walked around the reception room, looking for a bar, then spotted a waiter with champagne flutes. We both took one, and Billy tossed his drink down in one gulp, the glass toy-like in his giant hand. He grimaced at the taste and set his empty glass on the waiter's tray before grabbing a new one.

"It's bad enough we have to drink this crap, and then they only give you a mouthful at a time," he said. "I wonder where they're keeping the real drinks. Last year the bar was right over here." He looked around over the heads of the crowd, and I saw his eyes light up when he spotted it. He looked down at me. "Wanna wait here? I'll be right back."

I nodded, and he handed me his glass of champagne. He strode away, disappearing into the crowd. I found myself alone for the first time tonight and suddenly felt incredibly self-conscious. Having Billy nearby took a lot of attention away from me because of his size. Standing here alone, I was suddenly on display. I detected several covert and not-so-covert glances my way, and I could feel the color mounting in my face. I looked down at my drink and the extra in my other hand and felt a strong temptation to slam both of them to ease my nerves. The temptation passed, but I continued to keep my eyes down and away from people's faces, too embarrassed to look anyone in the eye.

I heard my name in the crowd and turned toward the person who'd called it, my mood changing to relief, but I didn't see anyone I knew. Instead, I met the eyes of several people clearly staring at me and flushed with embarrassment. I looked around again, trying to spot the person who'd called, wondering if they'd been waylaid on their way over to me. It had been a woman's voice—that much I knew—but I didn't recognize anyone around me. Far off, almost on the other side of the room, I recognized someone, but she was turned away from me so I couldn't see her face. Her figure and her posture seemed familiar from behind, however, and I watched her for a long time, hoping to see her turn my way. I was just on the verge of walking over to her when someone suddenly jostled me. Some of my champagne sloshed out onto my hand, and I just managed to stop myself from cursing.

"Oh, please forgive me," an elderly man told me. "I can barely see where I'm going in this crowd."

"It's no problem," I said. "It's not very good champagne anyway."

He chuckled and moved on. When I looked back across the room, the woman I'd spotted was gone. I looked around again, hoping to see her, but in vain. Whoever she was, she'd disappeared.

Billy came back then with two glasses of bourbon. We both

laughed at having two drinks in our hands, and Billy drank one of his quickly, setting the glass down on a little table nearby. I followed suit, and he grinned.

"You're a lot more fun than anyone Amelia's dated before," he said. He seemed to realize his mistake immediately, as his face reddened perceptibly.

I felt a sweeping thrill of curiosity. On the whole, Amelia avoided talking about her exes. She had a lot of them, and I'd learned that in the past she generally didn't keep girlfriends around for very long, but so far, I'd gleaned very little information about any of them. I knew, for instance, that until she met me, Amelia had never brought a girlfriend to meet her parents before, but that same rule had clearly not applied to her siblings. Emma and Bobby had mentioned meeting exes, and I'd gotten the impression from both of them that they hadn't really liked any of them very much or at all. It was too awkward to ask Emma or Bobby about them, but as Billy had also been around long enough to meet some of them, maybe I could use this opportunity to get some information. Amelia wouldn't like it, but the champagne I'd just gulped down was making me feel a little reckless, so I decided to ignore my misgivings.

Billy looked uncomfortable and guilty and wouldn't meet my eyes. He clearly regretted speaking up. I touched his arm and he looked down at me, his face grim.

"I'm sorry," he said. "I shouldn't have told you that."

"It's okay," I said, keeping my voice purposefully casual. "I'm just curious. Amelia won't tell me about anyone she used to date. Well, almost anyone. I know about Sara."

Billy rolled his eyes. "That woman was a piece of work."

I pounced on this tidbit. "How so?"

Billy shook his head. "They were together for a long time—well, long for Amelia anyway. A year? Year and a half? I don't remember. Amelia was clearly in love with her, but Sara was a wreck. All she ever did was lie and cheat. Broke Amelia's heart."

While it was reassuring to know that Amelia had at least one long-term relationship before me, I was stunned. I'd known she and Sara had been together longer than most of her other girlfriends, but I hadn't known Amelia actually cared for her. Most of Amelia's stories about her exes made it sound like they had endured for weeks at most.

Amelia had withheld almost all details about her past with Sara from me, but from what she had told me about her before, I'd assumed their relationship had been mainly sexual.

Sara had inserted herself into our lives last November when she assaulted me in the bathroom of a bar. She hadn't hurt me badly, but she'd definitely scared me. She'd threatened me and my family and warned me off Amelia. I didn't listen to her, and so far I hadn't heard from her again, but her phantom still lingered at the edges of my relationship with Amelia. Amelia was reluctant to talk about her more than she already had. The only thing I knew was that they'd broken up and then Sara started sending mysterious and sometimes threatening messages to Amelia's new girlfriends and to Amelia herself. She'd never gone further than that until she attacked me last autumn.

I was about to ask Billy more about Sara and the other exes he'd met, but we heard the sound of the band striking up "For He's a Jolly Good Fellow." This seemed to be some kind of cue for everyone to go into the ballroom. Billy motioned toward the open doorway and I followed him, reluctant to end our conversation.

The entire Winters family was on a stage at the far end of the room, and everyone joined in the chorus to sing to them. It was strange on many levels, chief of which was the fact that Amelia's mother seemed to think everyone was singing entirely for her and not for her children on their birthdays. The song continued into a third round, which was long enough for almost all of the attendees to finally gather in the ballroom and find their seats.

While my table assignment was surprisingly close to the stage, I'd been placed between two elderly women who refused to greet me when I approached the table. They both looked hostile, though as far as I knew I'd never met them before. My chair was also pointed away from the stage. I turned it around and sat down, and as I did, I saw both of the women on either side of me give me a dirty look. I smiled back at them with mock graciousness and then ignored them.

A few moments later, Hilda Winters took the center stage in front of the microphone, and the voices in the room gradually quieted as she waited for attention.

"Welcome all to the Winters Family Birthday Gala!" she finally said. Tremendous applause and a few whistles greeted her, and she flushed with pride.

"The celebration marks the thirty-seventh birthday gala, which has taken place in late January since our eldest son, Dean, was just one year old."

I found it strange that after the applause, Hilda didn't ask Dean to say anything. In fact, as mistress of ceremonies, she seemed reluctant to acknowledge that she was onstage with anyone else. The rest of the family stood a few paces behind her, all of them smiling like fools. A flash of hot anger swept through me at this whole charade. If Hilda wanted a party, I thought, why even pretend it was for her children? It all seemed so fake and pretentious.

Hilda cleared her throat. "Tonight's silent auction will be an ongoing affair throughout the evening. On your place setting, you will see a large envelope, and inside that envelope you will see a list of items our generous donors have contributed toward our cause. Simply make your bid and give the envelope to one of the stewards here in the room." She pointed them out. "If you would like to make a donation, please write the check to Art for the People. My beautiful daughter Amelia will tell you more about the organization now."

Hilda Winters was clearly reluctant to cede any of the attention she'd received, as, rather than rejoining the line with the rest of the family, she simply took a couple of steps to the left of the microphone. Amelia walked forward, and my heart gave a jagged leap when she took center stage. She was, as always, incredibly beautiful. I'd been so pleased to see her earlier in the receiving line that I'd barely noticed what she was wearing. Tonight her dark, wavy hair was arranged loosely on top of her head and held in place with what looked like pearls. They studded her hair and stood out in vivid contrast to her dark locks. Unlike her mother's light-blue and icy eyes, Amelia's are a startlingly dark, deep blue, like the ocean in a storm. She's almost exactly my height but slighter overall, with narrow hips and a slender waist. In her gorgeous red-silk gown, she was positively stunning. The crowd around me seemed to agree, as a kind of preternatural silence swept across the room at her appearance. Everyone was looking at her with awe.

"Thank you all so very much for being here tonight," Amelia said. She was clearly confident in front of a large crowd. Had I been up there, I would have been, at best, stammering, more likely speechless. She looked comfortable, more at ease than her mother, in fact.

"Art for the People is a local chapter of the national organization that brings art to children and teens. The wonderful pieces in the lobby are works created in part by the generous efforts of this organization with local primary and secondary schools. As you know, the Winters family has long been a patron of the arts, none more so than me. Studies have shown that children exposed to the creative arts at a young age are more successful in all subjects in school, and they are less likely to engage in petty or violent crime. Please consider the future of young people and art in our fair city when you make your donations tonight. A young da Vinci or Cassatt might be waiting for the paints or pencils your generosity could provide. Thank you."

While I am, of course, biased, I thought her speech was very nicely done, and I'm sure I clapped the longest and the loudest of anyone in the room. It had been informative but not didactic, pleading but not desperate. It was, like the woman who gave it, perfection.

Hilda closed the opening remarks with a few words of her own, and we were finally dismissed for the meal. I stood up and turned my chair around, once again noticing that the women on either side of me seemed put out to have me here with them. After I sat down, I glanced around the table, hoping for a friendly face, but no one looked at me for more than a moment except to glare. They clearly all knew each other and had apparently decided to pretend I wasn't here. Rather than let it bother me, I took this dismissal as a gift, as it meant that I wouldn't have to make small talk with anyone. I did enough of that at work.

Simply to have something to do, I opened the envelope on my plate. Inside was a long list of items donated for the auction tonight. I noted that Amelia had given several paintings to the cause, all of which I recognized as coming from her personal collection. Her parents, brothers, and sister had also contributed, and though Michael and Emma's respective gifts of music and film memorabilia were clearly more modest than those of their elder, wealthier siblings, I was still pleased to see that their names had been included.

People outside of the family and a few organizations had also donated items and event tickets, but the one that grabbed my attention had been donated by a local travel agency: a six-night trip for two to Puerto Vallarta. While I knew I was lucky to live in such a warm climate, and I knew our cold snap was likely to pass any day now, the thought of basking in the warm sun on a sandy beach made me yearn for it in a kind of hungry desperation. I hadn't actually been to a beach in years. Between graduate school and internships, I'd barely had a vacation longer than a couple of days since my undergraduate years. Amelia and I had been working long, back-to-back days almost since I started working with her. Except for a few days during the holidays and my illness last week, I hadn't had a single break.

This didn't, however, mean that I had the money to outbid anyone for the trip. Between setting up my apartment and paying off some of the debt I'd accumulated as a graduate student, I was still fairly tight on money most of the time. Working for Amelia meant I was very well paid, but it would be a long time before I had enough extra money set aside for a vacation. Sighing, I returned the auction card to my plate and took out my checkbook. I could make a small donation, at the very least.

Dinner was served soon after this, and no one spoke to me the whole time we ate. By the time the cabernet sorbet was served, I'd been sitting there in relative silence for almost an hour, and my carefree façade was beginning to crack. To pass the time, I'd read the auction sheet to myself so many times I must have looked like a crazy person. There simply wasn't enough information on that piece of paper to warrant a twentieth read, but it gave me something to look at. Sighing, I set it down for the last time and stood up. The movement caught my tablemates by surprise, and I smiled at them.

"Such a pleasure," I said, loud enough for all of them and nearby tables to hear. I saw a couple of the people I'd been sitting with flush, but I wasn't in the mood to feel bad about my rudeness in the face of theirs. I needed some air or I might start tearing my hair out. I pushed my chair in and walked away as quickly as I could. One of the waiters saw me looking around, and when I told him what I needed, he directed me toward a large purple curtain that had been hung in front of the back exit. I thanked him and went out into the cold night.

I walked across the patio, rounded a corner into the back flower garden, and found the darkness back there thick and deep. Clearly the family had not anticipated anyone coming out here on their own, as the garden lights were off. Safely hidden from the people in the ballroom, I took several long, deep breaths and closed my eyes. A moment later, I heard something snap off to my left and jerked my eyes open.

"Hello?" I asked, peering into the dark. "Is someone there?" I couldn't see anything or anyone. I stood there for a long time, squinting and looking in the direction of the sound, but nothing was there.

Shivering now from the cold, I decided to head back inside. The last thing I wanted was to go back into that room with all of those terrible people, but at least I might get to see Amelia again. I took the long way back and reentered the house from the side to avoid any curious questions.

❖

Sara let out the breath she was holding when Chloé finally went away. She'd seen her leave the party through the back door and had raced out here from the side so she could watch her from the garden. To her surprise, instead of staying on the patio, she started walking toward Sara. For a moment, Sara was certain that she'd been spotted, that Chloé was coming to talk to her, so she'd decided to hide in the farthest reach of the garden. It was so dark there, no one would be able to see her.

When Chloé came around the edge of the hedge, however, it was clear that she wasn't looking for her. She was out here on her own for some reason, and Sara watched her stand there by herself for a long moment and take deep breaths. Chloé closed her eyes, and Sara's heart leapt at her luck. She hadn't planned to do it tonight, but she couldn't ignore an opportunity when it fell in her lap. She reached in her purse for her little pistol and took a step forward from behind the tree, but she stupidly managed to step on a branch, snapping it. Chloé jumped and looked directly at her, but the darkness still hid her. Sara stopped completely and held her breath, not wanting to give Chloé a reason to investigate. After a while, Chloé relaxed and then shivered, rubbing the cold from her bare arms. Finally, she turned and walked away.

Sara cursed herself. She'd almost blown the whole thing. When she'd heard about the gala tonight, she'd been reminded of how Amelia had refused to let her attend when they were together. Amelia's excuse at the time had been her parents—they wouldn't want to rub a lesbian in their guests' faces. Yet here was Chloé, greeted by Ted and Hilda and the rest of the family like an old friend. Naively, Sara hadn't expected to see Chloé here. She'd come only to see Amelia, knowing that she might not get another opportunity before she had to leave New Orleans again. She'd been invited to the gala by Daphne Waters—a family friend of a Winters—but when she and Daphne got out of the car in front of the mansion a couple of hours ago, she'd been flabbergasted to spot Chloé sneaking in ahead of her. She hadn't been able to stop herself from calling her name, and it had taken a series of deft lies to Daphne to cover up her stupidity.

Inside, she simply avoided the receiving line, walking past the whole family without notice. She'd waited in the reception room and watched Chloé come through the line, and then she hid in the crowd when she saw Chloé coming her way with that giant oaf of a man Emma was still seeing—Timmy or Jimbo, or whatever his name was. He'd been rude to her when she met him a few times years ago. And to be perfectly honest, his size also intimidated her, so she patiently waited until Chloé was alone again before calling her name once more.

All evening, she knew she was courting disaster. Any moment then or now, someone would recognize her, and it would cause a scene. More than the scene, however, Sara was afraid of putting Chloé or Amelia on the lookout for her again. They'd clearly forgotten about her at this point—that whole disastrous slipup at the bar last November was safely in the past. Sara knew that surprise was the only thing she had going for her, and she was on the brink of showing her hand.

She didn't want either Chloé or Amelia to know she was coming for them. She wanted to ambush them when they least expected it.

There was, however, one last thing she needed to do before she left the party, and she grinned wickedly. Tonight was, after all, a charitable event, and she hadn't bid on anything from the auction. If she was careful, she could sneak in and do it now before anyone noticed her.

CHAPTER FOUR

When I came back into the ballroom, I walked right into a crowd of people milling around Ted Winters. I tried to move around them, but he spotted me and called me over. Every person near him turned to look at me, obviously curious, and my face heated as I walked closer. Ted held out an arm, and I came near enough for him to put it around my shoulders. He squeezed me once, tightly. He had a glass of bourbon in his free hand, and I could tell from his ruddy face that it wasn't his first drink.

Ted addressed the men and women around us. "And this little lady is the newest addition to Amelia's fantastic company. But she isn't just an employee. No, this young beauty here has captured my daughter's heart."

My face couldn't have been hotter if I were on the surface of the sun. Ted, however, was oblivious to my embarrassment. "We're all just so glad they found each other. Amelia has needed to settle down for some time now."

The people around us looked embarrassed for me, and I only just managed to give them an awkward smile.

"Jesus, Dad," a voice said behind us.

Ted turned with me, his arm still gripping my shoulders, and we both saw Bobby a few feet away.

"Can't you see you're embarrassing her?" Bobby asked. His face was red, too, but from anger.

Ted squeezed me tighter and laughed. "Oh, come on. Chloé knows I'm just playing around. Don't you, honey?"

They were both looking at me, Bobby's face serious and hard, Ted's open and clearly drunk.

"Sure I do," I said, smiling up at Ted to reassure him.

"You're just being kind," Bobby said. He'd kept his voice as quiet as possible, but I could see the people around us stirring uncomfortably.

Ted let go of my shoulders, and it was all I could do not to run away. I took a couple of steps from him, closer to Bobby, and saw Ted's expression falter a little with embarrassed dismay. The expression faded, however, and he turned back to his guests, effectively dismissing us.

Bobby took my arm in his and steered me away from the others and toward the bar in the corner of the room.

"Jesus, I'm so sorry," he said. "Dad always overimbibes at these things. I think it's the only way he can stomach my mother's antics."

"Don't worry about it," I said. "At least he was saying good things. It could have been worse."

Bobby laughed and grinned at me. "That's a nice way of looking at it." His expression sobered a little. "I guess I should tell you that the longer you're around our happy little family, the more you'll see how unhappy we really are—especially my parents."

Over the last couple of months, I had come to wonder about the two of them. Ted was sociable, kind, and forthcoming, welcoming me from day one with genuine warmth. He seemed to be this way with everyone, but I could tell he actually liked me. Meanwhile, his wife was brittle and cold toward him and the rest of the family, and phony and happy with anyone in public. They clearly shared few interests and, for the most part, spent entire parties like this and their anniversary in different places. I didn't know until now, however, that their differences were causing marital problems.

We were in line for drinks now, and Bobby was still holding my arm in his. We'd received a few curious stares as we walked over here, and I could almost hear the confused gears turning in people's minds as people tried to figure me out. Bobby is, in fact, a very handsome man and an eligible, rich widower. While he'd been having some troubles recently keeping a long-term girlfriend because of his children, I was sure plenty of women in this room would be willing to overlook some inconvenient kids for a chance to spend his fortune. Yet here I was on his arm, monopolizing their chances. The rumor mill would surely be grinding by the end of the evening. Bobby, however, could apparently care less. Amelia would be amused to hear that some people not in the know obviously thought he and I were together.

Bobby got me another glass of champagne and a gin and tonic for himself. Together with our drinks, we walked over toward a little raised table by a small dance floor and watched several couples twirling around. We didn't say anything. He seemed to be thinking about something else—his parents, most likely—and, after the disastrous, nerve-racking dinner, I was relieved to have someone friendly to stand near for a while. I turned toward him to chat, but his eyes were fixed on the stage. I looked up to see Hilda Winters take the microphone again. After she was greeted by a long chorus of applause, she took a slight bow.

"Once again, thank you all for coming. Cake will be served shortly. My daughter Emma will now read the names of the highest bidders for our auctioned items. Whether you won tonight or not, please remember to take a moment before you leave to make a donation to Art for the People."

Once again, she seemed reluctant to give up her position at the center of attention, but Emma managed to take the microphone from her a moment later. She was holding a piece of paper and began reading off the names, items, and prices people had paid for them. I was flabbergasted by the amounts people had bid for the auction items and quickly lost track of how much money was raised. Instead, I listened in mounting disbelief as each item's winning bid was read. Even Emma's donation—a Tarantino film poster signed by the cast and director— went for tens of thousands of dollars. I wasn't the only person in the room to be impressed by the totals, as everyone began clapping louder and louder the longer Emma read. There were a few whistles from the crowd at the biggest bid—over a hundred thousand dollars—on a tiny Calder painting Amelia had donated.

"Finally," Emma said, and then paused, waiting for the room to quiet down a little. "Finally, the last item, donated by the New Orleans Travel Group: an all-inclusive vacation to sunny Puerto Vallarta." She paused, and then her face broke into a wide smile. "The winning bid of twenty thousand dollars goes to Dr. Chloé Deveraux."

I was stunned. I'd donated a hundred dollars to the general fund, but I certainly hadn't made that bid. I looked over at Bobby, and he was grinning widely, clapping as loudly as everyone else in the room. He must have seen something in my face, as I saw his smile falter. He stopped clapping and leaned closer to me.

"Is something wrong?"

"I didn't make that bid, Bobby," I said. "I don't have twenty thousand dollars."

His face clouded with anger. "What the hell?"

I shook my head. "I don't know what happened. Is someone playing a joke?"

He sighed. "I hope not." Seeing my dismay, he patted my arm. "Don't worry about it, Chloé. We'll get to the bottom of it."

Despite his reassurances, my stomach was a sudden knot of tension. I excused myself and walked as quickly as I could out of the room just to get away from everyone. Of course I knew that I wouldn't be accountable for money I hadn't bid, but that didn't help me feel any better. What bothered me primarily was the thought that someone had done this to me. I'd known since we got together that being with Amelia meant sacrificing a lot of my privacy—we would always be in the public eye. But until now, I'd never recognized that it was more than having my picture in the paper all the time. It also meant incurring the petty meanness of the public. Someone had done this to me simply because I was with Amelia. The thought was sickening and sad.

I had to search the ground floor for a while to find somewhere to be alone. Staff members were walking around, busy moving trays of plates and glasses from the dining room. I remembered a little butler's pantry down the hallway to the kitchen and found it blissfully empty. There was a little stool in there, and I sat down on it heavily, putting my face in my hands. A moment later the door opened and Amelia came in, looking upset. She walked the two or three steps and then knelt in front of me despite her gown. She clutched my hands in hers.

"Chloé, I'm so sorry. Bobby told me what happened."

I shook my head. "It's not your fault, Amelia. Someone just has a sick sense of humor."

"That doesn't make it right. I can't imagine why someone would do this."

I sighed. "I can: jealousy. They see us, they know that we're happy, and they're jealous of our happiness. People can't stand it when other people enjoy themselves when they're miserable."

"Well, you don't have to worry about the money. Bobby is talking with the auction committee now, and he'll explain what happened."

A little tension went out of my shoulders. I'd known the situation would be taken care of, but it was still nice to hear. But then I suddenly realized just how terrible Amelia looked up close. In the forgiving light of the ballroom and the reception hall, she'd looked tired and worn, but here in the harsh glare of the light in this pantry, I could see that the problem was deeper than that. She was clearly exhausted. She'd done what she could to hide her fatigue with makeup, but her eyes were deeply sunken and bloodshot. Her face looked strained and wan.

"My God, Amelia," I said. "You look like you're about ready to drop."

Her shrug was unconvincing.

"I mean it. You should be at home in bed. Why don't we just leave?"

Her laugh was bitter. "I wish we could, but really, I can't. This event is mostly mine, after all. I still have to get people to open their wallets for my cause."

"Can't you put your cause to rest for the night? You've already made so much money. You're going to make yourself really sick if you keep pushing."

I saw temptation pass in and out of her eyes, but she finally shook her head. "It will be at least two more hours before we can call it a night." She got to her feet and held out her hand. "Come on. We have some people to schmooze together."

I took her hand and stood up, smiling. "We can go out together now?"

She smiled weakly. "I no longer care what my mother thinks. We've been following her rules all night, and I'm sick of it. I told Emma to go find Bobby, too. My mother's being ridiculous, as usual."

Amelia moved toward the door, but I grabbed her arm to hold her back. She turned, obviously confused, and I grinned at her.

"Do we have to go back so soon?" I asked. "Couldn't we hide in here for a while?"

Her face lit up, and she stepped closer before slipping her arms around me. She kissed me gently, then nibbled on my bottom lip, and a little sigh of pleasure escaped my throat.

"We might have a couple of minutes to ourselves," she whispered.

"Only a couple?"

She met my eyes, her expression dark with desire. "I don't think it'll take longer than that, do you?"

My stomach dropped, and I swallowed before shaking my head. She was right—it wouldn't take long. Between not seeing her for the last two weeks and being kept apart all day today, my body had been clamoring for her for what felt like decades. Generally, as long as I kept my mind off her, I could keep myself under control, but when I was around her, all I wanted to do was tear our clothes off and ease my wild craving for her.

She moved her lips back to my neck, and I lifted my chin to give her access to my exposed skin. Her kisses felt incredible, but I couldn't help but feel a pang of guilt. She was obviously exhausted. Still, I didn't think I could make it all night without something like this.

Her hands slid my dress up, bunching it at my waist and exposing my legs. Finally, her fingertips brushed the outside of my underwear. My entire body jolted at her touch, and she chuckled.

"A little worked up?" she whispered.

I could do nothing but nod, my desire so strong it was choking me.

She knelt to pull my underwear off, flinging them into a corner of the pantry. She stayed down there on the ground, her hands on my thighs, just looking. I put my hands on her shoulders, forcing myself to just keep them there. I was trembling, and some of my anxiety clearly communicated itself to her. She gave me a wicked grin and then leaned forward for a taste.

I could have screamed when her lips touched me. Just about anything would have set me off right then, and her kiss and her strong tongue instantly drove me crazy. Knowing that a crew of busy people was walking by, mere feet from us out in the hallway, I only just managed to stifle a moan. I had to put my hand over my mouth and bite down on my palm, hard, to silence myself.

Amelia's fingers started tracing up my legs, and when she finally slid one finger up inside me, I immediately started to come. The sounds escaping me were muffled and strangled by my hand, but still audible. The pleasure was so glorious, at that moment, I would have screamed and shared it with the world if I hadn't had my wits about me. The orgasm pulsed through me, fast and hard, my insides clenching around Amelia's finger. Finally, the shudders of my climax began to lessen.

She stopped and I sagged onto her, bracing myself with my hands on her shoulders. A moment later she rose, her smile so self-satisfied you might have thought she'd just won the lottery.

"See," she said. "I told you it would be fast."

I clutched at her, drawing her into a kiss, and maneuvered a little so I could rub on her leg. She let me continue for a moment and then stepped back, laughing lightly.

"You'll have to wait for more, my darling. Don't you remember? We're supposed to be somewhere right now."

I could have cried in frustration. "But, Amelia—"

She lifted a finger to my lips. "No buts. There's more where that came from when we get home tonight. Now let me help you put your hair back in place."

After we helped each other look as composed as possible, we were ready to exit the pantry. She'd insisted on leaving my underwear here— she'd pick them up later. She told me she wanted to know I wasn't wearing any as we walked around her parents' house.

We pushed open the door and stepped into the hall, and I met the eyes of several guilty-looking staff members. They all tried to pretend they hadn't been listening to us and scurried away, and Amelia gave me an amused glance. I was mortified, but it takes a lot more than that to rattle her.

Back in the ballroom, I saw heads swivel our way as we passed several tables, the two of us holding hands. Hot under their gaze, I was still fixated on what had just happened. I couldn't tell if everyone knew what we'd just done, but it seemed like all of them did. Rumors spread quickly in this kind of crowd. Also, the confused gears were clearly in motion again, judging by some baffled expressions. It would appear to strangers that I'd moved from Billy to Bobby and then on to his sister, and I couldn't help but feel a twisted sense of satisfaction. It served them right for making assumptions.

Head high, oblivious to the looks we were getting, Amelia led me directly toward the largest group of men, all of whom were milling around Hilda Winters. Hilda's face fell when she spotted me with Amelia, but she quickly covered up her dismay with a phony smile.

"And here's my lovely daughter and her...friend," she said, gesturing toward us.

The crowd opened up a little to allow us entry, and all of their faces turned toward us with unconcealed curiosity. Amelia clutched my hand tighter, her palm a little sweaty, and I was surprised to realize that she was nervous, too. Just looking at her would suggest that she was unfazed by anything or anyone, but, as I'd come to understand the last few months, a lot of her confidence was simply a very good front for her real feelings.

"Gentlemen," Amelia said, "thank you so much for attending. I'm here with Dr. Deveraux here to answer any questions you might have about Art for the People."

About half an hour later, she'd managed to get a check from every single person there, and as we walked away, we also left Hilda behind us, looking deflated and lessened by the experience. Her daughter was clearly better at this than she was, and she knew it. I couldn't help but worry that this might cause some strife later, but for the moment, it was good to see Hilda put in her place.

Amelia handed the pile of checks to one of the stewards, and we turned around together just as Bobby approached us.

"It's all taken care of," he said, handing Amelia a small envelope. He turned to me. "So don't worry about it anymore, okay?"

"Did I miss something? What's taken care of?" I asked.

"The auction," Amelia replied. "I asked Bobby to sort out your fake bid."

"So what happened?" I asked.

He shrugged. "We don't know who actually made the bid. The handwriting on the form looked feminine to me, but I can't be sure. I asked the committee to talk to the stewards to see if anyone remembers something, but I'm not holding my breath. We probably won't ever know who did it." He looked back at Amelia. "Anyway, I simply exceeded the next highest bid, and the auction committee was satisfied. They told me we don't even need to announce the change since it was clearly a fake."

"Wait," I said, confused, "what do you mean?" Suddenly, his words came together in my mind, and I realized what he meant. I looked back and forth between the two of them several times, alarm mounting. "You mean you had to *pay* them? Why couldn't it just go to the next-highest bidder?"

Bobby shook his head. "We tried that, but he didn't want the trip anymore. The committee told me it often works that way when mistakes like this happen. People bid, but they're also sort of relieved to be outbid, too. Anyway, he didn't want to pay, so I covered it."

"Just let me know how much, and I'll pay you back," Amelia told him.

"Wait, wait," I said, a hand to my forehead. "I still don't understand. If the next bidder didn't want it, why not just tell the travel agency what happened?"

They were both staring at me as if I'd just suggested that they drive over someone's cat. They glanced at each other, seeming equally confused.

"Because if we did that," Amelia said, choosing her words carefully, "they'd never donate anything to our charities again."

"And if we reneged on payment altogether, we'd have the auction committee after us."

I was floored. Somehow in their world, paying for an item none of us had bid on—a situation that was clearly a poor practical joke or worse—was still more important than looking bad to strangers. It was a mind-set so foreign to anything I'd grown up with, I could barely fathom it. And yet, to judge from their expressions, it was so normal for them as to seem utterly obvious.

"So how much did you have to pay them?" I asked, anger mounting despite myself.

Bobby's face broke into a wide smile. "That's the real beauty of it. The next highest bidder was much lower than the fake bid. I had to go over it by only a hundred dollars, and the committee called it even."

"You still haven't answered me." Something in my voice must have finally made both of them realize how upset I was, as I saw their eyebrows lift in surprise, but they still looked confused.

"Eight thousand, one hundred dollars," Bobby said.

"Eight thousand dollars!" I shouted. I was loud enough to cause several people to look our way, and I lowered my voice. "Eight thousand? Are you kidding me?"

He shrugged. "It was fair, Chloé. And remember, all of that money goes to charity. So Amelia gets a tax write-off, and you both get a trip out of it."

I was speechless. My mouth opened and closed as I tried to speak, but no words came. Amelia touched my shoulder, and I turned toward her so quickly she actually flinched.

"Do you have any idea how ridiculous this is to me?" I demanded.

She nodded but looked uncertain. "I'm starting to see that, honey, but I don't understand why you're so put out. There was a problem and we solved it."

"With eight thousand dollars," I said. "For a trip we didn't want."

"Actually," she said, "I did want that trip. I bid on it myself."

"For how much?"

"Seven thousand." She said this in the same way I might say twenty or thirty dollars, and I was once again struck by the vast, immeasurable distance between our two stations in life. She'd grown up with a kind of wealth I could barely understand, and she'd also made a fortune as a businesswoman. Amelia had never been in a position to worry about paying rent or making a car payment or paying a bill, and even if she stopped working today, she would never be in that position. She could live on what she had right now for the rest of her life and several subsequent lives, comfortably. Seven or eight thousand dollars wasn't even a drop in the bucket for her. In fact, the thousand-dollar difference between seven and eight thousand hardly registered. While I could understand this mind-set intellectually—after all, it wasn't her fault she was born into wealth—that didn't necessarily help me feel entirely easy with her solution. Many, many times we'd had little and sometimes large misunderstandings entirely related to the fact that she was wealthy and I was not. I knew I could be with her for years and years and never understand this part of her fully.

My anger deflated, but I still felt sickened. Someone had pulled a joke on us, and we were stuck paying for it. Someone, perhaps someone looking at us right now, had seen our happiness and decided to throw something at it. We were lucky Amelia could meet this challenge without batting an eyelash, but it depressed me, too. Would we always be under scrutiny like we were now? Would there always be people trying to wreck things for us?

I'd been quiet long enough that both Amelia and Bobby were beginning to look nervous, as if I might fly off the handle at any moment. I gave them both a weak smile and shrugged.

"I get it," I told them. "I don't agree with it, but I get it."

Amelia's face brightened and she gave my hand a quick squeeze. "I'm glad. It's only fair, after all. And don't worry—if I find out who put that bid in for you, I'll sue her so fast your head will spin."

I laughed and hugged her, some of my uncertainty melting with her ruthlessness. I'd read about some of her lawsuits and knew she always won. That was the kind of person she was and the kind of lawyers she kept.

"And hey," she said, meeting my eyes, "there's a silver lining here, too. Now we get to go to Puerto Vallarta."

I laughed. "You know, when I saw that trip on the auction form, I had a fantasy of us down there on the beach together. I didn't think it would come true."

She took a step closer to me, her voice dropping a little. "I wanted us to go for Valentine's Day. How does that sound?"

I closed my eyes, picturing white, sandy beaches and cocktails under palm umbrellas. Amelia would be next to me, her smooth, lean body clad only in a swimsuit. I opened my eyes, and this time my smile was genuine and full-hearted.

"It sounds like heaven."

CHAPTER FIVE

The day before Valentine's Day, we left New Orleans for Puerto Vallarta on a commercial flight. The sky was leaden with clouds and rain, and the fog was so thick it took us ages to drive to the airport despite the light Friday-morning traffic. It warmed up a little after our cold snap in January, but it was still bitter when the wind blew. Amelia and I were bundled to the gills in heavy coats and hats, and the idea of arriving somewhere with actual sunshine seemed more like a fantasy than a reality.

We had more reasons to be grateful for leaving New Orleans than the weather, though. Part of why I'd been so excited to leave was to avoid the Mardi Gras celebrations in New Orleans this weekend. Most locals have a very torn relationship with the holiday. On the one hand, lots of people get some or most of the week off, like a second Christmas. The weeks leading up to Mardi Gras—Carnival—are graced by beautiful balls, fantastic parades, and gorgeous costumes. On the other hand, in the final days of the season, including the day itself, the city is deluged with hundreds of thousands of drunk tourists, all of whom have decided that puking, peeing, and defecating in the street are part of the fun. For several days every year, it's difficult to get anywhere, especially downtown, and if you have to go down there for any reason, you have to fight through crowds of rowdy, drunk people. As I now lived next to the French Quarter, I was anxious to get out of town. I'd enjoyed the parades as a child but had started to dislike most of the celebrations as a young adult, especially the main attractions in the tourist parts of town. The Marigny has some smaller, mainly local parades and events that I like to attend when I can get to them, but that is really the only part of

Mardi Gras I enjoy anymore. Living in Paris as I had the last few years, I hadn't celebrated in a long time, but I hadn't exactly missed it, either.

Also, we were exhausted. We'd spent the weeks between the birthday gala and our trip working, almost nonstop. The day after the gala, we both had to get to the office the moment the shipping company in town opened, just after dawn, and we worked all morning, afternoon, and into the late evening. This happened almost every day, including weekends, until we left. Most of our efforts dealt with arranging, storing, and cataloguing the massive shipments of artwork from Montreal, but we were also wrapping up several long-term, large-scale projects, including one of my original sales with Brent Cameron. The Cameron sale was our largest project for the last quarter of 2014 and the first quarter of 2015, but I was so tired of the whole job that by the time I was overseeing the final installation of artwork a few days before our trip, I felt neither jubilation nor joy. I was simply too tired to care.

We had also experienced several delays at our newest project at Teddy's, and it seemed like I spent at least an hour on the phone every day with someone about it between the gala and our trip. It took eons to get the artists' work and then another era to try to figure out a time for the installation that would serve for us and for Teddy and her staff. Nothing had panned out. Finally, after days and days of back-and-forth phone calls, we'd settled on a delivery date after the trip. Still, I strongly suspected, based on what had already happened several times, that the date would end up moving again before it actually happened.

Amelia had come back from Montreal in desperate need of a break, and the long hours and frantic pace of our work didn't make things any better for her. By the time we left for Puerto Vallarta, she looked harrowed and ill. She'd lost weight and had battled her cold and a sore throat on and off since she returned. I didn't look much better than she did by the time we climbed onto the plane to Mexico, and both of us quite literally passed out when the plane took off, too exhausted to be excited. When we finally walked off the plane, out onto the tarmac in the blazing sun of a Mexican winter, both of us were still blinking away our sleepiness, befuddled to find ourselves there already.

Puerto Vallarta is a city divided in more ways than one. Obvious divisions exist, as in most resort towns, between tourists and locals. There are also divisions among locals: those with lots of money, those with a basic standard of living, and those crushed by institutionalized poverty. Even among tourists are divisions, and the divisions are, much like those of the locals, arranged geographically. On one side of the Río Cuale, newer resorts and American businesses crowd the beach in tacky, offensive blandness, appealing to U.S. travelers that want all the conveniences of home in a new place. Tourists that want to go to Walmart and KFC are welcome to stay in a Holiday Inn and feel like they never left home.

On the other side of the river, where we were staying, is the Old Town, Emiliano Zapata Colonia. There, smaller, off-brand hotels attempt to blend in with the older part of the city by borrowing design elements of the original architecture. There, the restaurants, stores, and shops are generally locally owned and singular, with none of the banal Americana available a couple of miles away. Many of the streets in the old part of town are still cobblestoned, and it's easy to imagine why old Hollywood used to flock there for getaways. Emiliano Zapata is also Puerto Vallarta's gay neighborhood and is generally considered one of the safest places for gay and lesbian tourists in Mexico.

Our limo driver offered to give us a driving tour, but both of us were too worn out to want one. Instead, he dropped us off in front of our hotel, a small bed-and-breakfast. It was less than a block from Playa Los Muertos, the ghoulishly named but gay-friendly beach. Our room was a penthouse suite with a large balcony overlooking the water, hemmed in by tropical plants and flowers like a little private oasis. We could see the crashing waves and the beach below, but it would be difficult for anyone to see us from any direction. We both stared at the water for a long moment and then collapsed into the two Adirondack chairs there on the balcony without saying a word.

After watching the water for a few minutes, I began sweating heavily. I'd expected it to be warmer here, but it was actually hot. Our balcony was shaded with palm trees and large-leafed bushes, but even in the shade I was uncomfortably warm in my heavy winter clothes. I'd flung my coat onto the bed when we came into the room, but I needed to get out of the rest of my winter things. I was about to suggest this change to Amelia, but when I looked over at her, I saw that she'd fallen asleep. Her face was drawn and pale, and the lids of her eyes looked purple and bruised. She'd pulled off her sweater and was clad only in a light cotton button-up shirt and slacks, so it was safe enough to leave her out here in the shade for a little while. She appeared so tired, I didn't want to wake her. I rose as quietly as possible and went back into our cool, dark room.

A bottle of champagne and an assortment of fresh fruit stood on a little table, with instructions to call for more when needed—no extra charge. Several bottles of beer and water were in a little mini fridge, and the freezer held ice and *paletas*, Mexican fruit popsicles. I opened and drained half of a large bottle of water and then stripped down completely. My bra and underwear were damp with sweat, and once I removed them, the cool air felt marvelous on my hot skin. The floor was a beautiful blue tile, and as I walked over to the bathroom, my bare feet, clad in woolen socks for the last few weeks, felt remarkably unconfined.

The bathroom was a modern wonder, done in the same blue and white as the bedroom. The fixtures were marble and stainless steel, and large, flowering plants served as decorations. The shower had a slightly raised lip on the floor to capture the water, but it was deep enough to have no curtain or door. I turned the water on and left it cold, jumping in with a little shriek as it hit my hot skin.

I'd just finished washing off the last of the soap when I saw movement in our bedroom. A moment later Amelia was walking into the bathroom, still wearing her clothes but without shoes. Without saying a word, she came into the shower with me, fully dressed. Her face seemed almost grim when she met my eyes, but I quickly realized what I saw there wasn't anxiety or anger, but raw desperation. The water hit her clothes, plastering them to her as she slid into my arms. She crushed my mouth under hers, bending my head back. Her excitement was so frantic and stark she seemed to want to spend it all in her lips. I let her kiss me a while longer before meeting her a little and then a little more. She clutched my breasts, squeezing them painfully. I groaned and she squeezed harder, making my vision cloud with pain and pleasure.

My hands were on her back, and I hesitated for a moment and then let go before backing up a couple of steps. Her hands dropped to her sides as I stepped too far away. She blinked at me a few times, her eyes still clouded with desire, and it seemed to take her a moment to realize I was no longer in her arms. She frowned slightly in seeming confusion, and I hesitated for a moment before reaching up to undo the top button of her shirt. I saw her go rigid and I stopped after the first button, resting my hands on her hips. She seemed to shake herself a little, and some of the tension went out of her shoulders.

With a barely perceptible nod, she gave me permission to continue, and that was all it took. I quickly unbuttoned a couple more and then helped her wrench her wet shirt off and over her head. We flung it out of the shower and she stood in front of me, breathing hard, her eyes smoldering with heat. Then she moved her hands to the button on her slacks. The action made me gasp with shock. While I'd seen Amelia in just her lingerie more and more frequently over the last few months, it certainly wasn't a regular occurrence, and she rarely did it without significant coaxing. A moment later, slacks yanked down and slung aside, she stood in front of me, glorious in her bra and panties. She moved to take a step closer, but I held up a hand to stop her.

"Wait a moment," I whispered.

Even when she did undress this far, she generally didn't let me stare at her like I was doing now, and I could see her mounting frustration as I continued to gaze at her. Her body seemed to thrum with suppressed energy, her shoulders and hands literally shaking. She often teased me by making me wait, and I was enjoying the reversal. She looked almost angry.

"Nice," I said. I ran my fingers up and down her arm, light enough to draw goose bumps. She took that as a sign of permission and leapt toward me. I slipped to the side again and held up a hand. "Did I say you could move?"

"But, Chloé—"

"Quiet."

She finally caught on, and I saw her relax a little. A sly grin rose on her lips, and she put her hands on her hips.

"You want an eyeful, is that it?"

I nodded. "And I plan to get it this time. You have to wait until I'm done looking at you."

Her smile widened, and then her hands moved around behind her, and she unclasped her bra. I was stunned. In all the months we'd been together, and in all the times we'd made love, she'd removed her bra two or perhaps three times, always in the dark or when we were in the middle of things, making it difficult to look at her clearly. I went cold and then hot with surprise, and she looked gleeful at my reaction.

Too stunned to react, I didn't stop her when she stepped closer to me, pulling me into her arms.

Our breasts crushed together, almost painfully, and I moaned into her as she kissed me, her mouth rough on mine. Her lips moved to my neck, and she bit down. My shriek echoed off the tile, and we both jumped a little in surprise. She met my eyes for a second, amused, and went back to my neck, nibbling a little more tenderly and sucking gently as her kisses moved across the sensitive skin on my collarbone.

My mounting desire was making it hard to stay on my feet. My fingers and toes had gone slightly numb, and it was as if electricity were racing up and down my arms and legs. Every time Amelia's hands moved on my body, I jerked toward her, clutching her sides, drawing her toward me, wanting to absorb her into myself. My hands rose, almost as if by their own accord, and rested on her breasts. She went completely stiff under my fingers, and I almost wrenched them away, suddenly aware of what I was doing. Then she relaxed again and continued to kiss and fondle me. Permission given, I let my fingertips explore, for the first time, her magnificent breasts.

My hands had brushed her nipples and breasts before, but being allowed to explore them like this was a revelation. Though we are nearly exactly the same height, Amelia has a much slighter build than I do. Her breasts are also two cup sizes smaller than mine, but perfectly proportioned to her slim frame. Her nipples, however, are surprisingly large and pert, and they responded to my touch immediately. Feeling them quicken under my fingers made me gasp with surprised excitement, and Amelia was likewise surprised into a reaction. She tilted her head back for a moment, her eyes closed, and I continued to roll her nipples in my fingertips. I watched her face quickly shift from pain to pleasure. She grimaced as I squeezed them especially hard, but then her face relaxed into a smile. Her eyes opened just slightly, and she smiled wider when she saw me watching her.

"I like that," she whispered.

With these words, a heat like fire raced through me, and without pausing, I impulsively leaned forward and slipped one of her nipples into my mouth. Again, she stiffened in surprise. Her hands froze for a moment, and then she was clutching at the back of my head, encouraging me to go on. For months I had been desperate to do this, and I sucked on one nipple, hard, before biting it slightly. Amelia groaned—a sound like nothing I had ever heard from her. Encouraged, I shifted my attentions back and forth between her breasts for the next few moments. I'd wanted to pleasure her in some way since we got together, and being allowed to do it for the first time was one of the most erotic things I'd ever experienced.

Finally, as if no longer able to control herself, Amelia pushed me back against the shower wall, her mouth meeting mine in a brutal kiss. Our breathing was jagged and harsh, both of us so turned on we were shaking all over. Her hands were on my breasts, and mine on hers, and then she was sliding hers down toward my hips. She slid her foot between mine and roughly shoved one of my legs to the side. Obediently, I slid my legs apart, bracing myself on the shower wall behind me, and a moment later, her fingers slid between my legs.

"So wet," she whispered, grinning at me.

I could only nod, dumbly, as her fingers began to explore. She often began this way—gently, teasing me—and it was all I could do not to scream at her to give me what I wanted. I'd learned through extended experience not to rush her, however, as that generally made her go even slower. I stayed rigid as her fingertips brushed my lower lips and parted them, gingerly. She ran a finger up and down, just inside the folds, from my clit to my opening, and I shuddered. I squeezed my eyes shut and bit down on my lip, trying not to say or do anything to extend this wicked torture. Still, she stopped moving, and when I opened my eyes, she wore a devilish grin.

"What would you do if I left you here? Alone?"

I almost sobbed, not sure if she was serious. "I'd die."

Her grin widened, and then her fingers continued to move, slowly, languidly, only briefly touching the places where I wanted her to focus. I moved my hands up to her shoulders, and I couldn't help but relay my desperation as I squeezed them, hard.

"Gently, Chloé, or I'll leave you here to 'die.' " She had the nerve to wink at me, and I couldn't help but almost growl at her. She looked delighted with my anguish and continued her slow gentleness between my legs.

"Amelia, please," I hissed. I shifted my hips a little, hoping to force her to speed up.

She drew her hand back, and this time I did almost scream at her. I managed to muffle my response at the last second, and a kind of strangled mewl came out of my mouth. As if sensing I could wait no longer, she shifted from amused anticipation to something harder, more determined. Her blue eyes seemed to go a shade darker, her pupils widening. Finally, she put her fingers between my legs again, touching, gently, and then they were plunging inside me.

My head whipped back of its own accord, hitting the tile behind me, and my eyes squeezed shut in pleasurable anticipation. The angle was somewhat awkward, but I could move my hips up and down a little to meet her fingers inside me, and the feeling was so incredible I almost melted into her right then. My orgasm began building instantly, and Amelia paused again.

My eyes opened and I looked at her, too incredulous and angry for words.

She smiled again. "Not so fast. Just wait a moment more, darling, and it will be even better."

Again, I knew better than to argue with her, and we both stood there, staring at each other, not moving, eyes locked. Her fingers were still inside me, and I could barely stop myself from shifting to meet them. Despite trying to wait and keeping myself still, the orgasm was building inside of me anyway, and Amelia, finally realizing the futility of holding me back, began to move her fingers again.

My pleasure, as it crested over me, was so vast, so engulfing, I lost all sense of self. I was dimly aware of screaming, of yelling, of throwing back my head again. My eyes were shut and tears leaked from them. Blood was rushing through my head so quickly, it drowned out sound and sense. The pleasure pulsed behind my eyes, and I could hear and see nothing—only feel. At some point my legs unhinged, and Amelia and I were falling down together, onto the tiled floor. The orgasm faded into delicious, sensuous ripples inside me, and she then pulled me into her arms, the cold water of the shower still falling on us from above.

I came back to myself slowly, still trembling all over. I don't know how long we lay there, but for a long while I was incapable of doing anything but staying where we were. I finally began to return to myself when I realized that my back was aching from the hard tile. Also, I was beginning to get cold. I wriggled out of her arms and stood up to turn off the water. She watched me from the floor with hooded eyes. She was still in her panties, but they were so wet from the shower I could see the outline of her sex and some of the dark curls of hair down there.

Despite the fact that we'd been together for months now, I'd only seen her completely naked a few times—when she was going in and out of a shower, for example, never when we were having sex. In general, she liked to leave most or all of her clothes on when we made love, and it was a rare day that I could get her to remove both her shirt and her pants. She'd taken her bra off a couple of times, at my insistence, but only once or twice of her own accord, and she'd never let me touch her breasts before. Today marked significant progress toward achieving my ultimate relationship goal with her: making love with Amelia and not simply receiving it.

"Are you just going to stare at me, or are you going to help me up?" she asked, her mouth fixed in a wry grin.

Realizing I'd been staring, I laughed and reached down to grab her hands, hauling her up. We both slipped a little on the wet tile and laughed, bracing ourselves on the walls to keep from going down again.

"I'm actually cold now," she said, shivering.

I rubbed her arms. "Me, too. Let's dry off and get some clothes on."

We both toweled off and then put on the thick terry-cloth robes provided by the hotel. They were lush and soft, and in no time I was quite cozy. Coziness turned to overly hot fairly quickly, and I replaced my robe with a long T-shirt. Ever the lady, Amelia disappeared into the bathroom for a while, coming back dressed in red-silk lingerie. She looked good enough to eat.

We both went outside to lean against the railing for a while to cool off, watching the waves crash on the beach. Then, after a short, nearly wordless conversation about it, we went back inside to take a nap, lying down as far apart as possible—too hot now to cuddle.

We slept most of the afternoon. A loud gull woke me, and when I opened my eyes, I could tell that a few hours had passed by the light on the ceiling.

Still on the far side of the bed, Amelia had propped herself up on her side to look at me. Her face was still pale and fatigued, but her cheeks were flushed and pink for the first time in weeks. She had a merry twinkle in her eyes I hadn't seen in a long time, either. I didn't know how long she'd been awake and staring at me, and I felt myself blush with pleasure as she continued to stare.

"I'm starving," she said finally, breaking eye contact to yawn.

As if in response, my stomach growled, and we both laughed.

"Did you make a reservation for dinner?"

She shook her head. "I forgot. But I have some options." She sat up and counted off on her fingers as she began her list. "One, we could go to a little place on the beach that does fresh seafood."

"Sold." I made a cutting gesture. "Don't give me any more choices—I'm too hungry to make choices."

She scooted over to the edge of the bed and stood up, her lingerie clinging to her sweaty body. I watched as she shimmied it off and over her head. I couldn't keep my eyes off her naked ass and was still astounded to see her display her body so openly. She went into the bathroom, and I heard the shower turn on.

She reappeared a moment later, grinning at me. "Are you going to join me?"

My heart leapt. Until today, we'd never taken a shower together, and now she was offering it twice in one day—this time completely nude. I rocketed to my feet and raced over to her, and she threw back her head and laughed as I skidded into her arms.

"You're like a kid on Christmas," she said, then lightly kissed my lips.

I kissed her back and drew her naked body toward mine, locking my lips to hers. I continued to kiss her, and when I finally moved back, her pupils were wide beneath her hooded eyes.

"If you keep kissing me, we'll never make it to dinner." Her voice was quiet, serious.

I laughed. "Who needs food?"

By the time we finally made it to the restaurant, the sun was setting over the water. We'd been inside all afternoon, so even the dim light hurt my eyes a little. We were both wearing sunglasses as if to hide hangovers, and the truth was, I was a little hung over. My body ached, my head was woozy, and all I wanted to do was cram food into my mouth. A day of heavy sex does wonderful and terrible things to the human body.

Amelia had chosen all of my clothes for the week, and I was wearing a new cotton skirt, a short-sleeved, button-up shirt, and open sandals. All of these were a dark pink I would never have chosen for myself, but Amelia liked me in the color. She was in solid white, which brought out the pallor of her skin a little too much for my taste, but contrasted nicely with her dark hair. I knew she would look a little less sickly once we both got some sun, and already the afternoon had brought some life back into her eyes.

The seating for the restaurant was directly on the beach under an enormous palm canopy. Each table was raised on a little wooden platform, but we had to trudge through sand to get to ours, leaving my feet grainy and hot. There was a two-for-one drink special, and we both ordered piña coladas. I was surprised when they brought out all four drinks at once, but Amelia seemed game, grabbing both of hers and clutching one in each hand like they were gold. Her silliness was surprising. Generally she struck most people as overly serious with, at best, a dry sense of humor that rarely appeared. I'd seen her playful a few times, but it was usually in the bedroom, not in public. The cause, I realized, was very likely our work. This was, after all, our first extended trip away with no work responsibilities to speak of. Amelia hadn't mentioned a recent vacation when we'd first met, so she and I were both in desperate need of a few days off. Part of the reason we'd worked so hard the last three weeks was to make time for this trip, and now we finally got to receive dividends.

The restaurant was crowded at this hour. The waiter explained that all of the beach-front restaurants and bars were full around this time, everyone wanting to watch the heartbreakingly beautiful sunsets over the ocean. We were given a table toward the middle of the seating area, but we could still see the water. We both moved our chairs around to face the view, sitting elbow-to-elbow. After we ordered, I stared out at the waves, mesmerized. Going to the beach was not something my Aunt Kate enjoyed, so I'd rarely gone as a child despite its close proximity to New Orleans. School and internships had kept me busy for the last ten years, leaving little time for vacations beyond visiting family. The fact that I was here in this beautiful place with a woman I loved was entirely novel. I looked over at Amelia to share this insight with her and found her gazing at me, a dreamy expression on her face.

I couldn't help but blush and look away. Here we were, in one of the most beautiful spots on earth, and she would rather look at me than the scenery. Her attention was unnerving and deeply flattering.

She took my hand and kissed it, sending chills up and down my back. I glanced around surreptitiously, a little worried about a public display like this, but was pleased to note that we were surrounded almost entirely by gay and lesbian couples. Another thing I noticed was that, though the majority of the people eating here were also Americans, at least three couples looked like locals. I'd read that Puerto Vallarta was also a getaway for local gay travelers and was pleased to see that this was true.

I leaned close to her ear. "So is this gay paradise?"

She looked around and then smiled at me. "It seems so."

Our food arrived a moment later, and I had some of the best fish tacos I'd ever eaten. After I gushed about the food to our waiter, he told us that their fish was caught daily, and I believed him. Amelia was eating with quick relish, her usual casual gracefulness at the table discarded because of her hunger.

Finished with dinner, we both sat back to stare at the water a while longer, and our bill was delivered after we finished our cocktails.

After a long, peaceful spell of quiet contemplation, she sat back and motioned to the waiter with the money for the check and then looked back at me. "I want you. Now. In bed with me."

A new flush of excitement rolled through me. I swallowed hard and nodded in perfect agreement.

CHAPTER SIX

We made it back to the hotel as quickly as we could, the two of us speed-walking the whole way. The elevator was slow, so we raced up the stairs together, hands clutched, giggling like girls. Amelia fiddled with the key for a while and then flung the door open for us, pulling me in behind and putting the *No Molestar* sign on the outside of the door before closing and locking it. Then she turned toward me, grinning.

I leaped at her, and my quickness caught her off guard. I kissed her like she'd kissed me earlier, hard and brutally. She seemed too surprised to stop me and let me control her through my mouth. I pushed her into the wall behind her and heard her back slap the hard surface. Moving my lips from hers, I trailed downward onto her neck, feeling her racing heartbeat in her pulse. Her breathing was ragged and harsh, and her clear excitement made me feel powerful and sexy. She let me continue to kiss and suck on her neck for a moment, and I risked reaching up under her shirt to touch her breasts again. I was used to her resisting this move, but now, for the second time in one day, she let me touch them. Her nipples were hard under her bra, and when I touched them, she groaned with something like true yearning.

This went on for a long moment until, as if she couldn't stand it anymore, Amelia seemed to wake out of her pleasured daze. Before I knew it, she was pushing back with her mouth and hands, maneuvering me farther into the bedroom. My legs hit the edge of the bed behind me, and then we were falling, Amelia on top of me and between my legs. We made out for several minutes, pausing to fling off various pieces of clothing, until I was naked and she was down to her underwear.

Having so much of her skin against mine was different and extremely distracting. I wanted to stop her and kiss every inch of her.

Her kisses were starting to hurt, but it was exactly the kind of pain I like—mixed with pleasure. Because of Amelia, I'd finally begun to explore some of my own, long-suppressed sexual cravings, chief of which was rough sex. We'd experimented off and on with another one of my secret cravings, some elements of S&M. Our S&M, however, had no rigid rules and wasn't implemented every time we made love. I simply liked to be teased to distraction, tied up, and spanked. We'd talked about going a bit further than the riding crop we occasionally used, but I was leaving that up to Amelia. Often, we were so overcome with desire, we didn't have time to put many of the props we owned into our foreplay.

Today, however, Amelia was clearly in the mood for something a little different. After kissing me long enough to make my lips feel bruised and hot, she sat up and then got out of bed, walking toward her suitcase. I knew without speaking about it that she was getting something to use on me, and I took the opportunity to climb farther onto the bed, away from the edge. She turned around, holding two pairs of metal handcuffs, a set of metal ankle shackles, and something black and plastic. We'd used scarves and silks to tie me up before, but never anything so rough and menacing. I couldn't help but flush dark with desire. I gave Amelia a slight nod to let her know I approved, and she walked toward me, slowly, her expression sly and mischievous.

She reached the foot of the bed and held out one of her hands, and I lifted one foot obediently. She locked my foot into one of the shackles, and the chill of the metal on my skin intoxicated me. A moment later she held her hand out for the other foot, and I raised it for her. She locked my other ankle in the second bracket, and my feet were very effectively locked together. I could spread my legs a little—slightly more than shoulder width, but no farther. The metal, unlike the silks we normally used, had absolutely no give, and the idea that my legs were locked in place was so exciting, my skin prickled with heat.

"You like that?" Amelia asked me, one eyebrow raised.

I could only nod.

"Good. I'm going to fasten the chain between your ankles to the bed. You won't be able to move. Is that okay?"

Again, I nodded.

Ankles chained together and to the bed, I was effectively pinned from the waist down. I could still twist and move my upper body, but not for long. A moment later, Amelia was slapping the handcuffs on my wrists, attaching them to the bedframe behind me. Completely chained up, I could hardly move anything except my torso.

Finally, she held up the last thing: a pair of darkened goggles. She pointed at the lenses. "These will make it impossible for you to see." She pointed at the sides, which had two thick pieces of cloth along the earpieces. "And these will make it hard for you to hear."

She waited again for me to nod and then slipped the goggles on over my head. The world went dark and quiet. I could still sort of hear her moving around. I wasn't completely deafened, but like she said, I couldn't see a single thing. Immobilized, blind, and deaf, I was at her mercy.

She made me wait a very long time—or at least what felt like a very long time. I didn't like to be gagged, and she liked to be able to hear my excitement, so my mouth was free, but I wasn't supposed to talk or ask questions. If I did, she would simply extend my torture, and I was already so worked up, I was on the verge of a spontaneous orgasm. I needed her hands on me, and I needed them soon, or I was going to lose it.

Something cold and thin touched my leg. Unable to see it, I had to guess, and after a moment or two, I surmised that it was our riding crop. I hadn't realized she'd brought it. My heart, already racing, began to pound, my excitement somehow rising despite its already ridiculous heights. A moment later the riding crop was slapping my upper leg. The pain sent a jolt through me, and I couldn't help but gasp and twist in my bindings. Nothing happened for a moment longer, and when she slapped my other leg, I let out a little shriek of painful pleasure. Part of what made this situation so delicious was not knowing what was coming. We'd used blindfolds before, but the device she'd put on me today was much, much better—I couldn't see a thing.

I was gasping now, the air whistling in and out of my lungs, and she left me there for a long time, my frustration building with each passing second. Finally, just when I thought I'd have to start begging her to touch me, her weight shifted to the foot of the bed as she climbed up onto it. She kept her hands on either side of me, an inch or two from my skin, as she crawled up the bed on her hands and knees. I could feel her breath on my face when she finally got there, but she wasn't actually touching or kissing me. She must have been holding herself above me with her arms and legs. We stayed that way for a long time, me gasping and her completely silent. I knew she was there, but I didn't know what she was doing. I was tired of waiting, and I had to bite my lip to keep from begging her to do something, anything. She would drag this sweet torture out if I said anything, though. Nevertheless, a high, shaky groan started to come out of my mouth, and I felt rather than saw Amelia react.

Her weight came down on me as she sat astraddle one of my legs. She put her hands on my stomach, just resting them there, and I squirmed under her, trying to get her to do more. She pinched my nipples in response, and I stilled. That was her warning. If I didn't let her do what she wanted, she would stop completely. I made myself go still and took a long, shaking breath. Whatever she had in store for me would be better than anything she would do if I rushed her.

Finally, as if hearing my silent assent, she began to trace her fingers up and down the skin on my chest and breasts. She would pause, playing absently with my nipples, and then continue, as if she didn't know how good it felt for her to touch them. At last, she pulled one of my nipples into her mouth, and I let out a long, satisfied sigh, relaxing a little. She moved back and forth between them, slowly, languidly, for several long moments, and once again, my tension started to ratchet up. I wanted what she was giving me, but her kisses made me want more, and the longer she took, the more desperate I became.

Her mouth busy with my nipples, but she finally began to trace her hand up and down my upper thigh. She was still sitting on top of my right thigh, so her touches remained exclusive to the left. I spread my left leg a little more to the side, my right pinned, but I could hardly move it because of my ankle shackles. Amelia's fingers stilled on my thigh, and then, becoming impatient, she finally touched me between my legs.

I couldn't help it—I shrieked. I also writhed, hard, and almost bucked Amelia right off me. I could move only my torso easily, so I arched my back, wrenching against my restraints with all my strength. The feeling of being nearly immobilized and the cold sharp bite of the metal on my skin only added to my excitement. I was so overwrought, I knew I wouldn't last long.

I didn't. Seconds after she began to touch me, an orgasm rose from inside me. I could no sooner have stopped it from coming than stopped breathing. Amelia could apparently sense it from the tension in my body. She hesitated for a second and then, as if recognizing the futility of stopping me, sank all of her fingers deep inside me. As much as my restraints would allow, I rose to meet her hand, thrashing around as much as I could as my orgasm built.

The next twenty seconds were lost in a haze of pain and pleasure as I came. I was screaming myself hoarse, so overcome that it never occurred to me that someone might hear me. I struggled and bucked under Amelia and jerked at the chains fastening me hard enough to make the bed creak in protest.

Just as the first wave of pleasure began to wane, something almost stopped me cold. Amelia still had her fingers inside me, but her hand had gone completely still. Instead, she was writhing against my leg as I thrashed around beneath her. She'd been sitting astraddle my thigh this entire time, her body weight almost like another restraint, and now she was rubbing on my leg. She'd clearly lost sense of what she'd been doing—her hand was completely still within me. Instead, she was focused on riding my thigh. In only her damp panties, her sex on my leg felt hot and wet beneath the fabric. This went on for a while, and she pushed down harder and harder. I would have given anything to see her face right then.

Suddenly, as if realizing what she was doing, she stopped completely, stilling on my leg. A moment later, her hand continued to move inside me, and, turned on by feeling her on me, a brief, light shudder passed through me as I had a final, shallow orgasm.

She climbed off me a few seconds later, and we lay there together, her head on my stomach as we caught our breath. What was she thinking about? Was she, as it seemed a few moments ago, as turned on as she'd felt riding me? A moment later, she was scooting away, and I waited patiently for her to return and release me. She unlocked my handcuffs first, then my ankles. I pulled off the goggles to smile at her, but she was distracted and her face was troubled. Then, sensing my gaze, she met my eyes and smiled back.

We rested for a while, lying on the bed as far away from each other as possible again. I was so hot, sweat was pooling on my stomach. I was aware of the heat, of my sweat, of my exhaustion, but most of me was basking in the memory of Amelia's excitement. I'd felt her pleasure before she seemed to realize what she was doing. I had to find a way to capitalize on the moment. She had slipped and enjoyed herself for the first time since we'd been together. This vacation, with all the time we'd get to spend together, might give us an opportunity to experiment and push her boundaries a little more.

I knew better than to talk about or even allude to what had just happened, however, as she would undoubtedly shy away from the conversation and become uncomfortable. Strong and stoic as she almost always was, she didn't like to discuss her sexual problems, and this was the last place on earth I wanted to make her uncomfortable. Something about being here on our own was seeming to make her body insist on what it wanted: me. Now it was just a matter of waiting to let her desire defeat whatever was stopping her from taking what she craved.

Amelia crashed hard and fast—falling asleep earlier than I did for one of the first times since I'd known her. As I watched her sleep, I knew she must have been faking most of her vigor earlier. I knew then that I should have insisted on staying in today and resting. Still, her face was clear and peaceful for the first time in weeks.

Back in New Orleans, on the rare occasion when I woke up earlier or stayed up later than she did, her face was clouded with anxiety and worry, even as she slept. It often seemed as if running her business was a bit much for her. She could easily delegate a lot of the tasks she took on to me or to other employees, but she seemed to want to do just about everything herself. I knew she was passionate about the Winters Corporation, but I'd never stopped to wonder before if she actually liked running it. She was very, very good at what she did, but it was too much work for one person. Imagining her slowing down, keeping normal hours, and sleeping every night like this made me a little sad, as I knew she would never do it. With Amelia, it was all or nothing.

We both slept very late the next day, and after a quick shower and a ridiculously delicious room-service breakfast, we both donned clean clothes and headed out to explore and shop. After the third or fourth boutique, I realized that Amelia was dead-set on buying me anything that even momentarily caught my interest. The storekeepers were delighted with her, but I found the extravagance tiresome, to say the least. To me, it's one thing to buy things that you truly like, but even if you have more than enough money to buy anything, it doesn't make sense to me to shop for its own sake. After the fifth store, Amelia began to sense my growing impatience, and I saw her put her credit card away with some reluctance. In the same way that I had problems accepting her largesse, she had problems keeping it to herself. All I could think about that morning and afternoon, however, were the late nights, early mornings, and anxious days it took for her to earn her money. I would rather have a happy, considerably less-wealthy girlfriend than a burned-out zombie.

Amelia had all of our purchases shipped home or sent back to our hotel, so we walked unencumbered up and down every street in the Old Town. Having never taken this kind of trip with her, I was surprised to see that Amelia was the kind of person who needed to take a picture of nearly everything and everyone she saw. I'd seen some of her photography before and knew she had talent for it, but I'd never anticipated that she was such an enthusiastic photographer. She took my picture several times until I objected, but I'm pretty sure she still managed to snap a few candid photos of me.

Eventually, we crossed onto the cute little island in the middle of the Río Cuale, famous for its art galleries. I could see Amelia struggling to simply look at the art rather than buy it all, but she knew the rules about this trip—no work or work talk allowed. I knew I would have to relent eventually, as some of the art we viewed was spectacular and just the kind of thing some of our clients would love. But for now, we were simply tourists, and I wanted to keep it that way a while longer.

We had a light lunch in a café by Nuestra Señora de Guadalupe, the large cathedral just beyond the river from our hotel. After lunch, we toured the cathedral, and I was surprised to see it decked out for Mardi Gras, much like St. Louis Cathedral in New Orleans this time of year. After I saw the decorations in the cathedral, I realized there were decorations all over Old Town. I'd simply overlooked them. It seemed that our attempt to escape Mardi Gras season would be a failure after all. Speaking in fluent Spanish, Amelia learned from a group of locals that the holiday, while a smaller celebration in comparison to the one in New Orleans, was still quite lavish. There were a few balls and a parade with throws, just like at home. Amelia and I laughed to think we wouldn't have to go a whole Mardi Gras season without plastic beads.

We'd intended to go to the beach before our Valentine's Day dinner, but by the time we headed back to the hotel, both of us were too exhausted and overheated to change and sit in the sun, beach umbrella or no beach umbrella. Instead, I ordered a carafe of iced coffee sent to our room and took my book out onto the balcony, appreciating a few hours of quiet nothing ahead of us. Amelia joined me a while later and promptly fell asleep again. For once, instead of her usual uptight, refined persona, she was a graceless, limp thing next to me, her mouth open and her hair unkempt. I loved it. It was like seeing a new person.

After a while, I dozed off, rising only when I heard the shower running inside the room. A little thrill of mischief and excitement raced through me at the sound. Yesterday, Amelia had joined me in the shower and then invited me in. Today, I decided to risk joining her without asking her permission. I'd never done that—had never even conceived of it—but after yesterday, it seemed like a risk worth taking. I shucked off my sweaty clothes and crept as quietly as I could to the bathroom, wanting to watch her for a moment before coming in. The door to the bathroom was partially closed, as if it hadn't quite latched, but I didn't know if that meant that Amelia had closed it to prevent me from coming in or if she'd closed it to keep the sound of the shower from waking me. I pushed it open as silently as I could and peered inside.

Amelia would likely have seen me if she'd been looking, but her eyes were sealed shut. She'd left the lights off, but plenty of sunlight was streaming in through the skylight in the middle of the room. I could see everything. Her chin was tilted upward, head thrown back, and water coursed down her tight, lithe body. She was biting her lip and her face was flushed. Her left hand clutched her breast, and I saw her squeeze and twist her own nipple. Her right hand was between her legs. She was sliding her fingers in and out of herself, pausing and teasing her body before speeding up again, only to stop once more to build tension. Eventually, her body simply wouldn't let her stop. She threw her head back farther, and her hand sped up, faster and faster. She came quickly, silently, her body hitching and shuddering, her face contorted in pleasure.

Her hands finally dropped, and a few seconds later her eyes flickered open. Vision blurred with her orgasm; it seemed to take her a moment to realize who I was, and she blinked at me, still stupefied. Seconds later, I saw her realize what I had just witnessed, and her whole body actually seemed to flinch. Her face crumpled and she burst into tears, turning away from me and covering her face with her hands.

I didn't hesitate. I rushed into the shower with her and embraced her from behind. A moment later she turned and grabbed me, burying her face in my neck. The strength of her arms bespoke a clear sense of desperation, as if she clung to me for life. All I could do was hold her, running my hands up and down her back. I spoke some quiet nothings in her ear as she cried, but for the most part, I was reeling. I'd never seen Amelia so upset or so vulnerable. She held me so tight, I think she was afraid she might fall apart.

We stayed under the water long enough for it to start to turn cold, and, Amelia's arms now a little looser, I reached back behind her and turned it off. The sudden silence seemed to jolt her, and she pulled away from me and covered her face once more with her hands. She was racked with quiet sobs, and I rubbed her shoulders. Finally, she took several snuffling, deep breaths and let her hands drop. She still wouldn't meet my eyes, however, and she kept her face lowered.

"Let's get out of here," I said, grabbing one of her hands.

She followed me without comment, clearly too deflated to resist. I handed her a bathrobe and grabbed one for myself, then led her over to the little divan in the corner of the bedroom. Her gaze was rooted to the floor, and silent tears dripped from her eyes. I knew that I needed to wait—that pushing her would ruin whatever was about to happen. I grabbed one of her hands and held it in mine. We sat that way for a long time.

Finally, she took a shuddering breath and let it out. Her eyes flickered up to mine, and then she looked away from me. Then, in a voice so quiet and defeated it was barely audible, she said, "I'm so sorry, Chloé."

This whole time, her face had a strange expression, and with these words, I finally recognized the expression as guilty shame. I grabbed her chin, forcing her to look at me. "There's nothing to be sorry about, Amelia."

The flicker of hope in her eyes was replaced a moment later, again with doubt and guilt. She'd glanced away again, and once more I moved her face to make her look at me.

"Damn it, Amelia. Listen to me." She looked surprised at the anger in my tone, but she finally met my gaze and held it. "You have nothing to be sorry about. I swear to God."

She burst into tears again and launched herself into my arms. The tears passed a little faster than before, and when she pulled back, she seemed quieter and more relaxed. She was still having trouble meeting my eyes, but she was doing so more often. She seemed to be looking at me to see if I was being honest, so I tried to smile with every bit of reassurance I had. Tears were still falling from her eyes, but she reached up to wipe them away.

"You're so good to me, Chloé. I don't know what I did to deserve you."

I laughed. "What you did to deserve *me*? I don't know what I did to deserve *you*."

She looked troubled, and that worried line she had almost all the time appeared between her eyes. She looked up at me and met my eyes firmly for the first time since this conversation began. "You deserve better. I'm hoarding you for myself when you could be so much happier with someone else."

It was hard not to laugh again, but I could see that she was deadly serious. I took both of her hands in mine and met her eyes. "Amelia, I've never been happier in my life. I couldn't be happier."

Worried doubt and guilt passed across her face once more, and I touched it with my fingers. "I love you, Amelia. Don't you see? When you love someone, you accept them. You don't have to be perfect, and I don't expect you to be. I love you for you."

Her face crumpled again, but she shook her head as if to clear away the tears. She seemed deep in thought, and I let her absorb my words without saying anything more. I wanted her to hear them and believe them, and nothing more I said would help.

Finally, she sighed and gazed at me again. "I love you too, Chloé. And I'm sorry I'm so fucked up. I don't know why I did what I did. In the shower, I mean. And I don't know why I won't let you touch me that way. I wish I knew."

We had finally come to it, and my heart skipped a little with anxiety. We never talked about this. We'd fought about her reluctance to be touched a couple of times when we were first together, but we'd both dropped it since then. I think she was relieved not to discuss it, and I didn't want to cause another fight by forcing her to confront whatever it was. I'd been pushing, very gently, for months now, when we made love, but I never brought it up anymore. I realized now that something like this scene had been building for a while now. I cursed my own previous cowardice, recognizing that we should have been talking about it all along. Problems don't go away just because you refuse to face them. In fact, they fester.

Whatever I said next would be important, so I took a deep breath before beginning. "Amelia, you don't owe me anything. Your body is *your* body, understand? Of course I'd love to make you feel the way you make me feel—I want that very badly. But it might be my own selfishness, my own vanity that wants it. When you're ready to share yourself with me, I'll be over the moon. But it's *your* body—not mine."

We were quiet again, and I could see her weighing my words, testing them for sincerity and looking for flaws. She was staring at her hands again, but I wanted to let her talk in whatever way she needed to, so I didn't force her gaze.

"I almost never do that, you know," Amelia said, so quiet I almost didn't hear her.

"Do what?"

She looked up at me again and quickly glanced away, her face clouded with shame again.

"I almost never touch myself like that," she said, her voice a little firmer. Her expression was dark, almost livid, and I realized she was angry with herself for what she'd done.

"I wish you would, Amelia, if you want to. You should do whatever you want with your own body."

Her tears passed more quickly this time, but they were ferocious. Once again, Amelia clung to me, but I knew this time it was from relief. After she pulled away, I brushed her tears aside with my thumbs, and then we kissed, long and gently. We were quiet after that, both of us thinking our own thoughts, processing a momentous experience. The tension, however, was beginning to get to me, and I wanted to lighten the mood.

"I touch myself all the time," I told her.

She looked up at me, clearly shocked. "You do?"

"Of course! Especially when we're not together. You should have seen me when you were in Montreal. I could barely keep my hands off myself. I actually strained my wrist at one point."

Her laughter was genuine: warm and infectious. We giggled together, and my heart lifted at the sight of her joy. The tension was gone now, and we'd said what needed to be said. We could move on from here and progress—I knew it.

She wiped a couple of tears from her eyes and then paused, raising one eyebrow. "Wait a minute. You said you did it *especially* when we're not together. Does that mean—?"

"That I do it when we are together? Of course!"

She barked a laugh. "When? Where?"

I paused, wondering how truthful to be. She saw my reluctance and grinned widely before shaking a finger at me. "Hey—no cheating! You brought it up, Chloé. Tell me everything."

I held up a hand and started counting. "Well, just recently, I did it in the office at work."

"No!"

I nodded and held up more fingers. "I do it a lot when I'm waiting for you in the car. Or if you're on a phone call at my place. Or if you're in the shower, or making breakfast, or anywhere in the house when I can't get at you."

"Really?" she asked, looking doubtful. "You really do it so often?"

I grinned. "All the time."

Her expression darkened. "Don't I, I mean don't you get enough from—"

Realizing where she was going, I held up my hands. "I get plenty from you, Amelia. That has nothing to do with it. You satisfy me in every way. I could never do what you do to me, even if I tried."

"So why?"

She was clearly still doubtful, so I chose my next words with care. "I do it because I want to. I do it because it makes me feel naughty— dirty in a good way. It excites me to sneak around a little. A few times you almost caught me. Just recently, I was sure you knew what I was doing when you came to bed after me, but you never said anything."

"I didn't know at all."

"Good," I said. "I like that."

She still looked confused, so I tried to think of a way to make it clearer. "I do it, Amelia, because I can and I want to. There's nothing wrong with it, and it feels good. It gives me pleasure, and pleasure is too rare in this world to deny myself."

I let her mull that over for a while, and I could see that she was beginning to accept my words on faith. Her expression was clearer now, her tears dry.

Finally, she looked at me, grinning. "Can I watch you sometime?"

I grinned back. "Of course. You can watch me right now, if you want to."

Her grin widened and she nodded. Rather than moving to the bed, I opened my robe right there on the little couch. She was surprised but pleased, and she leaned forward a little as if watching something interesting on television. The experience was novel for me, too, and I found it incredibly sexy.

My excitement was there, instantly, with her eyes on me. When I snaked my fingers down between my legs, I was wet and hot. Amelia was staring at my hand, not my eyes, but I wanted to see her watching me, so I kept my eyes open. I moved my other hand between my legs, one set of fingers going in and out of me, the other toying with my clit. Amelia's eyes were dark and hungry, and seeing her excitement made my own increase exponentially. I was slipping over the edge quickly, my breath coming faster and faster, almost in gasps, and I saw Amelia's eyes flicker up to mine and then back down between my legs, almost as if she couldn't help but look. I pushed my fingers inside a little deeper and couldn't suppress a groan. At that sound, my insides began to quiver against my fingers, and I sped up the pressure on my clit as I came. My eyes closed of their own accord, the blood rushing through my head in a roar. Finally, I could hear myself moaning, and the pleasure between my legs turned to painful intensity. I stopped and opened my eyes, dropping my hands to my sides in exhaustion.

Amelia was flushed pink, her lips parted. Her pupils were dilated, and she was breathing heavily. Her robe had come open a little, and I could see one of her breasts, the nipple puckered with excitement. I leaned forward and kissed her, and her hands were on me instantly, exploring my breasts with her nimble fingers. We continued to kiss as she fondled me, her mouth hot on mine.

Finally, almost as if we were afraid of taking things too far, we both pulled away from each other, panting. I was trembling all over, a dull, aching pain between my legs. I knew it was too soon to ask her to touch me again—it would be painful for a while yet—but that didn't stop me from wanting her with a deep, yearning hunger. We stared at each other, and her eyes seemed to mirror my longing.

"Jesus, Chloé," she finally said. "That was the most erotic thing I've ever seen."

I smiled. "I'm glad you liked it."

"'Liked it' doesn't begin to describe how much I enjoyed watching you. It was everything I could do not to jump in and take over. I had to sit on my hands there at the end to stop myself."

"Well, maybe next time I'll let you play, too. If you're good."

By mutual, unspoken agreement, we got up off the couch simply to gain a little distance from each other. I was still quaking with desire and knew I wouldn't be able to stop myself if we sat close for much longer, pain or no pain. Amelia seemed to be having a similar experience, as she went directly to the balcony a moment later.

I decided to take a quick, cold shower, and when I came back out into the room, Amelia was still on the balcony, leaning on her elbows and looking out at the sea. She must have heard me enter the bedroom, but she didn't turn around. I decided to let her alone for a while until she was ready to come in on her own or call me to her. She stayed out there a long time, quietly meditating, and didn't join me until I was already dozing in bed. She seemed at peace with herself, from what I could tell, but we didn't talk about what had happened.

In the end, we decided to stay in for dinner instead of go out again, ordering fried food and cheesecake delivered to our room. It was the best Valentine's Day I'd ever had.

CHAPTER SEVEN

The rest of the trip was relaxing and less emotional. We slept in every day, ate a lot of great food, had a lot of sex. We spent most of the trip in our hotel room, but we made an effort to leave a couple of times a day to eat or sit on the beach. By Monday, Amelia was starting to look like herself again. Her complexion became a natural pale pink again instead of the greenish gray it'd been for the last month. She was absolutely rigid in her use of sunscreen and insisted I wear a heavy SPF as well, but we both managed to get a little color anyway. My usual summertime freckles appeared, but Amelia thought they were darling and insisted on kissing every one of them she could find.

On Wednesday, I finally let her do a little reconnaissance work at the local galleries for her business, but only with the promise that she would spend a single morning working. She followed the letter of the law, if not the spirit, by getting up before dawn and heading out before I'd even woken. She was back at exactly noon, and I gathered from her enthusiasm that she'd basically bought everything in town. She was already planning an art show with the work she'd gathered and thinking about how to bring some of the artists to New Orleans for it.

I interrupted her after listening to her gush for half an hour. "Hey, hon—I realize you're excited, but this counts as work, you know, and I gave you only the morning. We'll be back soon enough."

She sighed. "Tomorrow."

I sighed, too. "Tomorrow."

It wasn't that I was dreading going home, precisely—I enjoyed my job with Amelia for the most part. Also, Amelia had already given me the rest of the week off. We flew back tomorrow, Thursday, and then

I had three days to recover after the trip before returning on Monday. So it wasn't work that I dreaded; rather, it was difficult to share Amelia with her job. It consumed her so wholly. It seemed like I'd spent more time with her in the last few days than we'd spent as a couple during the last three months. And it wasn't as if I could ask her to go in fewer hours. Her passion for her job devoured her life. I knew, however, that I should begin to exert some small amount of pressure to get her to stop working herself into literal illness, as she had before this trip. It wasn't good for her or us. I promised myself that if I saw her get that way again, I'd try to get her to put the brakes on and take it a little easier.

The cold snap was still in effect in New Orleans when we landed. The skies were heavy with rain, and the fog was dense and chilly. Amelia dropped me off at my apartment, and we spent a significant amount of time saying good-bye to each other on my front porch. She had a lot of paperwork to go over before heading in to the office tomorrow, and she wanted the evening to get started. She'd given me an extra day off, but she herself couldn't afford to let things slide through the weekend.

"You should stay here with me," I told her, kissing the end of her nose. "Screw work. Screw everything and stay here with me forever. Better yet—let's go back to Puerto Vallarta."

She laughed, but I could already see the tension creeping back into her face. She'd been quiet on the plane, likely planning all the things she needed to do once we were home, and now it was clear her thoughts were already at the office.

I sighed and relented. "Okay, Amelia, you can leave me. But promise you'll call me tomorrow. I'll even stay at your place if it means actually seeing you."

"You'll make that sacrifice? For me?" She batted her eyelashes.

I laughed and pushed her arm. "Well, go on then. You clearly want to leave."

"It's not that I *want* to, Chloé. I have to."

"It's okay."

She didn't seem to hear the defeat in my voice as she kissed me one more time and dashed away, trotting back to her car. I unlocked my door and picked up my little suitcase, dropping it just inside the door. My face was chilled from the exposure to the bitter cold, and my apartment didn't feel much warmer. I turned up the heat and then went in search of my phone. I'd given the number of the hotel to my Aunt

Kate in case of emergencies, but I'd left my cell phone at home and made Amelia do the same thing. When I turned it on, I found several messages.

The first was from my friend Meghan. "Hey, chica, it's me. Just got back from my tour. Give me a call."

The next was also from her. "Hey, lady, it's me again. I just bumped into your aunt and she told me you were on a trip. Give me a call when you get back. I want to hear all about your wacky sex-capades."

The third message was from my Aunt Kate. "Hey, honey, it's Aunt Kate." I grinned at this. She always spoke on the phone as if I could mistake her voice for anyone else's. "I just wanted to see if we could have dinner this weekend—Friday, Saturday, or Sunday, whatever works for you. Me and Jim are wide open. It's been ages since I saw you, and I want to hear all about your trip. We could invite Meghan and her Zach, too, if you like." Finally, she added, "And Amelia, of course."

While things were better between my aunt and Amelia, they weren't altogether easy, either. Amelia had managed to mend some fences when she'd gotten my aunt involved with a big surprise for me—my new apartment—but one would still hardly call the rapport between them friendly. Aunt Kate was still a little leery of her for some reason. I'd tried broaching the topic a few times to see if I could figure out what bothered her, but I'd gotten nowhere. I could only hope that her usual warmth and friendliness would win out in the end.

"Anyway," she said, "call me when you can."

The next message was from my friend Lana in New York. Lana and I did our doctorates together in France, and while we'd been friendly when we lived there, we'd recently become much closer. She'd become something like my go-to guide for all things lesbian, as she was engaged to a woman herself.

"Oh my God, pick up the phone! I have something amazing to tell you."

I could see that her next message was only a couple of hours after the first. "Seriously, Chloé, call me back immediately. You are not going to believe who I just met, and what I just did for you."

And a few hours later: "Where are you, lady? Do I need to contact the Louisiana National Guard? Was there a hurricane down there I didn't hear about? Are you dead in a ditch? Call me. Now."

I couldn't suppress a stab of guilt. Somehow I'd neglected to tell

Lana I'd be out of town. All of her messages were from at least two days ago.

The next sounded even more frantic. "I seriously just talked with the morgue down there, Chloé. Where the hell are you?"

And the next: "Do I need to fly down there and start looking in the river for bodies? What is going on? Does Amelia have you locked up in some kind of sex dungeon?" She paused. "Maybe you'd like that, you saucy minx."

She was calmer in the next message. "Thinking about Amelia got me thinking about her business down there, and so I dialed the main office. Apparently you two are on some kind of romantic sex getaway until Thursday. I'm glad to know you're alive and having orgasms somewhere hot and tropical, Chloé, but for the love of God, please phone me the second you hear this message. You'll never believe the news I have for you."

Lana's messages were the most insistent, so I called her first. She picked up on the first ring. "Oh my God, you're finally home."

I laughed. "I literally just walked in the door. I called you first, since you sounded like you're ready to piss yourself."

"I am ready to piss myself, and you will be too once you hear this news. Are you sitting down?"

"Would you just tell me, for Christ's sake?"

"Okay, okay. Are you ready?"

"Jesus, yes! Just tell me!"

"Okay. How would you like to be the new assistant professor of art history at New Orleans State University?"

"What?" I shouted. "What are you telling me right now?"

She laughed. "Listen up. I've been running these workshops here at MOMA for educators. I told you about them."

"Yes."

"Anyway, last week I met this guy from down there, and we started talking. It turns out that he's the new dean of arts and sciences at New Orleans State. His name is Christophe Montmartre. He used to be the chair of art history, and now that he's moved up the administrative chain, there's an opening in his old department. He wants to meet you. Immediately."

I was sitting now, my legs having turned to jelly. "Holy shit, Lana. I can't believe you did this for me."

"I know! I'm the best."

I couldn't even laugh at that, as it was true. Working for a university was my absolute dream job, and she knew it. I'd been educated and trained to be a professor. I'd moved back to New Orleans knowing I would have to sacrifice that dream for a long time, perhaps permanently, and now it seemed like it might happen after all. The idea that I could stay in New Orleans and still achieve my ambition was hard to believe.

"Hey," Lana said, "are you still there?"

"Yes," I said quietly. "Lana, do you know what this means? Do you know what you've done for me?"

"I do, Chloé. I do. And I'm glad I could help, even in this small way. You can't keep working as Amelia's lackey forever."

The thought of Amelia immediately dampened some of my excitement. She would, no doubt, be excited for me—she knew how much I wanted to become a professor. She'd even promised to help make it happen at one of the private colleges in town. But we both thought it would be years from now, if ever. Even with her family's influence, we needed to wait until a position opened, and that meant waiting for someone to retire or die. Still, Amelia liked working with me and would likely be disappointed.

"Anyway," Lana went on, "it's not quite a sure thing. You still have to be interviewed, but I think you can get your hopes up more than a little. He seemed very interested to meet you and was excited to hear that you're from town. You need to contact him and set up an interview, and then he said something about a teaching demonstration. He'll give you the details when you call."

I took down his information on a notepad with a shaky hand, so flabbergasted I had to have her repeat the number several times. She didn't give me a hard time about it, seeming to understand how important this chance was for me.

Once off the phone, I contemplated calling Amelia immediately but decided that it wouldn't hurt to wait a little while longer. After all, it wasn't as if I'd been offered the job. I had a momentary pang of guilt hiding it from her, but on the other hand, I didn't want to tell her about a job offer if it came to nothing—that seemed cruel, somehow. Hands still shaking, I took a deep breath and dialed Christophe Montmartre. It took a while to get through the various levels of administrative assistants, but he was apparently expecting me, as they passed it along until he answered the phone. His words were heavily accented, and we switched to French immediately after greeting each other in English.

"Your French is beautiful, Dr. Deveraux," he told me.

"Thank you, sir." I shivered a little with suppressed joy and excitement. It's always a good move to impress the person who's going to interview you.

"I am so glad you called. When I met your friend in New York, I could hardly believe all of the lovely things she told me about you. I hope you don't mind, but I already did a little digging just to make sure she wasn't overstating your case, and I'm pleased to tell you that she wasn't. In fact, judging from the information I found, she was, if anything, underselling your qualifications. But that's a good thing. I like to be surprised. I read your article on *Nouveau Réalisme* this morning and enjoyed it immensely."

I was floored. Already, this phone call suggested that he was serious about my candidacy, as it would take a bit of work to find my article, let alone all the information about my education and background.

"When can you come see our little department in person?" he asked. "Is tomorrow too soon? Or we could do Monday. I understand from your friend Lana that you're just back from a trip, so perhaps you still need some time to recover."

"Tomorrow is perfect," I said, almost interrupting him in my haste and excitement.

"Excellent. Most of the department is still off for Mardi Gras, but all of us in administration are here today and tomorrow. I'll call in some of the other professors to meet you as well. No rest for the wicked."

My heart sped up with anxiety. "What can I expect?"

"Tomorrow? Just a couple of quick meetings—two, three hours tops—with me and some of the art-history professors, and possibly the provost. If we decide to move on from there, we'll set up a teaching demonstration next week when the students are back from break."

We agreed on a time the next day and hung up. My whole body was still thrumming with excitement and joy, but once again, I decided to put off telling Amelia. It seemed premature, somehow. I could share my news after the interview.

I called Meghan next.

"Hey, bitch," she said. "What's up?"

"Not much, cunt." Meghan and I always talked to each other like this on the phone—a habit from high school that drove my aunt crazy when she was around to hear us. "Actually, that's not true. I have some big news."

Meghan was silent, waiting for me to say something. This was confusing, as she would normally ask me a million questions about anything. "Aren't you curious to hear my news?" I asked.

"Just tell me, girly."

Her voice sounded strangely cold, and my confusion deepened. "I have an interview at New Orleans State tomorrow."

"You what?" Meghan cried. "Oh my God, Chloé! I'm so happy for you. I can't believe it!"

"I know, right?" I paused, remembering her earlier silence. "What did you think I was going to tell you?"

She laughed. "I thought you'd gotten engaged. You know— tropical vacation, lots of sex, pretty sunsets, Valentine's Day. It seemed likely that she'd popped the question."

I'd actually expected it myself. Amelia had made sure we spent most of our time alone, once or twice insisting on a table in a restaurant far away from other tourists. A couple of times, I'd been certain she wanted to tell me or ask me something, but nothing came of it. In some ways, I was relieved. We'd been dating for only a little over three months, after all, and an engagement would be a little premature at this stage. Still, I'd expected her to ask, and some small part of me had hoped she would. Meghan's somewhat cavalier and definitively cold expectation about the imaginary engagement, however, was a little hurtful. Like my aunt, she wasn't entirely sold on Amelia yet. If it wasn't for the fact that she couldn't get away with it, I was pretty sure Meghan would avoid her altogether. It didn't help to call attention to this hunch, however, as Meghan was always defensive about Amelia when I brought her up. Like with my aunt, I just had to hope things got better with time.

"I attended there briefly, you know," Meghan said. "New Orleans State, I mean. Before I goofed off too much and got kicked out."

"That's right—I forgot."

"It's a great school. It's not as fancy as the private colleges Uptown, but that's the beauty of it. People like us go there. You'll love it."

I laughed. "I don't have the job yet, Meghan."

"Is there any doubt you'll get it?"

I paused before responding. In truth, I didn't think there was. Unless I completely screwed up tomorrow or botched my teaching demonstration, I was pretty sure the job was mine. This caused another pang of guilt, as I realized that I really should tell Amelia, and soon. While I wouldn't start until summer at the earliest, more likely autumn, she would need some time to find my replacement.

As if reading my mind, Meghan asked, "So what's Amelia think about it?"

"I-I haven't told her about it."

"Why not?"

I had no response for her straightforward question. "I guess I wanted to make sure I got it first. I don't want to bother her about it unless it's real."

Meghan blew out a low whistle. "She's going to be pissed off if you hide it from her, Chloé. I would be if I was her. You really should tell her now."

"You think?"

"I do. But that's just my opinion. You don't have to listen to me."

I knew she was right. My guilt the last hour was entirely derived from my instinct to hide this opportunity from her. It didn't make any sense to hide my news. She should have been the first person I called. As usual with Amelia, pure cowardice had led me to cover it up. It would be much worse to tell her after I'd been offered the job, and I knew it. Still, it was my decision to wait or tell her, and I needed to think about it a while longer. I changed the subject.

"Anyway, Aunt Kate wanted to know if you and Zach could come to dinner this weekend."

Meghan sighed. "I don't think so. I just got back a couple of days ago, so I can't take another night off so soon."

I remembered then that she'd been gone for the last month. Meghan is in a jazz-and-bluegrass band, and she and her band had been on their first tour together. I could have smacked myself for being so self-centered. "Jeez. That's right. You just got back from your tour. How was it?"

"It was great, Chloé. We went all over the South. We were in a different place every night, just about. Nashville was our last stop, and it was fantastic. We got to play in this cute little honkytonk on Broadway—Robert's—and the crowd was great."

"That's so awesome. Are you sure you can't come to Kate's? What about tomorrow? I want to hear all the details, and I'm sure Kate would, too."

"I guess I could if we had an early dinner—like four o'clock. I have to be at the bar by seven."

"Four should be perfect. My interview is in the morning, and I can fill you and Kate in about it and my trip, and I'm sure she wants to hear about your tour, too."

"All right. I'll tell Zach about it now. I think he has to work, but I'll ask him."

"Great. I'll see you then."

"Oh, and Chloé?"

"Yeah?"

"Good luck tomorrow. At the interview, I mean. You deserve it."

"Thanks, Meghan. That means a lot."

We hung up, and I called my Aunt Kate, letting her know about my interview and Meghan's packed schedule. Luckily tomorrow worked well for dinner for her and Jim, too, and she promised to have it on the table when we arrived so we'd have plenty of time to talk about everything that had happened.

"Should I expect Amelia, too?" she asked.

"I don't think so, Kate. She has to work all day tomorrow, and I doubt she'll agree to leave the office so early just after our trip."

Kate clicked her tongue. "She works too hard, that one. She's going to work herself into an early grave if she isn't careful."

"Don't I know it."

She wished me luck, and then we finalized plans and hung up. I paced around the house for a while afterward, too anxious to settle down. I needed to call Amelia, if, at the very least, to invite her to dinner tomorrow, whether she would come or not. I also needed to tell her about my interview. I knew it would seem like I was sneaking around behind her back if I didn't.

Squaring my shoulders, I finally picked up my phone and dialed her number. It rang long enough for her message service to pick up— not a surprise when I knew she was working on something.

"Hey, Amelia. Aunt Kate wanted me to see if you might come to dinner tomorrow at four. I know you're busy, but I'd love it if you could try. Also, I have some big news. Call me back when you get a chance. Love you."

Too distracted to read, but too anxious to watch television, I decided that painting would be the best way to relax. I went upstairs to my bedroom, dragging my suitcase, then changed quickly into my painting clothes—a pair of old gym shorts and a ratty T-shirt so splattered with paint and turpentine, I wouldn't be caught dead in them outside. My new painting quickly absorbed me, and several hours passed without my realizing it. Only when my bladder started to actually hurt did I think to check the clock. It was after ten.

Confused, I looked at my phone, wondering why Amelia hadn't called. I realized I'd left it on silent and missed her twice. She left two messages.

"Hey, Chloé. Just calling you back. I can't make dinner tomorrow, but I promise I'll come to the next one. What's your big news?"

In her second message, she sounded tired. "Hey, hon. I just got home and I'm headed to bed. I can barely see straight. Sorry I missed you tonight. I bet you're in your studio right now with your head in the clouds, knee-deep in paint. Wish I were there to kiss you good night. I have an early morning conference, so catch me at lunch, okay? I want to hear your big news."

The second call had been an hour ago, which let me off the hook for responding. I relaxed. Telling her about the interview before it actually happened was now a moot point. She would be busy all morning, which wouldn't give me an opportunity. Part of me knew I was being a coward—after all, I could text or email her the news—but mostly I was so relieved that I was finally calm enough to head to bed. I stripped down and was asleep in seconds.

CHAPTER EIGHT

My interview went fantastically well. It helped that I went into it believing that I would be hired, and it also helped that everyone I met that morning seemed to think so as well. Christophe Montmartre, who'd arranged everything, managed to get just about every current faculty member from art history to show up. It wasn't a large department, and most of them had planned to come in to catch up on paperwork, so no one seemed to resent having to be there during a holiday week. The new chair of art history, Heidi Maslov, was so excited to have me as a candidate, she was actually trying to woo and flatter me. I might have told her that she needn't have bothered—I wanted the job so desperately I found it hard not to fawn all over everyone.

I was shown my potential office, given a quick tour, and then we all had a formal, sit-down conversation about my credentials and the job's responsibilities. Everyone was impressed with me, and I with them and the job. Christophe dropped by briefly to say hello at the end, and when we started chattering away in French like old friends, I was pretty sure I'd just nailed it. I walked back to my car certain they would call me to arrange the next step.

I'd texted Amelia just before going into the interview to let her know I was turning my phone off. This was a code between us that generally meant I was painting. This arrangement had been a hard-won battle, as Amelia thought it should always be possible to contact me. I didn't think there was a single emergency that warranted being in constant contact. We went back and forth about it so often I'd simply had to put my foot down—I could turn my damn phone off when I felt like it.

When I turned my phone on in the car, I found only a single response from her—a texted picture of some white roses from her garden last summer. The image brought tears to my eyes, as it spoke of all the progress we'd made since we started dating. The photo meant, simply, that she loved me and thought I was beautiful. As I drove back to my place, I tried to call her, but, as my interview had lasted into the early afternoon, I'd missed her mini lunch break.

Back at home, I took off my beautiful gray skirt suit, grinning at the memory of the interview I'd had last September. I'd shown up for my appointment with the notorious Amelia Winters wearing some of my Aunt Kate's old work clothes. They'd looked terrible and were ill-fitting, but as I didn't own anything suited for business, they'd been better than nothing. Now I had a whole wardrobe of fine clothes, many of them tailored, all thanks to Amelia. This thought gave me pause again. Amelia had bought all of these clothes for me, ostensibly so I could look the part as her assistant at work. She'd spent lavishly on them, and looking at them now, I realized once again the significant investment she'd made in me. If I left her employment, all of this would go to waste.

I shook my head, angry with my self-doubt. Yes, she'd bought me these clothes, and yes, they were for work, but I'd already made her company hundreds of thousands of dollars. As far as I was concerned, I'd earned them already. And anyway, when I'd brought up paying her back for the clothes out of my wages, she'd dismissed the idea, laughing. As far as she was concerned, the clothes were a gift.

Calmer now and more at ease with my decision to work for the university if they wanted me, I went back to my painting, becoming lost in it. By the time I snapped out of my dream world, I was running late for dinner and had to drive to my aunt's place to make it on time.

When I got there, at exactly four, I walked inside without knocking. I'd grown up here, for the most part, and Kate and I didn't stand on ceremony. The house was incredibly warm, and the scent of peppers and onions made my eyes sting the moment I walked in. Kate came bustling out of the kitchen in her usual cooking disarray, her graying hair wild and her apron splattered with sauces and flour. Neither of us paid attention to this kind of thing and hugged anyway, the tomato sauce on her hands smearing into my shirt.

"Oh my goodness! You're a sight for sore eyes," she said. "You look so healthy and tan!"

"All we did was eat seafood and drink piña coladas and margaritas." Among other things, I thought.

"Well, you needed it. You work much too hard, sweetie. You're going to burn out if you're not careful."

I let her little jibe slide, used to it at this point. She took every opportunity to criticize my work with Amelia, and Amelia's business in general. Despite my excellent salary, she thought it beneath me.

I didn't want to get into it, so I changed the subject. "Where are the others?"

"Meghan just popped out for some wine, and Zach and Jim aren't coming. Zach has to work, and Jim was just called out of state on some granite-countertop emergency or something with his company. It's just going to be us ladies tonight." Her eyebrows shot up. "Oh! Where's Amelia?"

"She couldn't come," I said, trying to sound casual. I hated the cracks about Amelia's company, but I especially hated it when Kate criticized Amelia for missing things like this. It wasn't as if she did it on purpose.

Luckily Aunt Kate seemed to know when to let it go, as all she did was shake her head. "Well, that's too bad. Maybe she'll make it next time. And anyway, it does seem like an age since it was just the three of us."

It did. Meghan and I became friends right before I moved in with Aunt Kate. We were both in middle school, and my parents had just died in a car accident. Meghan's dad had abandoned them when she was a kid, and her mom, a musician, was frequently MIA, so Meghan stayed at our place at least a couple of nights a week through high school. To some extent, she'd been like a second surrogate daughter to Kate, and lately it was rare that the three of us had a night together without someone's boyfriend or, more recently, girlfriend in the mix. Tonight was a good opportunity to catch up as a family again.

Meghan came in a moment later, and she and I greeted each other with a long, solid hug. I realized then that it had been almost six weeks since I'd seen her—a length of time that would previously have been unheard of. In high school and college, she and I had basically been attached at the hip, either seeing or calling each other every day. We'd gone to different colleges, but that didn't stop us from hanging out every weekend into our early twenties. When I'd moved to France for my graduate studies, we still had weekly phone calls and long visits during my holiday breaks. Things had changed lately with the introduction of Amelia into my life, and that change was rarely clearer than when I realized how distant Meghan and I had become. She'd cut her hair recently, and her clothes looked a little smarter than usual. It seemed like she was a different woman almost every time I saw her.

"You look great, Chloé. You really do. I haven't seen you this tan since the Jazz Fest disaster of 2010."

I laughed. We'd both been twenty-one, and both of us had gotten ridiculously drunk at Jazz Fest. We'd been too far gone to think about the fact that we were outside in the sun all day, and both of us had been sunburnt to hell, wincing and pussyfooting around in pain for days after.

"God, don't remind me," I said. "I still can't listen to Elvis Costello without wanting to smear aloe all over my body." We both laughed.

"What kind of wine did you get?" Aunt Kate asked, interrupting us.

"All of them," Meghan replied, holding up her bag. It held at least four bottles. "I thought we could take this opportunity to celebrate, just the three of us, since I know you both have some good news."

This was the first time I'd heard about Kate's news, but when I looked at her, she was glaring at Meghan as if to silence her.

"You're right, Meghan," she said, "but we have to eat something, too, and the food is almost ready. You should always have a wine cushion."

We followed Kate into the kitchen, and Meghan and I immediately started setting the table—our old chore as adolescents and young adults. I brought out wineglasses, and Meghan poured very liberal glasses of pinot grigio for all of us.

"I thought you had to work tonight," I said.

She shrugged. "I do, but I can always head in a little late—my coworker won't mind. It's the Friday after Mardi Gras. People are worn out. It's always a dead zone in there this weekend."

When Kate served the shrimp-and-crawfish étouffée, I began salivating before I even tasted it. Kate knew this was my favorite dish and served it only on special occasions. The rice was fluffy and spiced, the bread fresh and hot, and she'd whipped up her own homemade butter. It was, as usual, enough food for twice as many people, but the three of us did a fair job of decimating the spread. After we finished, the table looked something like a natural disaster. We kept the dinner conversation light, by house rules. Important or bad news had to wait until after the meal to avoid detracting from the food. Food in a Creole home should, according to Aunt Kate, be the center of attention at a meal.

We left the mess and headed into the living room with our second bottle of wine—this time a sparkling rosé. Meghan brought out champagne flutes, and she and I sat close to each other on the love seat. Aunt Kate sat in the nearby armchair, all of us close enough to brush legs.

"Okay," Kate said. "I want to hear about the interview. I can hardly stand the suspense."

I looked at the two of them with a serious expression, letting the tension build, and then broke into a wide smile. "It went great. More than great. I think I'll get the job."

Meghan and Aunt Kate were tremendously happy for me, both of them rocketing out of their seats and pulling me into a three-way hug. We danced around a little, and when we sat back down I told them all about the school and the department.

"I told you that you'd like it there," Meghan said. "I think I even took an art-history course when I went there. Well, maybe—I never went to class. But I signed up for it, anyway."

"Did they tell you what kind of classes you'd be teaching?" Kate asked.

"Mostly freshman- and sophomore-level courses for now. Introduction one and two, that kind of thing. But I'll get more advanced courses in time, once they can work me into the rotation."

Meghan squeezed my shoulders. "I'm so damn happy for you, Chloé. You've worked so hard for this—harder than anyone I know."

Aunt Kate touched my knee. "Me too, honey. I can't wait to tell everyone that my niece is a professor."

I held up my hands. "Let's not get too hasty. I haven't been offered the job yet."

"But you will," Kate said, nodding with certainty. "I know it."

Her confidence brought tears to my eyes, and soon all us were blinking and wiping our eyes. I had worked very hard at my various degrees and internships, and these women had been with me through all of it. They knew as well as I did that I wouldn't have made it without them. Their encouragement and devotion had made it possible for me to get where I was today.

I cleared my throat. "Okay. Enough tears. This is a happy occasion, and Meghan said you have some news, too, Aunt Kate. What is it?"

Meghan and Kate shared a worried glance, and my heart rate picked up. What were they hiding from me?

I must have looked apprehensive, as Kate laughed and patted my hand reassuringly. "Don't be worried, Chloé. It's good news. I'm just sorry I didn't tell you first. It happened when you were in Mexico."

"I just happened to drop by the next day, and she told me everything," Meghan explained.

"Just know I would have told you right away if you were here," Kate said.

"What? What would you have told me?"

Kate took a deep breath and let it out. "Jim and I are getting married."

The news was so surprising, I didn't know how to react. Before my parents died, my aunt had been married to a drunk who'd deserted her. They'd had a nasty divorce some years after he left. She'd spent most of my adolescence and early twenties telling me to avoid marriage at all costs. While I knew she and Jim had become serious—he'd recently moved into her place part-time—I'd never expected them to get married.

"Wow!" I finally said. "I never—"

"Right? Who would have thought? I know I told you for years how stupid marriage is. But I'll admit it—I was wrong. When he asked me last Saturday, I didn't even hesitate. It seemed like the most natural thing in the world." She paused. "I hope you'll be my maid of honor, Chloé."

"Of course, Aunt Kate! I'm honored! I'm so happy for you!"

We all stood up and hugged again, and Meghan told me that she was going to be the bridesmaid. The wedding was already scheduled for the first Saturday in April—just over six weeks from now. I found this timeframe shocking, but Aunt Kate reassured me. "We don't want it to be a big thing. We've both been married before, and a big wedding seems silly at our age. It's just going to be some close family and friends. We're doing the court thing on that Friday with just us, you girls, and his sons. Then on Saturday, we'll have the reception with everyone else downtown. Very casual—forty or fifty people tops."

I was crying now, openly, though my tears were entirely happy ones. When I'd moved in with my aunt, she was fairly young to be a legal guardian for a fourteen-year-old. She was much younger than her sister, my mother, and I think her guardianship of me had effectively ended what remained of her youth. She'd never resented me. She'd fought like crazy with the other aunts and uncles on my dad's side to get custody and eventually won. She needn't have done that. Our family is huge, especially on my father's side, and right after my parents died, I'd spent almost a year being shuttled between different aunts, uncles, and cousins as the legal battle raged. Many of them would have been happy to keep me, but my mom's little sister had insisted the hardest and the longest and won out in the end. Even as a young and selfish adolescent, I'd felt sorry for her, having to take me in like lost luggage, but she'd never shown a moment's hesitation. Despite their age difference, she and my mother had been very close, and as my mom's only sibling, she seemed to think it was her duty.

She'd dated, on and off, over the years, but she always seemed to back out right when things started to get serious, especially when I was younger. I'd also known her to break up with men when they'd seemed reluctant to accept me as part of her life. I'd felt incredibly bad about that for years. She was always quick to reassure me it wasn't about me at all, but I'd never quite believed her. Dating Jim, moving in with him, and now marrying him finally put that past to rest. She would have her own life now.

Kate told me a little bit more about the wedding. Jim's three sons would be joining us a week early, and she asked if I could put one of them up at my place, which was fine. Jim's brother would also attend, but Jim wasn't close with anyone else in his family, so his side of the guest list would be limited to his sons, his brother, and their various wives and girlfriends. While Aunt Kate didn't have any other siblings, she had a mountain of cousins, aunts, and uncles, and it would be hard to limit the attendees.

She paused, looking troubled. "There's one more thing, Chloé."
"What?"

"As you know, Jim's construction business is doing really well. He's been splitting his time between here and Florida since Katrina, but he's getting a little tired of going back and forth all the time. The work here is starting to dry up a little, which means he sometimes misses out on opportunities in Florida because he spends so much time here or in the car."

I knew where she was going with this, and my face must have reflected my dread. She smiled weakly and took my hand in hers. "Chloé, we're moving to Florida."

I couldn't help my response. "Oh no! You can't, Aunt Kate! You love it here! Your whole family is here!"

She nodded, her face still serious. "You're right on all accounts, honey. But we've talked long and hard about this. He's years from retirement, and it just doesn't make sense for him to move here right now. I'm still a relatively young woman, and I've been thinking of going back to teaching full-time. They're desperate for teachers in Florida right now."

I was crushed. While I was happy for Aunt Kate and recognized the sense in what she was saying, it was difficult to think of living here in the city without her. She and I were very close. Still, I knew I needed to put on a brave face. She'd given up some of the best years of her life to take care of me and was finally moving on. We stood up and hugged again, and I had to fight back my tears for a few minutes. The wine wasn't helping. In fact, it was starting to make me feel a little maudlin, but I let Meghan fill our glasses for a celebratory toast.

We talked of less-important matters for a while. I gave them their presents from Mexico, Meghan showed us some pictures from her concert tour, and Kate served pecan tarts with peach ice cream. Finally, after Meghan and I drank a couple of cups of strong coffee to sober up, we gathered our coats to leave. Meghan left before me, seeming to understand that I needed a moment alone with my aunt.

Once she was gone, Kate put her hand on my shoulder and made eye contact with me. "The move won't be immediate, Chloé. We're planning to live there half-time at first, every other month for a while, just to make sure it works. He has some projects here that won't end for another year, and I want to sub down there for a while before getting something more permanent. I'll still be around for a long while before I move for good."

"I'm sorry, Aunt Kate. I know I should be happy for you. It's just hard. You've always been here for me. But I don't want to be selfish, either."

"You aren't. And don't worry—I'll always be here for you. I just won't be *here*, here. But you can call me any time, and we'll visit each other all the time. Florida is just beautiful."

I nodded, holding back tears again.

"You'll see," she said, hugging my shoulders. "You'll be so busy with your new job you won't even notice I'm gone."

I brushed away a stray tear or two and laughed. "Says you. I know I'll be freaked out, and you won't be here to make me ice cream or tell me it'll all be better later."

"It will. And you'll be a great professor. I promise."

I grinned at her. "See! That's what I need. Someone with confidence in me."

She looked a little troubled, and I saw her weighing something in her mind. Finally, she made eye contact with me. "What about Amelia? Doesn't she support you?"

"Of course she does," I said, impatient and defensive about her, as always.

Her brow cleared a little. "Well, good. What does she think about this job opportunity, by the way? I forgot to ask earlier."

This time I paused, and my hesitance must have been clear as I could see Kate tense up. "Is she upset?"

"No." I paused, hesitating. "I haven't told her yet."

Kate was a quiet for a long time, her gaze sad and concerned. I could see that she wanted to say something, likely something very hurtful, but she kept her mouth closed, waiting for me to finish.

"She was working all night last night and all day today. I haven't had a chance." My excuse sounded even stupider spoken aloud, and my temper heated up at Kate's continued silence—it seemed to mock and accuse me.

"I'm sure she'll be happy for me, Kate. She's not some kind of monster."

Aunt Kate just shook her head and gave me a quick hug. "Well, you better tell her soon. Are you seeing her tonight?"

"Yes."

"Then tell her right away. Don't wait."

My temper flared again, and it was all I could do not to yell an angry retort. I excused myself as graciously as I could and stormed back to my place on foot, too angry and still a little too drunk to get behind the wheel of my car.

Aunt Kate's expression haunted me all the way home. I kept telling myself I was being silly, that of *course* Amelia would be happy for me, but it was getting harder and harder to ignore the growing kernel of doubt and guilt when I pictured telling her. Further, I couldn't quite explain to myself why I hadn't confided in her immediately. I could have tried harder yesterday and today, and I hadn't. Did that mean I was afraid of what she might say or do? Aunt Kate seemed to think so, without actually saying as much. I could tell that's what she thought. Was I worried about Amelia, too? I was certainly acting that way.

I walked quickly, angrily back to my place, and by the time I reached my apartment, I was ready to do anything to get rid of my growing fear and guilt. Amelia picked up the second I rang.

"My God, it's good to hear from you," she said. I could hear the fatigue in her voice. "I'm just wrapping up at work now. Can I come over?"

"Yes. Please. I have something really important to tell you."

"You sound so serious about it, honey. I hope it's good news."

"It is. At least, *I* think it is. Anyway, get here as fast as you can."

"I'm on my way."

CHAPTER NINE

I was disappointed to see that Amelia had already lost some of her vacation glow. Her eyes looked tired and strained, and she was wearing the same clothes she'd worn yesterday when she left. She hugged me long and hard and then kissed me, and some of my earlier doubts evaporated in her arms. She was always like this—ethereal and elusive when I wasn't around her, and solid and sure when I was. A lot of my fear, I knew, was based entirely on my own uncertainty about the possibility of a new job, not about Amelia. I'd simply projected some of my anxiety outward, and she'd become the target.

Though it was the last thing I needed, I poured us both a glass of wine, trying to whip up some liquid courage. When I brought it back into the living room, she had her head thrown back on the cushion, eyes closed. I sat down next to her, and she roused herself a little, blinking her tired eyes a few times and then focusing on me. She wore glasses at work, and little red ovals were imprinted on her nose, as if she'd had them on nonstop since I last saw her. In the dim light of my living room, her eyes were a dark, almost cobalt blue, and when she turned them to mine, a shiver of joy shot through me at her all-encompassing focus. This was one of her superpowers and possibly the single-most significant reason she was so good at her job. When she looked at you, the rest of the world seemed to drop away. You saw only her beautiful eyes.

"So tell me your news," she said. "I've been curious about it all day."

I hesitated, not certain how to begin. I knew I should just tell her everything from start to finish, but it was hard to know what to say. I chickened out and said the first thing that came to mind.

"Aunt Kate is getting married."

Amelia's face broke into a wide smile. "That's excellent news. It's been coming for a while now." She paused and grinned slyly. "I actually knew about this a couple of weeks ago."

I was stunned. "You did? How?"

"I helped Jim pick out the ring. He was clueless, and when he called me, he told me it was because he knew I had good taste."

This information was so shocking, it was almost hard to believe. Jim is a quiet, reserved man—a sort of Sam Elliott type. The idea that he would contact Amelia, who was essentially a stranger, to help him make such a monumental decision stunned me, to say the least. Still, the more I thought about it, the less surprising it was. I'd seen the two of them chatting at family meals a few times. In fact, I was pretty sure she'd talked to him more than I had. They were both outsiders, both the quieter partner in their relationship, so perhaps friendliness between them made sense. Still, I was very surprised he'd called her.

"So you knew this was going to happen?" I asked.

She shrugged. "I mean, eventually. He didn't tell me *when* he would pop the question. I suggested Valentine's Day. Is that when he did it?"

I nodded, mute with shock.

She laughed. "I'm sorry, Chloé. He asked me to keep it a surprise. I hope you don't mind."

I shook my head. "No. I don't mind." I paused and looked up at her. "Did you know that he and Aunt Kate are moving to Florida together?"

Now she looked surprised. She leaned forward and set her wineglass down before taking both of my hands. The gesture brought tears to my eyes. She knew how much the news would hurt me.

"No, honey. I didn't," she said. "I mean, he mentioned a couple of times how much he hated going back and forth, but if I thought anything, I guess I assumed they'd settle here. I'm so sorry to hear it."

I laughed and wiped away a couple of tears. "I'm being an idiot. I'm happy for her, for them, I mean, but—"

"You don't have to explain yourself, Chloé. I know how much she means to you."

We were quiet for a while as I composed myself, and then I told her about the wedding plans to date.

"So I get to sleep with the maid of honor?" she asked, grinning. "Nice."

I raised my eyebrows. "I take it this is not the first time you've achieved that goal?"

She pretended to think about it and then shook her head. "Been there, done that. First at my brother Bobby's wedding, and then at my brother Dean's wedding. Oh, and at my uncle George's wedding. I almost forgot about her."

I pushed her arm, laughing. "Tramp."

She held up her hands. "Guilty as charged."

We sipped our wine awhile, and I knew that this was the time to tell her. I'd stalled long enough.

"There's something else," I finally said, almost spitting out the words.

She looked confused. "Something else what?"

"I mean, I have some other news."

She seemed to sense my anxiety, as her brow creased. "What is it?"

"You know my friend Lana? In New York?"

She nodded.

"She got me an interview at New Orleans State University. For a position as a professor."

She didn't react except to grow incredibly still.

"I called the dean yesterday, and I had the interview this morning."

She was quiet for a moment before she asked, "And how did it go?"

"It went really, really well. I-I'm pretty sure I have the job if I want it. I'll have to do a teaching demonstration next week and talk with the other deans and the provost and whatnot, but I think they want me, Amelia. And I want the job, too."

She was still just staring at me, her body tense. Her expression was neither happy nor upset, but neither was it blank. She seemed to be stuck somehow, as if absorbing the information had short-circuited her reactions. My own anxiety skyrocketed, and I started blabbering to get her to say something.

"I mean, it won't be right away. They told me this morning that I wouldn't start until fall term. I'll have some meetings and things over the summer, but I wouldn't actually teach until after Labor Day. I can wrap up some of the projects at work before then, and we can still do the trip to Paris together in June. I mean, if you want me to. If that still works for you. If, if, you know, you don't want me to leave right away. I mean, I'd like to stay and work with you until I have to go. And even then, I could probably still help out a little after I start teaching. It's full-time, but I can help out between classes."

I might have rattled on like this forever just to fill in the emptiness in the room, but she finally seemed to shake herself awake. Still, her smile, when it came, was strained. I could see the pain in her eyes and in the way she was holding herself, but she leaned forward and drew me into a hug.

"It's great news, Chloé. I'm so happy for you."

I pulled back. "You don't seem very happy."

She smiled that same strained smile and looked away. For a moment I thought I saw tears in her eyes, but they were gone before I was sure I'd seen them.

She looked at me again. "I'm just surprised, that's all. Of course it's an amazing opportunity."

"But you're disappointed." I said this rather than asked it, as the answer was obvious from her expression and body language.

She sighed and then rubbed her tired eyes. "I don't mean to be disappointed, Chloé, but I am. I love working with you. You're amazing at what you do, and I like being able to see you every day. Of course I knew it couldn't last forever—you told me that the first time we met. I just thought I'd have you with me for a while longer. Another year or two, maybe." She shook her head. "But that was stupid of me. I should have known that someone with your talents wouldn't sit on the shelf for long. And I'm very glad it's here in New Orleans and not somewhere else."

"So you're not upset with me?"

She smiled weakly again. "Of course I'm not, honey. I'm upset with myself. It was stupid of me to get my hopes up. I'd almost convinced myself you would stay forever."

I couldn't help the stab of guilt that followed her words. I knew how much she appreciated me at work. She'd told me time and again over the last few months how impossible things would be without me. And I also knew it would be difficult to find someone to replace me.

"I'm sorry, Amelia. I really am."

She laughed. "I'm the one who's sorry, Chloé. You're excited about your new job, and I'm shitting all over it. Don't worry about me, for God's sake. I'll be fine." She shook her head again. "I should be celebrating with you, not complaining."

"Well, I don't have the job quite yet. I mean, it's not official."

"But it will be," she said. "I know it will. They would be stupid to pass up the opportunity to have you in their department." She stood up. "In fact, this calls for a celebration. Do you have any champagne in the house?"

"No, I don't." I didn't like the strange, almost maniacal look in her eyes.

"Damn," she said, looking incredibly put out. "How can we celebrate without champagne?"

"I don't need champagne, Amelia. Please just sit down and talk about this with me for a moment."

"Are you crazy? After all these years, and all your schooling, you just want to sit and talk? We should be celebrating! Let's go dancing somewhere!"

I could tell she was saying all of this and acting this way to distract us from her real feelings, and I wouldn't have it. We'd come too far together to beat around the bush this way. We would have an honest conversation or we would fight, but we wouldn't avoid this issue.

"Sit down, Amelia. Please."

She looked surprised and then upset, but I saw her try to calm down before sitting next to me again. We sat there in silence for a while, and then she laughed, bitterly.

"What a fuckup I am, Chloé. I'm sorry. You see right through me now."

"I should hope I do. Love sees all, and I love you, Amelia."

Her eyes flickered up to mine, hopeful. "Even when I'm a complete asshole?"

"Even then."

She sighed and looked me straight in the eyes. For the first time, I could see the depth of her pain. "I want to be happy for you, Chloé.

I really do. And I know I will be—eventually. It's just a shock, that's all. And I shouldn't be shocked. Like I said, I knew this was coming. Eventually."

"But you want me to take the job?" I couldn't keep the note of pleading from my voice.

She smiled, and this time the smile seemed more genuine. "Of course I do, Chloé. Of course. I would never, ever want you to change your plans for me. You've worked so hard for just this kind of thing. You deserve it. And I know you'll be great at it."

I met her smile, my eyes welling with tears. She'd finally said exactly what I needed to hear. We could move on from here and be stronger for it. I knew it.

"I love you," she said. "I just want you to be happy. I'm sorry I didn't think of that first. That's all that matters to me."

I stood up, and she looked surprised.

"Come on," I said. "I want to show you something in the bedroom."

When I woke up the next morning, I was disappointed to see Amelia's side of the bed empty. She sent me a text explaining that she'd gone into work, the time mark on it long before the sun rose. Although she and I had been incredibly busy before our trip, our time away had still put several things behind schedule. I was a little guilty about not joining her today to help out, but on the other hand, I wasn't about to turn down a couple more days off. This was the busy season at the office, and I would be back at it soon enough. God knows when I would have another day off.

I spent the day in my studio, happy to have time alone to paint. I didn't worry about Amelia until much later, when I realized she hadn't called or texted me all afternoon. That was unusual for her. Even on a busy day, she would send me an update or two, and today I had nothing from her. By dinnertime, I was getting anxious, and by late evening, I was really starting to panic. Unless her phone was dead, this was incredibly unlike her. I couldn't help but think it might have something to do with our conversation the night before. She was likely still smarting from the idea of my departure and didn't want to upset me by being less than supportive.

It hurt to know this about her, but on the other hand, I understood all too well that it was possible to be both happy and disappointed about a situation at the same time. Aunt Kate's upcoming wedding presented the same situation for me. While I was excited and happy for her, I was also deeply hurt by the idea that she was going to move away. It was selfish of me, and I knew that, but that didn't necessarily mean I could bury my hurt feelings immediately. The best thing I could do now, I knew, was simply avoid seeing Kate for a few days until I got used to the idea. I was pretty sure Amelia was doing the same thing.

Amelia finally texted close to midnight, apologizing for her silence. She blamed it on work, but I knew that wasn't the whole story. I decided to let her have a day or two and then confront her if she didn't get her head out of her ass.

My resolve to wait faltered on Sunday afternoon. I'd spent so much time by myself the last couple of days, I was actually starting to get lonely. Meghan was working all weekend, and I wasn't ready to see Aunt Kate again, but mostly I wanted to see my girlfriend, and I wanted us to get past this. I put real clothes on for the first time in two days, and just as I was pulling on my jacket, my phone rang. I didn't recognize the local number calling, but as I got so many work calls on my cell, I answered it anyway.

"Hello?"

"Chloé? This is Daphne Waters. Amelia's friend?"

It took me a moment to remember her. I'd met her once in New York at an extravagant dinner. She was a rich, older woman and a friend of Amelia's family. She'd shown up at a party in New York with a posse of young, handsome men, all of whom were apparently paid arm candy to make her look powerful and attractive. I'd found her amusing and harmless until she set Amelia up with her ex-girlfriend Sara for a surprise lunch. Amelia hadn't explained why she'd done this, but I'd gathered since that Daphne and Sara were old friends.

It took a lot of willpower to keep my response civil. "Hello, Miss Waters. How can I help you?"

"Ooh, *Miss* Waters, no less. You are a charmer. I haven't been a 'miss' for twenty years or more, at least according to French custom."

"Is there a purpose to your call?" I asked.

"Well, you have no reason to be so snappish, darling. This isn't a social call. Amelia gave me your number."

I was stunned. "Amelia did what?"

"She gave me your number because I'm doing a little work with her, silly. Didn't she mention this to you?"

She hadn't, but several months at Winters Corporation had taught me to play along with almost anything customers said. It didn't pay to look like you had no idea what was happening in another part of the office. Still, I decided to remain a little evasive.

"What can I help you with, Ms. Waters?"

"Well, you see, darling, there's a problem. Amelia told me she had you scheduled for a consultation with me this Wednesday, but I'm going out of town on Tuesday. It's a last-minute thing, you see."

"I'm sure if you call the office, Janet can reschedule at a time more convenient for you."

"That's just the problem. I've been calling and calling, and I can't seem to get anyone on the line, and when I do, I get put on hold. I don't know what's happening over there at the office, but y'all need to get some more help to answer the phones. Anyway, I was hoping we could reschedule, just the two of us, and cut out the middleman, as it were."

I was annoyed. This happened, occasionally, when a client was pushy enough to get my phone number, which was why I always asked Amelia and Janet to withhold it in almost every case. I could only imagine that Amelia had agreed to give it to her because she was a family friend.

"Okay, Ms. Waters. Let me get my schedule out, and we'll see what I can do."

"Oh, that won't be necessary," she said. "I'm calling because I wanted to see if you're available now."

"Now?"

"Yes. I'm swamped before my trip, but I have the afternoon free today. I thought I would call and see if you're busy."

I hesitated before answering her. Technically, I was free, but on the other hand, I hated to set a precedent with any client that I could drop whatever I was doing and come at will, especially on a weekend. Still, I knew Daphne Waters was incredibly wealthy. I'd seen her entourage of followers, her gowns, and her jewelry, and I knew she had a large house in the French Quarter. For customers with that kind of money, it was usually worth being a little flexible with your schedule since it flattered them. Being rude to her might ruin the sale.

"Yes, I can meet you now," I told her. "Shall I come to your house?"

"Oh no, that's not necessary. I'm at the Club right now. Can you meet me here?"

"Certainly. I can be there shortly."

"That's wonderful, Chloé. Thank you so much. I'll give your name to the gate."

"I'm not really dressed for anything fancy. Is that all right?"

"Completely. It's Sunday afternoon. The rules are relaxed around here now."

"Okay. Give me fifteen minutes."

I walked out the door a moment later and headed for my car. The New Orleans Country Club was actually somewhat close to work, and I headed in that direction on autopilot. While New Orleans has several more exclusive social clubs, any socialite like Daphne Waters nevertheless stayed on the rosters at the Club, for mostly sociopolitical purposes. It looked good to be on the books there, even if you weren't interested in golf or tennis. I knew, for example, that Amelia and her entire family were lifelong members because of their generous donations and patronage, though I was pretty sure none of them set foot in there on a regular basis. Brushing elbows with the wealthy elite over the last few months had taught me several things, prime of which was that they liked to spend money on things that made them look good to others.

My name was indeed listed at the gate, and I think it also helped that I was driving a new Mercedes. Despite all my recent time around this kind of people, I still had terrible imposter syndrome. I was always terrified lest they see the real, near-impoverished me and drive me away like the poor cousin I was.

I held out my keys to the valet, who gave my clothing a once-over before taking them. While my outfit was nicer than the paint-splattered rags I'd been wearing the last couple of days, I was dressed very casually. I had on an old, comfy pair of jeans, a green canvas coat, and a blue pashmina. Trying to shrug off my appearance, I walked up the little stairs and inside, asking the host directions to the bar. He too looked me up and down before pointing the way, and I couldn't help but flush warmly at the rudeness.

When I entered the bar, I was surprised to find it nearly empty. The sun was shining outside for the first time in days, and I'd seen several people on the golf course, enjoying the warmth. Then I remembered what Meghan had told us the other night about the weekend after Mardi Gras and wondered if it was also the case here. After drinking heavily for four or five days straight, people were taking the weekend off.

I spotted Daphne immediately and was surprised to see that she wasn't alone. The person she was with had her back to me, and the sunlight coming in through the windows made it hard to see either one of them for a moment. Something about the set of the woman's shoulders rang a dull bell of recognition in my head. I'd seen her somewhere, recently.

Daphne spotted me and waved, and as the other woman turned, the sunlight hid her features for a second. Then it all came together. It was the woman from the birthday gala—the one I'd seen several times from behind.

It was Sara.

CHAPTER TEN

For a moment, I could barely breathe—the sight of Sara knocked the wind out of me. I realized then just how badly I'd been duped and how stupid I'd been to fall for Daphne's scheme. She'd done exactly the same thing to me as she'd done to Amelia, yet here I was, walking into the same trap. Amelia would never give my number out to someone without asking, or at least telling me about it, family friend or not. I'd let my insecurity blind me to a very obvious ruse.

Daphne was all smiles, beckoning with wild, waving arms. Sara was looking at me evenly, her expression impossible to read. I wanted to turn around and leave. It would have been the smartest thing to do. I would still look like a fool for showing up, but I wouldn't be fully manipulated into whatever these women were planning. However, my anger got the best of me, and I marched directly over to them, my feet pounding on the polished wooden floor.

"How *dare* you?" I said, my voice just lower than a shout. Only a few other patrons were in here, but they all turned to look at us.

Daphne colored slightly but gave me a wide smile. "Chloé, please be civil. I'd hate to lose my clubhouse privileges over a little… misunderstanding."

"Misunderstanding? Are you kidding me? And I could give a damn about your privileges."

We'd caused enough commotion to bring the host to the doorway of the barroom, and Daphne waved him away. "We're okay!" she said to him. She looked at me. "Aren't we?"

I didn't respond, too angry to speak without shouting. Daphne sat back down in her chair and indicated the free one next to her. I stared at her for a long moment, feeling mutinous enough to slap her in the face. I spent a long moment marshaling my anger. While I was angrier than I think I'd ever been, I was also curious. Sara had physically assaulted me, and she had haunted my dreams and nightmares for months. Yet here she was, sitting as casually as if we'd once been introduced at a party.

The last time I'd been close to her, she'd seemed unhinged, deranged even. Here in this exclusive place, she looked unruffled, casual. I put one hand in my purse on my phone, ready to pull it out in an emergency, took a deep breath, and made my way to the other chair directly across from Sara. Her face remained calm, and she and I simply stared at each other without speaking for a long pause. Her eyes looked a little amused, but her expression was otherwise blank and composed.

"There now," said Daphne, clearly pleased. "That wasn't so hard, was it?"

I broke eye contact with Sara and looked at Daphne. "Just what the hell do you want to prove by bringing me here?" I gestured toward Sara. "After the way she acted the first time we met, I should be calling the police." I managed kept my voice low when I spoke, but only just.

"I wanted the both of you to clear the air a little. Like I said, there's been a kind of misunderstanding. Sara is a dear friend of mine, and I don't want you to get the wrong idea about her."

"She attacked me!" This time I did shout, and several people looked over at us again.

Daphne held her hands up toward them and me defensively. "I'm not saying what Sara did was right. But she regrets it. She's told me as much."

I looked at Sara. "So she speaks for you? Why aren't you saying anything?"

Sara shrugged. "I told Daphne this was a stupid idea, but she insisted. I knew you wouldn't want to talk to me."

"I don't."

She shrugged again and looked at Daphne. "This is a waste of time."

"Now, ladies," Daphne said. "If you both attempt to be a bit more civil, we can make some real progress today. Shall I order us some cocktails?"

I glared at her, and she held her hands up again. "Okay! No cocktails. It was just an idea. Help break the ice and all that."

I looked back at Sara. "I still don't understand what this is all about. The last time I saw you, you threatened my life. And my aunt's life. Why should I speak to you?"

Daphne broke in again. "Like I said, it was all a misunderstanding. Though maybe that's not the best phrase here. Call it a misstep, if you will. Sara was…let's just say she was a little worked up. Not thinking clearly."

I glared at Sara. "That's putting it mildly."

Sara rolled her eyes. "Daphne, this is ridiculous. It's obvious this woman can't listen to reason."

Daphne tutted and touched Sara's shoulder. "Patience, my dear. I respect Amelia too much to dismiss this girl out of hand. There's clearly more to her than meets the eye. Wouldn't you agree?"

Sara hesitated and then nodded, though obviously reluctant to admit as much.

"So if we know that, it might behoove you to try, *n'est-ce pas*?"

Again, after a pause, she nodded.

"Good. Then it's settled. Now I'm going to absent myself and let the two of you get better acquainted. I hope you'll both be on your best behavior." She stood, her bangles and jewelry ringing together on her arms and fingers. She walked directly over to the bar proper and sat down, out of earshot but within sight, possibly in case something happened.

Sara and I continued to regard each other in cold silence. This was the first time I'd gotten a good look at her since she attacked me, and she seemed completely different in this context. Her face was narrow, with high cheekbones and flawless, olive skin. She had beautiful dark, shoulder-length wavy hair, which she'd brushed back from her face. Her lashes and brows were also very dark, framing a pair of deep-brown eyes. Her clothes were tasteful, clearly tailored, and she was wearing a band of platinum or white gold with little diamonds on the ring finger of her left hand. Though darker overall, she reminded me strongly of Amelia's mother. She had that same cold, remote beauty.

She was obviously absorbing me in the same way I was absorbing her, going so far as to lean forward onto her elbows on the table to get a better look at me. Finally, she sat back, her face finally showing some emotion—confusion.

"Well, I suppose you're pretty," she said. "In a girl-next-door kind of way."

"Is that supposed to be a compliment?"

She shrugged. "Take it as you will. I just don't get it."

"Don't get what?"

"What Amelia sees in you."

"And how is that any of your business?" I asked.

She didn't immediately reply. Instead, I watched as her face shifted briefly from anger back to calm again—the rage there disappearing almost as fast as it'd appeared. The transformation and cover-up were terrifying, and my heart rate picked up with fear. She was like a coiled snake. She sat forward again but kept her hands in her lap, clasped together as if to keep them controlled. After simply staring at me quietly, something else crossed through her eyes—sorrow. Her eyes welled up with tears, and for a moment I was sure she would start crying. She blinked rapidly a few times, looked up at the ceiling, and then wiped her eyes.

"I'm so stupid, Chloé," she finally said. "I don't even know why you're sitting here listening to me."

"I'm wondering the same thing."

She still looked hurt, but she nodded. She stared at me evenly before going on. "I was going to do something stupid again. Like the last time I saw you…but to myself. In front of you."

That was possibly one of the worst things I'd ever heard, and my heart swelled with pity. I certainly didn't want her to hurt us or herself—in fact, that was the last thing I wanted.

"But you decided not to?" I asked. I wanted her assurance that she wasn't suicidal.

She hesitated. "I probably would have gone through with it, but Daphne figured it out. I've been staying with her this week, and she saw something…she talked me out of it and helped arrange this little meeting to clear the air."

My fear was back, tempered by anger. This woman had hurt me and wanted to hurt me again. Yet I sat listening to her as if she deserved an audience for her lunacy. I needed to leave, and I needed to call the police. It was madness to be here.

I shifted as if to get up, and Sara grabbed my arm, the movement viper-like in its quickness. I froze, halfway out of my chair, her fingers digging into my skin.

"Please," she hissed. "Please just listen to me. If you listen to me now, I'll never bother you again. I swear it." Her voice caught and she swallowed a few times, choking back tears. "If I don't talk to you now, I-I don't know what I'll do."

I was looking into her eyes as she said this and finally saw the depth of her pain and panic. All of the casual nonchalance of the last few minutes had been a front. She was deeply, unmistakably wounded. I also thought she might be telling the truth. If I listened, this could all be over.

I took my seat again and watched as she calmed down. Once again, that composed mask slipped back into place and her tears dried up. Her madness, if that's what it was, was hidden again, but the earlier illusion was shattered. I knew now what was underneath her calm veneer, and I couldn't help but pity it, at least in part. This was a woman in pain.

She couldn't meet my eyes anymore, clearly embarrassed by her outburst. She stared down at the tabletop, playing with a fork on the table. I could see her willing herself to speak, and I waited, knowing words would come when she was ready. Finally, she stopped fidgeting, took a long, calming breath, and looked up at me.

"Let me tell you a story. About a girl, younger than you are now."

I nodded, trying to keep my expression neutral. I wanted her to have her say and be done with it. It was already clear she was talking about herself, but she could tell me the story any way she wanted to—that was her choice.

Sara looked as if she couldn't quite believe I was willing to listen to her. She went on.

"This girl grew up here in town. She was lucky. She was born into wealth and privilege. She attended all of the best private schools, grew up in a large house in the best part of town. She spent summers in Europe and the Caribbean. She had simply to ask and she received. She even had a coming-out party at a debutante ball, if you can believe it."

She had tears in her eyes and once again blinked them away before they fell from her lashes. She shook her head a little as if to clear it.

"As she got older, things changed. Her life was not as it appeared. For one thing, she wasn't interested in dating the young men her parents tried to set her up with. She knew at a young age that her interests lay elsewhere, were of a female persuasion, if you will. But she told no one.

"Finally, unable to keep her feelings to herself any longer, she told all to the only person she knew who would listen: an old family friend, Daphne Waters."

Ah, I thought. This explained their closeness.

"Daphne helped the girl accept herself for who she was and helped her come out to her parents." She paused and, her voice breaking a little, she then continued. "Daphne even helped the girl when her parents disowned her. She helped her through college, supported her through her first forays into love." She looked me in the eyes. "And she helped the girl land her first job out of the university."

I knew where this was going now, and while I didn't really want to sit here and listen to her anymore, I couldn't help but feel a surge of excited curiosity. Amelia had told me next to nothing about Sara or any of her other ex-girlfriends. Judging by Sara's violent behavior in the past, I knew she was a woman I shouldn't trust, but I couldn't help myself. I wanted to hear more about what happened.

"The girl fell in love with her new boss, and she fell hard and fast. And it seemed like her boss fell in love with her, too. The trappings of love were there, at any rate. Her boss showered her with gifts and vacations, took her to the best restaurants in town, introduced her to friends and family. Everything seemed to be going very well. The girl, who had held herself back all those years, terrified lest she be hurt the way her parents had hurt her, let herself fall in love completely, wholly."

This sounded eerily similar to my own experience with Amelia, and I shifted uncomfortably in my seat. I reminded myself of what Billy, Emma's boyfriend, had told me: that it was clear to everyone that they had loved each other, and for the first time, I was a little jealous.

"Then, out of the blue, a career opportunity for the girl presented itself. The girl had trained in business, and Wall Street came calling— recruited *her*, of all people. She'd only taken the job with Amelia's company as a stop-gap while she waited for just this sort of position to appear. When she told her boss about it, her boss seemed happy for her, even encouraging. At first."

She stopped long enough to drain the little glass of water in front of her, and when she set the glass down again, I saw that her hands were badly shaking. She clasped them again in her lap to hide them from me.

"As the moving date approached, her boss became more distant. Small changes occurred. Fewer phone calls and then fewer nights over. A missed night or two turned into three and four, and then a whole week could pass without the girl seeing her boss outside of work. Eventually the girl sensed a distinct coldness growing between them. Desperate to mend the growing gap, the girl offered to give up the job in New York, to stay in New Orleans and work for her boss forever, if that's what it would take. It didn't help—her boss had frozen her out.

"On the plane to New York, the girl knew she'd lost everything, all over a stupid job. She'd given up the love of her life for work, of all things. She tried to forget her first love. At times it seemed like she'd dated every available woman in New York. Nothing worked. Nothing helped her forget what she'd lost."

Then Sara was quiet and looked calm again. She stared outside at the golf course, her eyes distant and removed, locked in the past of her story. I was relieved, however, that I finally knew what had happened. It certainly didn't paint Amelia in a very good light, but I also knew that one of the reasons Amelia didn't like to talk about her ex-girlfriends was precisely because so many of her previous relationships had ended this way. Amelia had told me that she and Sara simply drifted apart, or at least it seemed so at the time, but clearly Sara remembered the breakup differently. It troubled me that Amelia hadn't recognized how badly she'd hurt this woman, but that didn't excuse Sara's violence and meddling. I didn't like the idea that Amelia had been so careless with her, but Sara had no right to try to cause us grief, either. Still, I couldn't help but feel a little remorse on her behalf. It must be galling to see someone else receive the love you thought you deserved.

I wanted this encounter to be over now, and I shifted in my chair to draw Sara's eyes to mine. Her expression was bleak, depressed. I held out my hand and after a moment of evident surprise, she took it in hers.

"Sara, I'm sorry Amelia treated you that way. You certainly didn't deserve it—no one deserves to be treated poorly. I don't excuse Amelia's behavior at all. It was cruel."

Her eyes filled with tears, and this time she let them fall, unheeded, down her cheeks.

"But you have to let it go," I said. "You have to let *her* go. And you have to leave us alone. It isn't going to help you to hurt me or try to hurt yourself. In fact, I can promise it will only make you feel worse.

"Get some help. Please. Find someone you can talk to about this—someone impartial. Not Daphne, not a friend, but a professional. I know you can get past this."

I stood, and she touched my arm one last time. Our eyes met.

"Chloé?"

"Yes?"

"Thank you. Really. You didn't have to sit here and listen to me." She paused, eyes welling with tears. "I-I think I understand why she chose you now. You're a good person."

"Good luck, Sara. I hope you find some peace."

I walked directly from Sara over to Daphne, who looked incredibly pleased with herself. My expression must have spoken volumes, as I saw her smile falter when I drew closer. I was calmer now and could keep my voice at speaking level, but I was absolutely furious.

"How *dare* you?" I told her. "Have you lost your fucking mind? Why on earth would you do that to me? Or to Amelia?"

She seemed far less certain than she had for the last hour, as if suddenly recognizing her tactical error. She shook her head, and then the faux confidence slid back into place.

"I care for Miss Sara very much. She's like a daughter to me. I'll do anything I can to help her—I always have."

"Well, this is not helping," I snapped. "And it's very, very clear that she needs psychological evaluation and treatment. Now. Immediately. If I were you, I'd take her to the hospital today."

She looked uncertain again, and I saw her eyes travel back to Sara, who was staring out the window again, appearing hunched and small.

"You think it's that serious?" Daphne asked.

"Of course it is!" I hissed. "She told me she was going to hurt herself in front of me. You don't think that's serious?" Daphne tried to wave the threat away, but I wouldn't have it. "She said you caught her and talked her out of it. What did she plan to do?"

Now she looked distinctly uncomfortable, even a little panicked. "Well, you see, I found this gun in her luggage yesterday."

My heart skipped a beat, and I stepped closer to Daphne, making her meet my eyes. "You found a *gun,* and you didn't do anything about it?"

"I thought it was a gesture—for show!" Daphne looked as if she barely believed this explanation herself.

I pointed at Sara. "That woman is suicidal. She had a gun and a plan. If you don't promise me right now that you're going to get her some help, I swear to God I'll call the police this minute." I held up my hands. "No—actually, your promise isn't enough. I want to see you contact someone right now. I'm sure you know some fancy doctor here in town you can get in touch with on a Sunday afternoon. After all, you seem to know everyone."

Daphne's eyes flickered back and forth between me and Sara a few times, and I finally saw her accept what I was saying. Her eyes suddenly filled with tears. She put a hand to her mouth to stifle a sob.

"My poor baby," she whispered, staring at Sara. "My poor darling."

"So you'll call someone?" I asked.

She nodded, quickly, with no hesitation. It was enough.

I started to leave, but she touched my sleeve. I turned to meet her tear-stained face.

"I have no right to ask you anything, Chloé, but do you think we can keep this between us?"

I shook my head. "I don't make a habit of hiding things from Amelia, Daphne, and I don't intend to start now."

"Well, do you think you could at least wait a couple of days? I mean, while I get Sara settled in a treatment center? Amelia can be a little…temperamental. I want Sara safe first."

I hesitated and then nodded. It wouldn't help to have Amelia on the warpath before Sara was tucked away somewhere.

"Thank you, Chloé. I owe you."

I pointed at Sara again. "You help that woman get her life together, and we'll be even."

I strode away and out the door before she could say another word.

CHAPTER ELEVEN

I waited too long to tell Amelia about my encounter with Sara—I'll be the first to admit that. I let several things distract me, accidentally on purpose as they say. For one thing, I had to go back to work the next day, Monday, and as I hadn't seen Amelia since Friday night, I didn't want to spoil our mini-reunion. Also, Daphne had asked me to wait a couple of days before I told her, so it was too soon the first time we saw each other to say anything anyway. At least that's what I told myself at the time.

Work was incredibly busy that week, too. After a couple of delays due to scheduling conflicts, we were finally doing the installation at Teddy's in the Marigny, and I was rushing back and forth between the office and the restaurant on Monday to make sure everything ran smoothly for the installation on Tuesday. It didn't. Three blocks from the warehouse, the moving vehicle managed to drive over several nails, puncturing almost every tire. I should have simply called our backup truck over and transferred everything, but I waited too long. By the time I realized they had to tow the truck over to the tire shop to get it repaired, our other moving van was out on a delivery.

I had to accompany the truck with the flat tires and our artwork to Peanut's Tires and sit there all morning and afternoon as the mechanics scrambled to fix them. Of course they didn't have the right tires in stock, and someone had to drive all the way to Baton Rouge to get more. By the time the tires were installed and the truck was ready to drive again, it was much too late in the afternoon to begin the installation. We'd planned on a one-day, morning-and-afternoon setup to help the restaurant avoid closing for dinner, so I had to call them and reschedule for the next day, which made me sound like an unprofessional idiot.

I had other distractions as well. On Wednesday, as I stood in the middle of Teddy's restaurant, directing the installation, I got the call I was waiting for. The art-history department at New Orleans State wanted me to come the next day or Friday for a teaching demonstration. I scheduled it sooner rather than later, wanting to get it over with, then immediately regretted my decision. I would be tied up at the restaurant all afternoon, and Amelia and I were going to receive a special early dinner at Teddy's today to celebrate. I wouldn't have any time to prepare. Still, I decided to forgo sleep rather than call the hiring committee back. I'd be just as busy tomorrow evening, after all.

When the last painting was hung and the last sculpture was placed, Teddy invited me to join her at the bar while we waited for Amelia. The light was different from the last time I'd been there with Emma. We'd changed all the bulbs to a soft, low white. It's amazing how much a few lightbulbs can change an atmosphere. The artwork was also dramatically different, so between the lights and the art, the dining room seemed like a new place.

Teddy insisted on opening a bottle of champagne to celebrate, and we sat close to each other at the bar. She was already in her black chef's uniform, but despite this, her athletic frame was still visible under the heavy material. She rolled her sleeves, leaving her forearms exposed. I'd noticed her tattoos the last time I was here, but now, alone together and sitting down, I had the opportunity to look at them closely. She noticed my gaze and held an arm out for inspection. The tattoos had been expertly designed. Hers were uniformly black with lighter shading, clearly inked by a master. I don't have any tattoos myself, but I appreciate them if they're done well, and hers were beautiful.

"I'm friends with a tattoo artist here in town," Teddy explained. "She's the only person who works on me. She's incredible. I can get you her number, if you want."

I laughed. "Oh no. I'm much too chicken."

Teddy grinned. "That's what my wife said until she got her first one. Now she's catching up with me. It's nice, because I always know what to get her for her birthday or Christmas: another tattoo."

We chatted a while longer, and then I saw a flash of movement and dark hair outside. A moment later Amelia walked in through the front door. She took off her sunglasses and stood blinking for a moment, taking in the room. She and I had done the mock-ups of the space together, but she hadn't actually been in here since we started work on the project. I saw her look around, carefully, and then she moved around the room to inspect some of our choices. Finally, she seemed to sense our eyes on her, and she turned until she spotted us and then laughed before walking our way.

"I'm sorry," she said, holding out a hand. "I thought I was alone."

Teddy shook her hand, clearly appraising her as they greeted each other. Amelia was at her prettiest today. Her cheeks were rosy from the slight chill in the air, making her color much higher and brighter than usual. Also, knowing that we had this dinner with our clients this afternoon, she'd dressed carefully to highlight her best features. Amelia always looks great, but she looks especially attractive in dark gem tones. She was wearing a silk, navy blouse with pearl buttons and a charcoal-gray skirt and heels. She kissed my cheek and remained standing next to us.

"Please, sit down," Teddy said, moving to get up and give her the barstool.

"Oh no, Miss Rose. Please stay seated. I've been at the computer all day. I'd rather stand for now."

Teddy handed her a glass of champagne, and Amelia took a sip, closing her eyes and rolling the wine in her mouth. I was amused to see Teddy watching her every move. After a moment, she swallowed hard and wrenched her eyes away. I could relate. Watching Amelia enjoy herself, with food or drink or something more carnal, was intoxicating. It made you want to please her over and over again.

Teddy shook herself out of her trance and stood up. "Now I really must go, Miss Winters. I have some things to look over in the kitchen. Please take my seat. I'll be serving our dinner soon. My wife and I will join you then."

Amelia took her spot and then cradled one of my hands in hers. She was still a little chilled from being outside, and I chafed her hand to warm it. We were having another series of chilly days. While it wasn't as cold as it had been in January, it was unusually cold for us this late in February. Amelia had neglected to wear a coat, I realized, and I almost chided her for her oversight, but she looked so happy that I didn't want to say anything. Her eyes were dreamy, dazed almost, and her lips were curled into a loose grin.

"What is it?" I asked. "Why are you smiling?"

"Just enjoying the view. I love looking at you."

I couldn't help but color at her remark and glance down at myself. I'd dressed with more care than usual and spent more time on my hair and makeup in anticipation of this dinner, but I didn't think I looked that different. But perhaps that was the point of her compliment.

"Thanks," I murmured. "You're not half bad yourself. Did you see the way Teddy was staring at you?"

Amelia grinned. "I did. I've heard she's always been like that. But I guess she just looks now, seeing as she's married."

"Did you know her before?"

"I knew *of* her, anyway. I mean I remember seeing her around at clubs and bars, but we never met. She was much too intimidating. She was around and on the prowl way back—before the hurricane. I think she lived somewhere else for a while, but when she came back to town, just about everyone had a story about her. She always went home with the hottest woman in the room. New one every night."

"So you didn't have the pleasure?"

She laughed. "No. I wasn't cocky enough to approach her, and I was much too young at the time, anyway. That was what, ten years ago? Christ." She shook her head. "Where does the time go? I can't wait to see the woman who finally managed to capture her. She must be something else."

She didn't have to wait long, as Teddy and her wife Kit came out of the kitchen a few minutes later. I introduced Amelia to Kit and watched in amusement as Kit reacted similarly to her, staring a little too long and watching her a little too closely before seeming to snap out of it. Amelia has this effect on people. It's hard to tear your eyes off her. I was, however, having a similar reaction to Teddy, so I guess the attraction was a kind of mutual admiration all around. After introductions, the four of us walked around the room, examining the paintings. Amelia and I took turns explaining our choices and arrangements. When we'd finished, we all sat down in a comfortable, circular booth in the corner of the room to wait for the food. It was still an hour until they opened to the public for dinner.

"I love all the pieces in here," Teddy said. "I'm more pleased than I can say. I knew we had a lot of talented artists in town, but I had no idea how much I'd love seeing their work all together like this."

"We plan to invite some local media here to do a write-up on the show, so I hope that provides business for both of us," Amelia explained. "Not that you seem to need it."

"We're also going to rotate our artists every other month, if that works for you," I explained. "That way we can showcase almost everyone we work with in town."

"I still don't understand why you didn't bring that one painting we loved so much," Kit said, frowning a little. "I like it so much, I was thinking of buying it for the restaurant permanently."

She was talking about my painting. Amelia and I shared a glance, and I looked away quickly to hide my anger. I'd been very upset that she put my work in the portfolio and had demanded that she remove it from future sales pitches. Amelia had been put out, especially after I told her how well Kit and Teddy seemed to like it, but she'd had no choice but to listen to me. My artwork was not for sale.

Teddy must have caught something in our glance, as she chuckled softly. She touched Kit's hand. "I think you put your foot in it, honey. There must be a problem with the piece."

I looked at Amelia in a panic, but she remained unruffled. "There is a problem. I'm afraid the artist is not selling that painting. It was included in the portfolio by accident. My mistake."

Kit looked genuinely disappointed, and I couldn't help but feel a little flush of pride. I didn't show my work to a lot of people, and those I did share it with were close to me. To have an outsider deem it worth buying gave me a quiet sense of satisfaction. Amelia was staring at me, one eyebrow raised, and I knew exactly what she was thinking: I told you so.

"Well, if that artist does paint something new, please let him or her know that I'm very interested," Kit said.

"I'll do that." Amelia winked at me.

We had a very pleasant, extremely delicious meal together. Amelia discussed her plans for a new show she was putting on, which would highlight the Mexican artists she'd discovered in Puerto Vallarta. She invited Kit and Teddy, who seemed interested in it, which led us to talking about our trip to Mexico and how comfortable we'd been there.

"It's certainly nice to go somewhere that caters to us. I hate having to justify wanting one bed when we go most places," Kit said. "We stayed in a little lesbian B&B in New Hampshire last year after our wedding, and it was just marvelous. We went skiing and sledding—all of the stuff I grew up doing in Colorado."

We then started to talk about weddings, the four of us lamenting the fact that Louisiana would likely be one of the last states to legalize gay marriage. Not long ago, the state had been the last bastion of the Democratic South, but recent inroads by the religious right had changed all of that. Now the state was as red as its neighbors. New Orleans and some of the other cities in the state were different, but it would likely be a generation before we elected another Democrat for anything more powerful than mayor.

Other topics arose, including careers and schooling, and I was surprised to learn that Kit used to be a literature professor in California. She explained that she'd moved to be here with Teddy and had never regretted it. Amelia gave me a level stare, and I couldn't help but feel a little guilty. I hadn't yet told Amelia about my teaching demo the next day, but this wasn't the time to bring it up.

By necessity, our dinner had to wrap up once the public began to appear. Kit and Teddy immediately began to seem anxious, and Amelia and I excused ourselves as quickly and graciously as possible. We all agreed, however, to meet again soon, and Teddy promised to call us for their next get-together at their place in the Marigny. I was happy knowing we might finally have some lesbian friends in New Orleans.

Outside, the air had turned from chilly to downright cold. A slight hazy fog was in the air, and a few drops of freezing rain were falling. Amelia looked distinctly underdressed now without a coat, and I rubbed her arms a few times to warm her up.

"So, are you coming over?" I asked.

"I can't. I have that damn phone call tonight with our client in Hong Kong."

"That's tonight? I thought it was tomorrow."

"They rescheduled at the last minute. Anyway, I'm calling them at eight thirty."

"That's still hours from now. Can you come over for a little while at least? We've barely seen each other all week."

She looked uncertain but agreed. Despite the short distance, we took her car back to my place so she wouldn't have to walk back over here later. I have my own parking space—a rarity in any city, let alone near the French Quarter—and it's just big enough to park another car behind mine without blocking the sidewalk.

I'd left the heat blasting in my apartment when I left this morning, and it was almost hot when we got inside. I saw Amelia relax a little and rub her arms, and I was reminded of Emma. Not wearing a coat must be a genetic predisposition.

I was strangely nervous with her and bustled around anxiously in the kitchen as she waited in the living room. Things had been a little off since our pseudo-fight last Friday, and neither one of us seemed to know how to get back to normal. It didn't help that I had two very awkward things to talk to her about: my demonstration tomorrow and my run-in with Sara and Daphne. Neither topic was likely to go well, but, coward that I am, once again I decided to lead with the easier one.

I brought our mugs out a moment later and found Amelia flipping through my sketchbook. I'd left it on the coffee table this morning. I wasn't exactly upset that she was looking at it—it was there, after all—but it reminded me of our earlier tiff about including my work in the local portfolio without my permission. My art was deeply personal. Even when I'd fancied myself something of an artist, in my youth and arrogance, I wouldn't dream of letting people buy it. It wasn't good enough to sell. I didn't even hang it anywhere in my house outside my studio—it was mine and mine alone.

She heard me and looked up, her smile changing to a slight frown. "Is something the matter?"

I shook my head, swallowing my annoyance. I needed to stay focused if I was going to get through this. I sat down next to her, handing her a cup of strong tea. She drank it black, and she rarely let it cool.

"So," I said, "I have some things to tell you."

She looked puzzled and set her tea down, turning her focus to me completely. Her eyes were beautiful, the color of her blouse making them seem even darker than usual.

"Shoot," she said.

I took a deep breath. "New Orleans State called me back."

She smiled. "Was there ever a doubt?"

I laughed, relief flooding me. "Of course. It was a formal interview, after all. They might have chosen someone else."

She kissed the tip of my nose. "Then they're smart. You're the best candidate anyone could ask for."

"I have a teaching demonstration tomorrow morning."

Her smile faltered and she looked away. We sat in silence for a long pause, and then she looked at me again. "So soon?"

A flash of temper sliced through me. I wanted and needed support. "Yes. I told you it would be this week."

She pushed a lock of hair behind one of my ears, her eyes definitely sad now. I could see her struggling with herself, and some of my anger died away. She clearly wanted to say the right thing but was having a difficult time.

Her lips were quivering a little when she spoke again. "And how soon will you leave me?"

I drew her into my arms and kissed the side of her head. I could feel her shaking, and she squeezed me back, hard. I drew away and met her eyes, and now I could see tears there.

"I'm not leaving you, Amelia. You know that. I love you. I'm not going anywhere."

She took a long, shuddering breath and blinked before laughing weakly. "I know, Chloé. I know. Well, at least part of me knows. But another part of me thinks that you'll start this new job, and I'll never see you again. It's stupid, but that's how I feel. I don't mean to be like this. I want you to have everything you want. I want you to be happy. I don't want to be selfish."

I squeezed her hands in mine. "I love working with you, Amelia. I love what we do together. Days like today—when we put up lovely pieces of art and a whole room is revitalized and everyone is happy—I didn't know I could enjoy myself like that in any job." I paused and made sure she met my eyes. "But I've wanted to be a professor my whole life. I worked very hard for this chance. And I think, no, I *know* I'll be good at it."

She took another long, deep breath. "You don't have to justify yourself to me, Chloé. I know you'll be an excellent professor. And I know you'll do great tomorrow." She paused and seemed to look inward for a moment. "I have a hard time letting go—that's all. I'm afraid you'll find something that will take you away from me. It has nothing to do with you. I'm just insecure. It's not your fault—it's mine."

I pulled her into an embrace again, and we stayed in each other's arms for a long time. I couldn't help but think of Sara. She had gotten a job out of town, and Amelia had basically shut her out of her life in response. Amelia's insecurity didn't seem to have spontaneously appeared. It appeared to be a long-entrenched defense mechanism. Where had it come from? Was it from someone before Sara?

Amelia sat back again and appeared much calmer. She was a little pale and a little sad, but I could deal with a mourning period. What I needed, however, was some support.

"So anyway, I won't be in to work tomorrow until after the demonstration," I told her.

"What are you going to teach them?"

"It's a contemporary art-history class, so I have a lot to choose from. The regular professor emailed me the syllabus, so I'll try to fit my choices in with his lesson plan as much as possible."

"I wish I could be there to watch you. I know you'll knock them dead."

It was the best thing she could have said. My heart swelled with happiness, and I gave her another long hug. She kissed me once, deeply, and my spirits lifted. Things weren't perfect yet, but maybe I shouldn't expect that from her. She was allowed to have mixed feelings.

When she sat back, her eyes were dark with desire, and my insides warmed up. She could clearly see the response in my eyes, and her lips twisted into a satisfied grin. She glanced at her watch and then cursed.

"Damn it! I have to go."

"What? Now?" I was still befuddled.

"I'm supposed to go over the contracts with one of our lawyers before the conference call. Something about a recent change in tariffs. He's going to be there at seven."

I gave her my best pout, and she laughed before kissing me and then stood up.

"Can you come back after?" I asked.

She shook her head. "It will probably go until at least midnight. We have to work through an interpreter, so it's going to take twice as long as usual. Let's have a long lunch tomorrow, and you can tell me all about your demonstration. I'll have Janet make a reservation somewhere."

I stood up and gave her one more hug. "I'll miss you."

"Me, too. I already feel like I need another vacation." She paused and linked her hands with mine. "And, Chloé? Good luck tomorrow. Really."

"Thanks, Amelia. I appreciate it."

"I always wanted to date another professor," she said and winked.

"Another?"

"How do you think I got such good grades?"

I was still chuckling as she walked out the door.

Much later that evening, surrounded by books and notes from graduate school, I remembered that I still hadn't told her about my run-in with Sara. I suppressed a twinge of unease but made myself dismiss it. I have enough to worry about, I told myself.

Only later would I realize how stupid I'd been.

CHAPTER TWELVE

I stayed up late preparing for the teaching demonstration the next morning. I debated with myself for a long time before settling on a topic. I would be taking over a section of a class for fifty minutes, and the professor I was standing in for had given me free rein. It was a survey class of contemporary art history, framed in the time period after World War II. From the syllabus, I could see that he'd focused primarily on American art, which gave me some options. I could continue to concentrate on Americans, or I could do something different. My specialty is European and French contemporary art, but I was schooled in American, too. After going back and forth with myself, I settled on French contemporary, guessing correctly that they had discussed very little about it in the class so far. I was up quite late getting my slides together, and when I finally went to bed, I tossed and turned most of the night.

I rose early and dressed carefully, and as I drove to campus I was quaking with nerves. I met the hiring committee in the parking lot, and all of us walked to the classroom together. They kept the talk light, clearly sensing my nervousness. When we finally stood outside the classroom, I had to suppress the desire to run away. I was that scared.

The moment I walked through the door to the classroom, however, things changed. My confidence returned almost instantly. I was still shaking a little when I handed my slides to the TA, but by the time the class officially started—the hiring committee sitting at the back of the room—I hit my stride. I managed to make a quick joke that broke the ice and jumped into my lecture immediately. I had left blank periods in my talk for discussion, and the students immediately raised their hands, clearly wanting to help me out. The entire class period passed quickly, and I was amazed to find myself running out of time as we got close to wrapping up. After the students left, I could see the committee chatting with each other quietly at the back of the room, and when they got up to come greet me, they were all smiles. The professor for whom I'd taught today walked me back to my car, asking insightful questions about the art I'd shown to his class. When I drove off campus, I was certain they would offer me the job.

Janet had texted me the information for lunch today with Amelia, and I arrived just as she was parking. She waved as she got out of the car, and I walked over to meet her. We kissed briefly, and then she held my shoulders, looking me in the eyes.

"I'm trying to tell if this is the face of a professor," she said.

I laughed. "I think so. That is, I hope so."

"Let's get inside, and you can tell me all about it."

Despite the fact that it was a weekday in a neighborhood far from the business district, Café Degas was bustling and busy when we walked through the door. Designed like a French bistro, the space is tight and cozy, with large windows and intimate tables. The food is French with a New Orleans kick, made fresh with local ingredients and by local bakers. I hadn't been there in a few years, but I was pleased to find it exactly as I remembered it. With so many changes in the city lately, it was comforting to find that some things stayed the same.

The menu was a little different from the last time I was there, however, and it took me a long time to choose between the appetizing options. Amelia, who always picks the first thing that looks appealing, watched me debate with myself with a grin. When the waitress came back for the third time, looking distinctly annoyed with me, Amelia finally chose for me and gave her our menus.

"Thanks," I said. "We would have been here all day."

"I figured." She paused and lifted her eyebrows. "So? Are you going to tell me about it or what?"

I launched into the story of the demonstration, sharing every little detail. I described my nerves and my shaking hands and how all of that had disappeared once I stood in front of the class. I described the bright students and how helpful they'd been, as well as the clear approval I'd sensed from the hiring committee after I was done.

She was smiling widely at this point, and when I finished, she took both of my hands in hers, squeezing them. "I knew you'd do well. I bet you anything they call you tomorrow with a job offer."

I sighed. "There's actually one more step before that happens. If they call me back, anyway."

"What? Are you kidding me? Academia is ridiculous. What else do you have to do?"

"I have to meet with the provost and the dean. Officially. I met both of them briefly last week, but we have to have a sit-down discussion about salary and tenure and things like that."

She snorted. "The dean that set you up with the interview?"

I nodded.

She grinned. "So no problem, right? It's in the bag, honey. I know it is."

Her happiness for me was genuine, and I couldn't suppress a nearly overwhelming sense of relief. Some of this must have shown in my face, as I saw her expression change a little and guilt flash through her eyes.

She squeezed my hands again. "Listen, Chloé. I wanted to apologize for how I've been behaving this week."

"You don't have to—"

"But I do. I've been a complete ass. I should have been excited and happy for you, but instead I acted like you were taking something away from me. From now on, you have my full support—whatever happens. I promise."

Our food was delivered then, or I might have broken down right there in the restaurant. I knew it was hard for her to admit that she was wrong, and I'd given her time to get used to the idea, but I hadn't realized quite how much her reluctance had bothered me until it had been put to rest.

When our plates were taken away, we continued to sit there in comfortable silence. The weather had finally turned today, and although it was still a little chilly out, the staff had opened some of the windows, letting in a cool, nearly spring-like breeze. Amelia had her eyes closed, soaking in the sunshine streaming in, and I grinned like a fool as I stared at her. We'd weathered our biggest misunderstanding in months, and I was giddy. She opened her eyes and smiled when she saw me watching her.

Amelia paid the bill, and we walked out into the afternoon

sunshine. It actually felt distinctly warm now for the first time in weeks. We both stood there on the sidewalk in front of her car, soaking in the sun.

Amelia sighed. "Makes me want to take the rest of the afternoon off."

"Can we?"

She shook her head. "No, not right now. But there's a light at the end of the tunnel. Almost everything major should be wrapped up by the middle or end of March if we keep pushing like this. Maybe we can take another little trip after—somewhere close this time. Maybe the beach again. I've heard nice things about Ocean Springs in Mississippi."

I walked up to her and put my arms around her, snuggling into her neck. "Do you promise?"

She shivered. "Yes. Now we better head in before you tempt me too much. Where's your car?"

I turned to point, but Amelia's phone rang. She rolled her eyes, clearly annoyed, and dug around in her purse to find it. She looked at the screen and frowned before she answered.

"Yes, hello?"

I'd taken a couple of steps away to give her privacy, thinking it was a business call, but as I watched her face while she listened, I could see something was wrong. Her expression changed from vague annoyance to clear anger and then settled into an icy rage. She was staring at me as she listened. She said very little as the other party talked, simply agreeing once or twice with one-word answers. Finally, without saying anything to the other person, she hung up, dropping her phone back into her purse as if disgusted with it. She was still looking at me with hard, angry eyes.

My heart was pounding. I'd never seen her this enraged. "Amelia? What is it?" I took a step toward her, and she backed away from me. I stopped completely, startled by her reaction.

"That was Daphne Waters," she said quietly.

The sidewalk seemed to shift under my feet. Suddenly the world seemed completely unfamiliar, unrecognizable. Amelia's expression was so cold, so angry, I could hardly believe she was looking at me. Panic flooded through my body in flashing waves of heat.

"You have to let me explain," I told her.

"I don't have to listen to a goddamn thing you say," she spat. She had her fists clenched at her sides and seemed about to spring at me.

I flinched and actually took a step away from her, sure she was about to hit me. My reaction did nothing to soften her stance or her expression. If anything, her eyes became colder.

"How could you?"

I was so scared of her and how she was acting, I started to blubber. "Amelia, please! You have every right to be angry, but I don't understand why you're so upset. I know I should have told you that I saw her—"

She laughed, once, cutting me off. "Of course you should have told me! Goddamn it, Chloé! All you ever do is lie and hide things from me. How do you think that makes me feel?"

"Amelia, that's not true and you know it."

"Hmm, let's see. What happened just a few days ago? You lied and covered up the fact that you had a job interview. A fucking job interview! Like it was no big deal! Like I was the last person who should know!"

I flushed with shame, but a tiny flame of anger began building inside me now. "You know why I was afraid to tell you about it, Amelia. You're not being fair."

She continued as if she hadn't heard me. "I might forgive you doing that, just that, but now I find out you did it again two days later! You've been hiding a fucking criminal! Sara should be in prison, Chloé, not in some fancy nuthouse. Why didn't you tell me? What else are you hiding?"

I opened my mouth to begin to explain, and then she held her hands up, closing her eyes briefly before opening them and fixing me with a dead, cold stare. "You know what? I don't care. I don't want to hear it. I've done everything I can to get you to trust me, and you clearly don't. You trust Sara and Daphne Waters more than you trust me."

I took a step toward her again, my arms open. "Amelia, Jesus! Just listen to me for a minute. We can fix this!"

"No. No, we can't," she said, shaking her head. For a moment, I saw the depth of the pain in her eyes, but anger quickly replaced it. She turned and started walking toward her car.

I couldn't help but run after her. I grabbed her arm and spun her toward me. "For God's sake, Amelia! Just listen!"

She wrenched her arm out of my grip, and again that murderous hatred flashed through her eyes. I stepped warily away from her, once again certain she might hit me.

"You're a liar, Chloé. Maybe that's all you've ever been. Maybe this was all some big ruse." Her eyes narrowed, and her face, already pale, whitened perceptibly. "Was it the money? Is that what it was all this time?"

She might as well have slapped me. For a moment, I couldn't breathe. Deep rage instantly replaced my terror and fear. "Fuck you. You know that's not true."

She shook her head, her eyes dark and sunken. "I don't know anything anymore."

We stood there, staring at each other, for a long moment, our world collapsing around us. The look in her eyes was cold enough to freeze the sun, and its fury was so harsh the words dried up in my mouth. I couldn't think of a single thing to say or do that would make things right again.

"You've broken my heart, Chloé. You betrayed me deeper and more fully than I knew was possible." She paused. "Don't come back to work. I'll send your things to your apartment."

My heart lurched again in my chest, and I managed a single word. "Amelia!"

She shook her head, and the words died in my mouth again. There was no point—she wouldn't listen to me. She turned away and stalked over to her car. Even from where I stood, I could see that her hands were shaking, and it took her a while to get out her keys. She paused for a moment, still staring into her purse, and then she looked up at me.

"I have one more present for you. I've been carrying it around for weeks. Take it and pawn it, for all I care." She pulled out a little black box and threw it at me. I let it fall into the grass at my feet, not attempting to catch it and not looking at it. She shrugged and got into her car, started it, and drove away without another glance at me.

I was frozen to the spot. My insides were ice, and I was quivering with what felt like a physical cold. My mind, so overcome by what had just happened, couldn't accept it. Ten minutes ago we'd been happy, making plans. We'd cleared a major hurdle. We were moving on.

Now it was over.

"No," I whispered, shaking my head. No way could it end like this. Again, my mind revolted. I'd lied to her, yes, but both instances had been lies of omission. She had to know this. She had to accept that I hadn't meant to hurt her.

"No," I whispered again. Tears were falling down my cheeks, but I was still petrified with dread and horror over what had just happened.

Finally, I started to come out of my deep freeze, but I was in a daze. I looked around, as if to see if Amelia was nearby, but of course she wasn't. Instead, I was left with her empty parking space and the little black box near my feet. I stared down at it, knowing precisely what was inside. I'd seen boxes like that in the movies. Only one thing came in such boxes. I was tempted to leave it there. If I picked it up and opened it, I would fall into a million pieces. I was breathing, heavily, my heart pounding. I was faint and ill, and my ears were ringing. I simply couldn't accept that it was over, that my carelessness had cut off Amelia's love as if it had never existed.

Finally, I bent down, but rather than opening the box, I crammed it into my purse without looking at it. I couldn't leave it there, but I couldn't look at it, either. Maybe I would never look at it. At that thought, I finally broke. I'm sure I made a scene for anyone to see, but I didn't notice. I sank to the ground, sobbing, I might have even screamed a few times—I don't know.

A woman from the café came out after a while and helped me to a nearby bench, but I barely registered her presence for a long time. She sat there with me until I finally calmed down enough to leave. I don't know what she must have thought. Somehow I stumbled back to my car, my mind still in a whirl of pain and confusion. Stupidly, I drove myself back to my apartment. I was hardly aware of what I was doing until my front door was closed behind me.

Then I fell apart.

CHAPTER THIRTEEN

I'm not entirely sure what would have happened if I hadn't had my aunt or Meghan around to take care of me. At first, when they didn't know, I think I was as close as I've ever been to actual insanity. I didn't eat and I didn't bathe. I resembled some kind of wraith, wandering around my apartment in the middle of the night and sleeping all day. Those were the only two actions I was capable of at first—pacing or sleeping.

Things might have gone on like this indefinitely, but my aunt's sixth sense told her something was wrong. We normally talk once or twice a week but have no schedule per se. So the fact that I didn't contact her all weekend wasn't unusual, but she was worried nonetheless, especially as I hadn't told her about the teaching demonstration yet. After another day of not getting in touch, she started calling once an hour, every hour, and then, fed up, she showed up at my place on Tuesday morning. I didn't answer the door. I'm not sure if I was avoiding people or if I was even aware of the doorbell ringing—I don't remember. She had to go back to her place to search for the spare key, and when she came back, she brought Meghan with her.

"I don't know what made me so worried," Aunt Kate told me later. "I just knew I needed to get inside your place and that I needed to do it immediately."

I was very lucky she did. When she and Meghan opened the door, they found me, delirious, on the floor of my kitchen, quietly crying. I hadn't eaten in days, I was dehydrated, and I'd actually soiled myself. My aunt wanted to take me to the hospital, but Meghan talked her into letting them try to bring me out of it, a move I'm ultimately grateful for, even if it was dangerous. The two of them managed to get through to me later that afternoon, and it was like coming out of a fog. They spent the afternoon bathing me and feeding me broth and electrolytes.

"Finally, it was like the lights came on in your eyes," Aunt Kate told me later, tearing up. "You looked at us and you knew us."

"It was the scariest thing I ever saw—you were in a trance," Meghan said, shaking her head.

The story came spilling out of me—incoherently, I found out later, but the gist was clear. Amelia had broken up with me. They eventually got the story from me when I'd calmed down a little, but it took a few more days for me to tell them without breaking down again. Meghan and Aunt Kate had been taking turns staying with me, but they were both there the following Saturday—about a week after the breakup— when I managed to relate the whole story. First I had to back up and fill them both in about Sara. I'd been lying about her for some time now, I realized. Sara had put me in an awkward position with just about everyone I knew. While Meghan knew Sara had attacked me last fall, she didn't know that she was Amelia's ex. This was the first time Aunt Kate had heard anything about Sara, and she was appalled and clearly hurt that I'd hid it all from her for so long.

Amelia's reaction completely baffled both of them. Yes, I'd lied, and yes, I'd covered up for Sara and Daphne, but it didn't add up.

"There must be something more than that," Meghan said. "It's not enough. Is there something else?"

I shook my head. "Not that I know of."

She and Aunt Kate shared a look, and I was reminded of a hundred similar looks before this. I forced myself not to speak up in Amelia's defense. At this point I still had the instinct to stand up for her, but the words died on my lips. I had no reason to defend her anymore. She'd done exactly what Meghan and Aunt Kate had predicted all along— she'd broken my heart.

Aunt Kate looked at her watch and tsked. "Oh, crap. I'm supposed to meet Jim for dinner."

"Go, Kate, please," I said, trying to seem brave and settled. I glanced at Meghan. "You don't have to be here either, Meghan. I appreciate all you've done, but I don't need a babysitter."

She and Aunt Kate shared another look, and Aunt Kate patted my hand. "It'll make me feel better if she's here, Chloé. For now. Just until you get back on your feet again."

I knew they were both afraid I was suicidal, and, not sure if I was or not, I didn't bother arguing. After getting wearily to my feet, I walked my aunt to the door and kissed her cheek before she left. I closed the door and turned to see Meghan sorting through a pile of DVDs she'd brought over.

"I've got romantic comedies and regular comedies. Nothing ghoulish or scary, since I know you hate that stuff."

I had to smile. For Meghan to agree to watch something that wasn't a thriller or a horror movie was a true sign of how much she wanted to comfort me.

"I'm not sure I'm up for a movie tonight, Meghan. I'm pretty tired. I kind of want to go to bed."

She frowned. While she and my aunt agreed that sleeping was good for me, they both complained that I was sleeping too much. Still, I'd been up for several hours at this point and was exhausted.

"You need to stay up for at least a little while, girly. If not a movie, how about cards? Or a board game?"

I shook my head. "Too much thinking."

She sighed. "Well, at the very least you need to eat something. A few more days of the Amelia Winters Breakup Diet, and we're going to have to buy you a whole new wardrobe."

She was kidding, but her remarks hit me like a fist. I barely made it to the couch before my legs gave out, and I sat down heavily, sobbing.

Meghan moved closer, putting her arm around my shoulders. "Jesus, Chloé, I'm sorry. I shouldn't have said her name, and I shouldn't have joked about her. Are you okay?"

I nodded and then shook my head. "Just felt dizzy for a moment. I'll be okay." I desperately tried to blink my tears away but couldn't. Meghan pulled me into her arms, letting me cry into her hair. Eventually I calmed down enough to move away, embarrassed once again by my inability to keep my shit together.

"The wardrobe," I whispered, staring at my hands.

"What?"

"My wardrobe." My voice was a little firmer. I met her eyes. "Amelia bought me almost everything I own."

Meghan's face clouded with anger, and she looked away. I watched her expression morph from rage to pain, and then to sorrow as she tried to calm herself. She and Aunt Kate had been very careful not to say anything too deprecatory about Amelia this week, surely knowing that I wouldn't take it well, but it had been very hard for Meghan to swallow her anger. She's always been something of a hothead and was clearly having a hard time holding her reaction in. Finally, almost as if choking down a big bite of something she hated, she closed her eyes, breathed deeply, and looked at me again.

"Do you want me to get rid of it?" she asked.

"What?"

"Your wardrobe. All the things she bought you."

I laughed. "Hell, no!" She looked startled and I laughed again. "They're the nicest things I've ever owned. I should get something out all of this, right?"

She looked disbelieving for a moment, and then she laughed, too. This set us both into a volley of giggles, the two of us clasping each other in merriment. Eventually Meghan sat back, wiping her eyes and wheezing to catch her breath.

"Well, I'm glad to see you're starting to have a sense of humor about it, Chloé. I was really worried about you for a while there." She took my hands in hers. "I hope I can stop worrying now. I can, right?"

I took a long time responding, thinking about how I felt. I was still gutted—still hollow and bleak when I looked inside myself, but I didn't want to kill myself. I'm not sure I ever really wanted to on a conscious level. I had almost died, or at least hurt myself, from self-neglect, but that was passive. I finally met Meghan's eyes and nodded.

"You don't have to worry anymore, Meghan. I promise I won't hurt myself."

The relief in her eyes was obvious, and we hugged one another, hard. I felt guilty for putting her through this, but I also knew I couldn't send her away. Even if she believed my promise, she'd keep staying over until Aunt Kate told her it was okay to stop.

Meghan grabbed a movie at random after this, and we both zoned out as it played. Instead of watching, I began my own mental movie—a series of memories I couldn't let go, playing them one after another in my head. Meeting Amelia. Falling for Amelia. Kissing Amelia for the first time. Making love to Amelia. Sex, laughter, tears, fights, makeups, dinners, breakfasts—all of it was burned into my mind, impossible to forget. The movie ended, and as Meghan put things away and cleaned up a little, I continued to stare into space, locked in my memories. Eventually she sat down next to me, and I snapped out of it a little. She looked worried, and I grinned to reassure her. She frowned a little more.

"I was serious earlier," she finally said. "You should get rid of all the things she gave you. She accuses you of being a money-grubber—send it all back to her in boxes. Every last thing she bought you."

The little black box was still in my purse, and my stomach clenched with a sharp pain. I hadn't opened the box yet—doing that was much too painful to contemplate.

"In fact," Meghan said, "I know you love this place, but you might think about moving out. Lot of memories here."

I couldn't help a sad smile. "Actually, I'm going to *have* to move out of here."

"What? Why?"

I shrugged. "I won't be able to afford the rent. I have some savings, but not enough to make it until my new job starts in the fall, not unless I get something temporary, and soon. I'll have to move out at the end of April if I don't get some more money coming in."

Meghan sat forward, her brow furrowed. "Are you telling me that bitch not only broke up with you, but she basically evicted you, too?"

I didn't like her word for Amelia, but I nodded.

"Damn," Meghan said. "She really is cold." She blushed and looked sheepish. "I'm sorry, Chloé. I don't want to talk badly about her in front of you, but it's kind of true."

"Maybe you're right," I replied, too tired to argue. I was starting to believe that what she said was accurate. Maybe Amelia really was just a cold bitch.

Amelia's coldness had been there all along. I'd simply ignored it. When I heard stories about her past, when I saw her chill toward people around us, I'd accepted it as part of her defense mechanisms. She was, like all of us, afraid of getting hurt. Despite her seemingly infinite confidence, she was actually quite shy. She had few friends and even fewer confidants. She might have been warmer with me than most people, but she'd held me at a distance, too. I knew next to nothing about her past, after all, and she'd always given up the small amount I did know with true reluctance. She was, in fact, still mostly a stranger.

The acceptance of this truth this last week sometimes made me angry with her. After all, her lack of candor had led, in part, to what happened with Sara. I'd been curious to hear Sara's story in part because of what it would tell me about Amelia. Still, most of the time when I reflected on how little I knew about Amelia or her past, I was sick with myself for not pushing harder, for not forcing the issue. I had been a coward—I knew that now. I'd wanted to avoid making her uncomfortable, but I should have insisted she tell me about herself. I didn't entirely blame myself. I'm not a doormat. The truth was, Amelia was clearly a coward. Things had become a little rough and she'd simply bolted.

I couldn't tell Meghan any of this, however. Not only was it too complicated, but she was also simply too angry to hear any of it with an open mind. She would think I was defending Amelia, justifying her actions. That was partially true, but I didn't forgive Amelia, either. I was still too upset and hurt to forgive her, even if I could understand, in part, why she was doing what she was doing. Still, not being able to talk to anyone about what I was thinking was weighing on me. In addition to feeling awful—truly terrible—I felt frustrated and alone.

Meghan excused herself to go shower. She and Aunt Kate had taken turns staying overnight this past week, both of them sleeping on my little couch. I knew I couldn't convince Meghan to leave me alone for the night, even if I begged her, so I didn't bother to try. I waited for her, sitting on the couch like a stone. It had become my spot over the last week. If I wasn't there, I was in bed. I moved back and forth between those two places alone.

When the doorbell rang, I was startled but not surprised. My aunt had dropped by a couple of times this week to relieve Meghan last minute and stay over herself. I got to my feet, my joints almost audibly groaning, and made my way over to the door. When I opened it, however, my aunt wasn't waiting for me: it was Emma.

She looked terrible—almost as bad as she'd looked all those weeks ago when she showed up shivering on my doorstep. Instead of cold, however, she looked ill. Her hair was disheveled and her face a sickly, pallid green. We stood there, staring at each other silently, for a long pause.

Finally, she shook her head. "Well, at least you look terrible, too."

"What do you mean?"

She opened her mouth to reply and then shook her head. "Can I come in? I think you owe me that much at least."

"What's that supposed to mean?"

She looked angry now. "Can I come in or not?"

Meghan spoke up from behind me. "No, you can't."

Emma and I turned to look at her, and then Emma's face turned a dark shade of red. "Who the hell are you?" she asked.

I suddenly realized how this might look to an outsider. Emma and Meghan had never met, and Meghan was in a bathrobe, toweling her hair, clearly naked underneath her robe. She looked as if she were at home here in my place, which she was, especially after this last week. I was in pj's and a robe, which suggested we were heading to bed.

Emma looked at me. "I can't believe you, Chloé. I really can't. I thought—I thought…" She and shook her head. "I thought you loved her."

"I did love her, Emma."

Emma gestured at Meghan. "Then what the hell? You've been broken up for, what? A week?"

"That's not your concern," Meghan said, stepping up to the door and slightly in front of me, her face a mask of pure rage and hate.

Emma took a wary step back.

"I take it you're one of Amelia's friends?" Meghan asked.

"I'm her sister."

Meghan's face darkened. "Well, you can tell your sister to go to hell!" She slammed the door in Emma's face.

"Meghan!" I said. "What the fuck?"

"You don't need that shit, Chloé. She's trying to manipulate you. Screw her."

"Emma deserves her say, Meghan. She hasn't done anything wrong."

"Yet. She hasn't done anything yet, Chloé, but she will. Trust me. She'll do something to get you and Amelia back together."

"You seem to suggest I would be stupid enough to go back," I snapped.

Meghan laughed. "Well, aren't you? Wouldn't you go running if Amelia called you right now?"

I didn't answer, and after a long silence, Meghan nodded. "Exactly. Stay away from her, Chloé, and stay away from her family. Please. Let

Amelia rot in her own shit. She doesn't deserve you, and she never did."

It was out in the open now. All the peace I'd made between Meghan and Amelia in the past few months had been a façade. I wasn't surprised—I'd known all along that Meghan didn't like her and that she put up with her for my sake alone, but her hatred for Amelia was clearly very deep. I'd hoped it was simple antagonism, perhaps something like jealousy, that fueled Meghan's distaste, but this was much deeper, much darker than that.

"I never understood why you hated her so much," I said. "Or why Aunt Kate hated her. What did she ever do to you? Is it a lesbian thing?"

Meghan shook her head and sighed. "No, Chloé, it has nothing to do with that. I'm glad you've finally discovered who you are." She paused and looked at me evenly for a long moment. Finally, she shook her head. "I don't think I should tell you why. Not after the way you were acting earlier this week."

"Tell me what?" I asked. When she didn't answer, I touched her arm. "What are you hiding from me, Meghan?"

She looked into my eyes again, and as if seeing something reassuring there, she finally nodded. "Okay, I'll tell you. But you're not going to like it one bit."

"What, for God's sake?"

Meghan sighed and indicated the couch. "Let's sit down first."

We sat, and I waited as Meghan seemed to gather her thoughts. My apprehension grew the longer I waited, as she was clearly struggling to figure out how to tell me. It had to be big, I knew, if both she and Aunt Kate, who were both warm and friendly people, had been soured on Amelia because of it, whatever it was.

"First off—do you have a tablet or a laptop? I can use my phone, but a bigger screen would be better."

I was confused where she was going with this. "My tablet's upstairs in the drawer in my nightstand."

"I'll go get it." She stood up and went upstairs, taking two stairs at a time.

I waited, still confused by what all of this meant. I heard her open the drawer, but she remained upstairs for a couple of minutes before coming back down.

When she reappeared, her face was grim. "I wanted to find the articles first, Chloé, and they're worse than I remember. Did you say that woman's name is Sara? The one who attacked you?"

"Yes," I said, my heart racing.

"Take a look at this." Meghan handed me the tablet.

Meghan had opened three articles from the online version of the local newspaper on my web browser. When I saw the headline of the first, my heart clenched with shock. I read the whole thing quickly, barely believing my eyes.

LOCAL HEIRESS TO WED
September 10, 2012
Society Staff Writer

NEW ORLEANS—Amelia Winters, 26, one of the many heirs to the Winters family fortune and local businesswoman, has announced her engagement to Sara Felina, 23. Miss Felina is Miss Winters's employee and daughter of local businessman Chris Felina, CEO of Allbright Industries.

Miss Winters and Miss Felina have told us they plan to wed here in their home city, but with some reported estrangement between both women and their families, it remains to be seen if their wedding will merit the kind of pomp and circumstance we might generally expect from the union of these two illustrious families.

Neither woman would comment on a possible venue or date, but Miss Felina seemed to suggest to one reporter that we can expect a winter wedding. Smart move, say I! Leave summer weddings for northern climates.

The article was accompanied by a photograph of Sara and Amelia, both of them smiling widely. Amelia's arm was around Sara's waist, and she was young and happy—happier than I'd ever seen. Sara was gazing at her, eyes shining and warm, almost as if she didn't believe she could be so lucky. I read the article several times but kept returning to that photograph. It was unbelievable. If I hadn't known better, I might have thought it was all Photoshop.

I let the tablet drop into my lap and sat there, staring at Meghan. "I can't believe it."

"She never told you they'd been engaged?"

I shook my head. "Never. Sara didn't tell me that either."

"What *did* Amelia say? I mean about Sara?"

I paused for a long moment and then shook my head. "Not a lot. From what I remember, the first time she brought her up, she said they kind of drifted apart. Sara got a job in New York, so they decided to break up."

Meghan shook her head, disgusted. "Have you read the other articles?"

"No."

"It gets worse."

I didn't think it could, but I was wrong. When I opened the other tab, the second headline was staggering.

HEIRESS SUES FORMER FIANCÉE
January 10, 2013
Society Staff Writer

NEW ORLEANS—Amelia Winters, 26, one of the many heirs to the Winters family fortune and local businesswoman, is suing her former fiancée, Miss Sara Felina, 23, daughter of local businessman Chris Felina. The news came to our desk via court proceedings submitted by Miss Winters's lawyers earlier this morning. No details about the trial were forthcoming from lawyers, but the lawsuit appears to be related to the Winters Corporation, Miss Amelia Winters's business. With all of the money and influence the Winters family wields in the City of New Orleans, and with a team of power-hungry lawyers at her disposal, this reporter believes it will likely be an open-and-shut case, leaving the much-younger Miss Felina in dire straits.

A source close to the women has reported that their engagement was severed within the last week, but this same source was close-lipped about the cause. This writer, however, has no doubts: if you plan to sue your fiancée, you're not going to be engaged very long.

The final article reported that Amelia and Sara had settled out of court a few months later for an undisclosed amount of money, though it was reputed to be hundreds of thousands of dollars. I couldn't begin to imagine how Sara had paid, knowing that her family had disowned her. Perhaps Daphne had paid.

I reread all three articles several times. I'd been forced to look at the society page more often in the last few months than I ever had before, in part because Amelia and I were in the news so often. We usually made fun of it and laughed about it, but it could be infuriating to see some of the ridiculous things they wrote about us. I recognized the tone of one of the more aggravating reporters we'd run into before, a young man who could never quite keep his snide remarks to himself. Society pages are essentially editorials, after all, so he could compose his "news" in whatever fashion he deemed fit. That said, the facts here were still clear: Amelia had been engaged to Sara and then broke it off and sued her. She had never mentioned any of this to me. It cast my entire relationship with her in a new light. If she could lie about this, what else had she been covering up? Further, why had she sued Sara?

"I don't understand any of this," I told Meghan.

Meghan shrugged and then shook her head. "Neither do I, and neither does Aunt Kate. But it was in the news a lot when you were still in Paris. Then, when you came back and took a job with her, and especially when you started dating her, we both remembered this story. That was why we never really trusted her."

"Why didn't you tell me about all of this before?"

Meghan winced. "Well, at first, neither of us could remember the details about the case. I recalled that she'd sued some poor girl and won, and Aunt Kate thought she'd been engaged before. By the time we thought to look it up again, you and Amelia seemed to be doing so well that it seemed, well, petty to mention it. The trial was a couple of years ago, after all. And when I reread those articles a while back, it still isn't really clear what happened between them."

"No, it's not."

"But she was engaged. And she did sue her. And she never told you about any of it. I thought she might eventually—Kate and I both did. We thought we'd give her the chance to come clean."

I swallowed the hurt lump that rose in my throat. My eyes were burning with rage and sorrow.

Meghan touched my arm. "Are you okay? Was I right to show you this?"

For a long time I didn't reply. I stared straight ahead, mulling over all the little things that had seemed strange about Amelia's story regarding Sara. She'd hesitated to bring it up, and when she did, she'd given me few details. It had seemed strange to me that she hadn't called the police right away when Sara started threatening me or Amelia's previous girlfriends. The fact that Sara was an ex-*fiancée*, not just an ex-girlfriend, made her hesitance a little clearer. Whether Amelia still loved her or not, she'd probably wanted to help her avoid going to jail, if, at the very least, to avoid embarrassment, if not something more severe. Judging by the engagement photograph, they obviously had, at least at one time, cared about each other, loved each other. Amelia looked positively radiant in the photo, clasping Sara like a prize she never wanted to let go.

I finally gazed at Meghan. "Yes, you were right. And you and Aunt Kate both were right to wait. She should have told me and she didn't. She was lying to me the whole time."

Meghan pulled me into her arms for a hug. I was still stiff, unyielding. I was so hurt, I was like a statue. She continued to hug me anyway, and eventually I relaxed into her, gripping her back. My eyes, however, stayed dry.

I was too angry for tears.

CHAPTER FOURTEEN

I'd been extremely fortunate during my mini-breakdown. The provost at New Orleans State had been out of town, so the final part of the hiring process had been delayed. Christophe, the dean, called me Sunday afternoon to set up the final meeting for Monday, and Aunt Kate helped me get ready before I drove up to campus. Even with her help, I still looked terrible. Staying inside for over a week, barely eating, and oversleeping had wrecked my looks. Even to myself, I looked like a changed person—sick and worn. I was still moving around with a kind of stiff pain, slow and unsteady as I walked.

I could tell that Christophe was shocked by my appearance, but he was too polite to say anything. Still, the meeting went extremely well, and I was offered the job on the spot. I'd promised my aunt not to accept immediately, as she wanted to look at the contract with me, and by the time I made it back to my apartment, she was almost as nervous as I was. A former teacher and current sub, Kate had some experience negotiating state budgets, and we talked about the contract together for a couple of hours that evening. I called them back the next morning with a counteroffer, and to my surprise, they met it. As of September 2015, I would be an assistant professor at New Orleans State.

Still, my depression took almost all of the joy out of this news. On Tuesday, when my aunt threw a small dinner party with some of our friends and family at my place, it was a bust. I tried very hard to be excited, but I could barely muster a smile for anyone. My reaction brought down just about everyone else my aunt called over to celebrate, and my appearance was so shocking that a few of our friends and family members took my aunt aside to ask if I was ill. I also still tired easily, so I was put in the awkward position of asking everyone to leave much earlier than my aunt had planned. She tried to shrug off her disappointment, but I could tell my mood was beginning to wear on her. When we were finally alone, she let me have it.

I very much just wanted to go to bed, but I forced myself to sit in the living room as she cleaned, feeling too strange to let her pick up dishes and wipe down the tables without, at the very least, being present in the room. It was ostensibly my party, after all. Her face, which had been carefully happy and relaxed with our friends and family, gradually became hard and angry the longer she worked.

"I've had just about enough of this, young lady."

"What do you mean?"

"You know exactly what I mean," she spat. "You don't deserve this, Chloé, and that woman certainly doesn't deserve to make you feel this way. She never did."

I opened my mouth to protest.

"No—I won't hear it! And I won't have you moping around here like someone died. You loved her—I get that. She hurt you—I get that, too. But you need to start living again, Chloé. You need to pull yourself out of this and start doing something again. Anything."

My eyes welled with tears, and she sat down next to me, sighing. She gave me a rough, one-armed hug and then let go. "I hate to give you tough love, Chloé. I always have. But you need to listen to me now, and listen good. It's not that I don't feel bad for you. I truly do. It's been an age, but I do remember my first love and how much it hurt when it ended. And it kept hurting for a long time. But you know what I did? I picked myself up. I dusted myself off. I started again. That's what you have to do, honey. That's all any of us can do."

Tears were running freely down my face. "But what if I can't get over her?"

My aunt shook her head. "Of course you can. Thousands of people, every day, are doing just that. It's part of the human condition, my dear. It's part of what love is. Love is happiness, but love is also loss." She paused, and sympathy replaced some of the anger in her eyes. She squeezed my hand. "I'm not asking you to get over her tomorrow, Chloé. Or the next day, or the day after that. But you have to start trying. You really do. At the very least, from what you've told me, you need to get a job soon, right? Something temporary until you start at the university?"

I nodded.

"Well, maybe that can be your first goal. Not to find one, necessarily, but to start looking. Maybe next week? Can you do that for me?"

I hesitated and then nodded.

She smiled. "Good. That's a start." She paused. "There's one more thing I want you to do."

"What?"

"Get out of the house. Make yourself do it this week. You've been stuck here too long, and I think you're in some kind of holding pattern. Even if it's just for a walk, try to get out a little every day. Can you try?"

Again, I paused, trying to decide. I didn't like to promise things I wouldn't do, especially to Kate, but I also knew she was right.

"I'll do it, Aunt Kate. I promise."

She smiled widely. "Okay. That's all I needed to hear. Now I'm going home tonight, if you don't mind. I think you're ready to be alone again. But if you start to get lonely, you can always call me or Meghan—day or night. Sound good?"

I hugged her, and we stayed like that, clasped together for a long moment. When we pulled away, we both had to wipe our eyes.

"Thanks, Aunt Kate. I-I wouldn't have made it this far without you."

"That's what I'm here for, sugar plum. Now I'm going to take one more look around, and you should go up to bed. And remember—get outside tomorrow."

"I will."

I took a long walk the next day, well, long for me in my current condition. I had to rest a lot, and my weakness more than anything else finally made me realize how run-down I was. By the time I'd made it to the Crescent Park, I had to sit on a bench there for twenty minutes to let my legs stop shaking. I was tempted to call a cab, but I made myself limp all the way back home, collapsing on my couch when I finally got there. I immediately fell asleep, and when I woke up, it was already dark out.

Wanting to keep myself honest, and curious about it anyway, I went upstairs to the bathroom and got on the scale. I'd lost a significant amount of weight. I peered at myself in the full-length mirror, not liking what I saw. I'd become a shadow of myself. More than ill, I looked desperately sick. My skin was papery and dry, my hair dull and lifeless, and for the first time in years I had a smattering of acne on my face and neck. I took a long bath to soak my tired muscles, and when I got out, I started making a list of things I needed to do to get back on track. I needed to eat more, that was clear, and I needed to start making goals for myself again. I was lucky that I had a job waiting for me in a few months, but I needed to do something concrete to help myself make it until then. I didn't want to have to move again. I wanted to keep this apartment. I loved it.

After my bath, I dressed simply and then went into my studio. The air in there had the odor of neglect, and everything seemed stale and dusty. Even before all of this upset, I'd barely painted in months. Amelia took up an incredibly large amount of my time outside of work, and work itself was so demanding that, on my free nights, I usually wanted to, at most, read a book and generally didn't even get that much done. I took stock of the room, looked at the painting I'd been working on, and decided to scrap it. I spent the evening cleaning my studio and the rest of my apartment, and by the time I was done, I felt remarkably better.

I might have gone to bed happy for the first time in over a week if Emma hadn't decided to call me just before I went upstairs to change. I held the phone in my hand for a long time, trying to decide what to do, but I waited too long. She left a voice mail. I spent most of the night tossing and turning, wondering what she'd said.

The next couple of days fell into a similar pattern, though I got up at an earlier and earlier hour every morning. By Friday, I was up by nine, and after a long walk along the river, I had so much time on my hands, I didn't know what to do with myself. I paced around my house, trying to decide what to clean, but it was spotless. I finally sat down on my couch to read, but I couldn't keep my thoughts on the page. I finally realized, after rereading the same paragraph for the fourth time, that I was restless. For the first time in two weeks, I actually wanted to be out in the world, and for more than just a walk.

Meghan was doing a set with her band that night at Mimi's, a little bar and tapas place not far away from my apartment. I decided on the spot to try to go watch her play. It would definitely make her happy to see me out in the world, and the idea of being in a public place made me feel better than I had in days. However, I still had the rest of the afternoon and evening to burn. Meghan and her band didn't start until nine, and it was only just after three now.

I picked up my phone and saw yet another message from Emma. She'd called three times now and had left a message every time. I let my finger hover over the Play button, but I couldn't make myself do it. I finally scrolled through to my contact list and called my friend Lana in New York.

I'd put off calling her since Amelia and I broke up. I was, I think, ashamed to tell her. Lana was my only close lesbian friend, and she and her partner were engaged to be married next fall. Telling her would throw my own failure into sharper contrast. She'd been the first person I'd told about my feelings for Amelia. She'd also been the person I'd called on and off over the last few months to talk about our relationship. Unlike Meghan and my aunt, she'd been over the moon about Amelia. She was happy, I think, to have her suspicions about my sexual orientation confirmed, but also, as she didn't know anything about Amelia's past, she took her as she was—a rich, gorgeous woman who was head over heels for me.

Luckily she picked up on the first ring, or I might have chickened out. She was overjoyed to hear from me, and she launched into a long tirade about her wedding plans and problems with her future mother-in-law. She talked so long I lost track of what I'd planned to tell her, so that when she finally finished her stories, I was silent.

"Hey! Chloé! You still there? I know I was talking forever. I'm sorry. I don't have anyone else to complain to. I hope you don't mind."

"Not at all."

"So what's been happening in your world? Did you get the job?"

Her words caused a stab of true guilt. She'd been the one to get me the first interview—she should have been the first person to know that I had the job. I'd been sitting on that news for days now, and it hadn't even occurred to me to phone her. I'd been so self-absorbed, so locked up in my own drama, it had simply slipped my mind. I made the choice then to lie by omission. She didn't need to know that it had happened days ago.

"I did, Lana, and it's all thanks to you."

She shrieked in my ear, and I laughed in response. I let her prattle on about how happy she was for me for a while, nodding along and agreeing as she spoke, but the subject I needed to bring up weighed on my mind.

I suddenly realized the line had gone quiet, and I snapped out of it. "Lana?"

"Chloé? You are still there. I asked you a question."

"I'm sorry. What did you say?"

"Is this a bad time or something? You seem distracted. I thought you'd be over the moon."

"I am. Really."

"Hmmph. You sound like you're expecting a root canal, not your dream job. What gives?"

I sighed, knowing I couldn't put it off any longer. "I'm sorry, Lana. I have some bad news, too. I just didn't know how to tell you about it."

"Did something happen?"

"Amelia and I broke up."

I could hear her breathing on the other line, but she said nothing for at least a minute.

"Oh God, Chloé. I'm so sorry."

I started crying then, sobbing into the phone. I'd managed to go most of this week without tears, so their renewal startled me, especially their vehemence. At one point I had to set the phone down and bury my face in my hands. But when I'd finally calmed down and picked up the phone again, Lana was still there.

"I'm back," I said, still snuffling. I laughed weakly. "Sorry for making you listen to that."

"Don't mention it. When did it happen? What happened?" She paused. "No, you know what? Don't tell me right now. You're obviously too upset. Just let me know when you want to talk about it. God, Chloé, I thought you two were doing so well, especially after your trip together. I'm so sorry."

"Me, too."

We chatted for a while after this, both of us avoiding the subject of Amelia or anything to do with her. She regaled me with another story of her future in-laws before we hung up, and when I set the phone down, I was actually smiling. Despite my outburst, I felt much, much better. I'd been embarrassed to tell her, and I'd been carrying around guilt about avoiding her. I could finally let it go.

I still had hours to wait until Meghan's set, but I went upstairs to take a shower and wash off some of the stress I'd shed talking to Lana. When I reached the top of the stairs, however, I glanced to my right, into my studio. The sunlight was perfect this time of day. The windows in there were the main reason I'd chosen the larger room for my studio instead of my bedroom. The blank canvas sitting on my easel looked appealing, inviting. Forgetting the shower, I went into my studio, picked up my palette, and started painting.

By the time I stopped, I was already running late for Meghan's first set, but I decided to go anyway. It was later than I'd stayed up in weeks, but painting had left me energized—excited in the way only working on a new piece can. I felt like I was taking my life back, once and for all. Amelia might take my happiness away, at least temporarily, but she couldn't have my creativity. That was mine alone.

When I got outside, it felt like freedom after a long confinement, and I walked quickly toward the bar. I could hear the music a block away, and as I fought through a jumble of smokers standing outside the door and went inside, the music from upstairs was still loud enough to be heard distinctly from down there. The place was packed, and I had to suppress a momentary urge to leave. I hadn't been around this many people in a long time, and the sounds and sights of a crowd were oppressive and hard to absorb. I squared my shoulders and shrugged off my reaction, pushing through them inside to the stairs at the back. I raced upstairs to the lounge.

Another large crowd was up there listening to Meghan's band, and once again I was tempted to turn around and leave. I paused at the far end of the room, looking for a seat. The crowd was significant enough to block my view of the little bandstand, and I didn't see a free table. Just when I'd given up hope of ever sitting down, a young woman at a nearby table caught my eye. She was sitting alone and had a free chair at her little table. It was too loud in here for words, but she gestured at the empty chair. I maneuvered around a group of young, loud men in my way and made my way over to her table. I mouthed a "thank you" at her and turned the chair around to face the band.

Meghan had been singing with different bands for almost a decade now. At first she worked as a backup singer in her then-boyfriend's band, but after she broke up with him, she set off on her own. She sings lead vocals, and she plays the accordion, fiddle, or the banjo in some of her songs. Her bandmates change over time, generally rotating every year or so, but last fall she'd begun playing with the four people on the stage with her now, and she and her band were finally getting the recognition they deserved. They were in high demand all over the city, and they'd been confident enough to book a twelve-city tour together. The tour had done well, and the band seemed to be on their way to relative, small-venue fame.

In Meghan's band, Amelia's brother Michael is the drummer and his girlfriend Jenna plays the stand-up bass. I'd been expecting to see them both here tonight, but I couldn't avoid a stab of pain, nonetheless. It was just another reminder of Amelia I would have to get used to. I didn't know if Meghan had talked to them about the breakup, or if it was causing problems with the band, and I didn't want to know. I was here only for Meghan. I mostly hoped Michael would leave me alone if he spotted me.

I glanced around the room, happy to see such a big crowd. Most people here had clearly come on purpose to hear them. Many were wearing T-shirts and hats from Meghan's tour. Despite my own depression, I couldn't help but be happy to see all of these people here for my friend. Meghan had always tried to seem as if she were happy being a bartender and playing with her band once or twice a week, but I always knew she wanted this kind of success no matter what she said.

Her boyfriend Zach was front and center by the stage. His face was one giant smile. Despite being back in New Orleans for six months now, I barely knew the man. It didn't help that Meghan was the more forceful personality in their relationship, but I knew that the main cause of my relative ignorance of him was Amelia. Meghan had rarely invited the two of us to her place or out on the town, and Amelia had never bothered to make either gesture to Meghan and Zach a single time. I'd spoken with Zach perhaps ten times since I'd met him. The reality of that neglect made my heart heavy. I'd been a terrible friend the last six months. Even before the breakup, I'd been selfish and isolated, and that was my fault as much as Amelia's. I should have insisted on seeing Meghan more often and not gotten so caught up in my own affairs. Tonight, I told myself, was my first step in making amends.

Their set ended about twenty minutes after I sat down, and the crowd visibly relaxed. Most of us had been listening intently, straining almost, to hear every note. I'd heard Meghan's bands over the last ten years, but with her current bandmates, they produced the best sound she'd ever had. Almost the moment the cymbals stopped ringing, I saw several people get up from their chairs to go purchase CDs and records.

Meghan and Zach were standing in front of each other, arms clasped behind the other's back. Meghan was looking at him with big doe eyes, and he was doing the same. They were talking to each other, but with the din in the room and the distance, I couldn't hear a thing.

"Hey, Meghan!" I shouted.

She flinched and looked over, and when she spotted me, her face lit up. She shrieked and ran over to me, several of her fans jumping out of the way. She threw her arms around me and kissed my cheek, jumping up and down a couple of times and squealing.

"I can't believe you came!" She looked as happy as I'd ever seen her.

I was a little embarrassed by the attention we'd drawn, but I tried to meet her smile as best as I could. "I didn't want to miss your triumphant return to New Orleans after the tour. I can barely believe how many people are here."

"I know! Isn't it amazing? The bar actually paid us to be here tonight. That's never happened to us before. We might, like, get paid to do this more often soon—I mean, more than the tip jar." She gave me a quick hug. "I've got to get back up there, but we should be done in an hour or so. Stick around and I'll buy you a drink."

The music started again a couple of minutes later, and I settled in to listen. I tried to keep my eyes rooted on Meghan as much as possible, but I did let them stray once or twice back to Michael on the drums. He didn't look anything like his sister, but his relationship with her was enough to get me thinking about her again. Meghan had caused such a scene earlier, he had no doubt noticed that I was here, but as he hadn't come over himself, I could only assume that he wanted nothing to do with me. Despite my earlier wish to be ignored, his evasion hurt a little, as I'd always liked him. But it wasn't hard to understand why he'd avoided me. I doubted very much if he and I could ever be friendly again.

After a couple of songs, I glanced down at my watch and had to stifle a yawn. I hadn't been up this late in weeks, and I hadn't had such a busy day in a long time. The last couple of days had started to make me feel human again, but I was still weak and easily tired. Though I wanted to stay and have a drink with Meghan, I knew I couldn't last that long, and I still had to walk home. The thought of my bed made me yawn again, and I decided to leave after the next song. I got to my feet right as people started clapping. I grabbed my purse and started making my way toward the stairs, and then someone touched my arm. I turned and saw Emma in the crowd behind me.

Like the last time I'd seen her, she looked sickly and worn. Her hair and clothes, normally neat and styled, were mussed and wrinkled. She looked as if she'd been sleeping in her jacket. Her eyes were red and sunken, and her face, normally open and guileless, was closed and pinched and almost shockingly pale.

She took a step closer in order to be heard. "Can we talk?"

I hesitated. I wanted very much to turn and leave, but Emma, like her brother Michael, had always been extremely sweet and kind to me, open and welcoming from the moment we met. She didn't deserve to be ignored, but neither did I want to hear what she had to say.

She sighed. "Look. I know you've been avoiding my calls, and I can't blame you. And I'm sorry about last week. I shouldn't have just shown up like that." She gestured at Meghan on the stage. "I didn't know who she was, but I should have known better than to assume you were sleeping around with someone." She shook her head. "I was just so hurt…I wasn't thinking straight." She paused again, meeting my eyes. "But things are really bad, Chloé. I mean really, really bad." Her eyes welled up with tears. "So can we talk? Please?"

It took all of my resolve to nod, and even afterward, as we made our way downstairs and outside of the noisy bar, I debated about whether to renege. I just didn't want to hear what she wanted to tell me.

We walked down the block a little, away from the noise and the smokers. Emma took a deep breath and rubbed her face. She looked as if she hadn't slept in weeks.

"Do you want to come back to my place?" I asked.

"That would be better than standing around here. Should I meet you there?"

"I walked over, so it might take me a little while."

"That's okay. I have to go tell Michael that I'm leaving anyway. I'll see you there soon."

Chapter Fifteen

In the brighter light of my living room, Emma looked even worse than she had at the bar. She also had a distinct odor—unwashed clothes and dirty hair. She glanced around the room as if surprised to find it unchanged. I gestured at the couch, and she walked over and sat down, her body stiff and closed in on itself. As I bustled around my kitchen making tea, I was reminded of the last time she was here with a sharp twist of pain. I had to stop and breathe deeply and evenly for a few breaths before coming out into the living room and sitting down across from her. She stared at me for a long time, her face hard and troubled.

"Do you know anything?" she finally asked.

"What are you talking about?"

"I mean, do you know what's happened recently? Anything at all?"

I shook my head. "I'm still not sure what you're talking about. If you mean Amelia, then no. I don't know a thing about her. I haven't seen or heard from her in over two weeks."

She stared at me intently, as if weighing my words, and then finally nodded. Her whole body seemed to relax a little. "I believe you. I don't know how you could have just let her go like that, but I guess that's what happened."

"She broke up with me, Emma. What should I have done? Begged her to come back?" I couldn't keep a note of anger out of my voice.

She looked surprised for a moment and then shook her head. "It doesn't matter now. But it does make me feel a little better. I think if you'd known about everything that was going on and not done something…" She shook her head. "But you clearly aren't aware, so that's better."

"What the hell are you talking about?"

She opened her mouth as if to reply and then closed it, her brow furrowed. Then she shook her head again. "I'll tell you, but first I need some answers."

"Need I remind you that *you* have been the one calling me all week? You're the one that wanted to talk—not me."

She raised her eyebrows. "Touché." She paused and leaned forward, her elbows resting on her legs. "But the fact is, Chloé, the things I have to say are personal, private. They should remain in the family, or at least between people who care about us. And I'm not sure about you. I don't know if you care or if you ever cared."

I couldn't stop a flash of deep anger, and I snapped at her. "Goddamn it, Emma, you probably know better than anyone in your family how I felt about her. My aunt, my friend Meghan, just about everyone I know warned me to stay away from her. But I couldn't! I couldn't because I loved her! You know I did."

"*Did*," Emma said, emphasizing the word. "But you don't anymore."

"Christ, Emma, what do you want me to say? She abandoned me! She said horrible things, and she accused me of terrible things—things that weren't true at all."

"What kinds of things?"

"She told me I was a liar and manipulator. She said I was after her money."

"Weren't you?"

I stood up, my fury a fire in my chest. "Get out of here right now," I said, pointing at the door. "How *dare* you accuse me of things you know nothing about! You don't know a fucking thing about me!"

She held up her hands. "Back up a minute. Maybe you're right, Chloé. Maybe I've misjudged you. But can you blame me?"

"I still don't know what the fuck you're talking about."

She stared up at me for a long time, her face a kaleidoscope of feelings, changing moment by moment. Finally, I saw tears in her eyes.

"Please, Chloé, sit down. Just answer a couple of questions, and then let me have my say. After that, if you still want me to, I'll leave. Okay?"

It took me a long moment to collect myself, but I finally nodded and sat down.

She blinked her tears away and rubbed her face again, her weariness so deep that for a moment I was moved with incredible pity for her. It was obvious she hadn't slept well in a long time, and whatever was bothering her was clearly destroying her health.

"What do you want to know?" I asked.

"First of all, I want to hear your side of the story. I've barely gotten anything out of Amelia. She's…well, more about that later. I want to hear it from you. Please."

I shared with her the version I'd told Meghan and my aunt. I described how upset Amelia had been when I'd neglected to tell her about my interview, and how worried she'd seemed to be that I was going to leave her. I told her about my meeting with Sara and admitted that, while I'd promised to wait a day or two, I should have told Amelia about the meeting long before she found out about it on her own. I went into detail about Daphne's phone call and Amelia's response. When I finished, Emma was looking at me with a deep frown.

"That's it? That's the whole story?"

I nodded.

"But it doesn't make any sense. Why would she break up with you over that?"

I shook my head. "I don't know."

"And you didn't think to ask?"

"You weren't there, Emma. You didn't see the look in her eyes. I was afraid she was going to hit me. Or worse." I swallowed, the memory of that expression almost too much to bear. "I knew there wouldn't be any point in arguing with her."

"So you just let it go? Just like that?"

I shook my head. "It wasn't 'just like that,' Emma. I was a wreck. I had something like a nervous breakdown. I don't know what would have happened if Meghan and my aunt hadn't been here to help me. I don't think I would have killed myself, but I might have died or hurt myself out of neglect."

She looked at me, still uncertain, but her eyes moved up and down my diminished body. I think, for perhaps the first time, she understood how truly awful the experience had been for me. It was written on my body and spirit like a sign. Some of the distrust died from her eyes.

"I-I think I believe you," she finally said.

I shrugged. "Good. It's the truth."

"Still, I need to know one more thing."

"What?"

"Why did you believe Sara's story? Why did you trust her?"

I opened my mouth to respond and then snapped it shut. In that split second, the weight of my mistake crashed over me. Sara's story, after all, made absolutely no sense, especially considering what I'd learned since. Never once had she told me that she and Amelia had been engaged, and never once had she mentioned that Amelia had sued her. If she'd left those major elements out, what else had she neglected to tell me? Had any of it been true?

"I don't know," I finally said. "I don't know why I believed her. You're right. There's no reason I should."

She nodded. "Every word out of that woman's mouth is a lie, always has been. And what I don't get is why you would trust her more than Amelia. Why didn't you ask Amelia about her right away? And not just when you talked with Sara, but before? When she attacked you last fall?"

I shook my head. There was no easy answer. "I don't know. I was scared, I guess, to push her. Amelia doesn't like to talk about the past."

Emma sighed and shook her head. "The two of you are hopeless. All of this could have been avoided if you both weren't so goddamn scared of each other, of your feelings, that you made room for doubt and mistrust. A simple conversation would have straightened this all out."

I couldn't help but doubt that it was that simple, but my own guilt now felt much heavier. For the last two weeks, I'd been baffled by Amelia's reaction. I'd assumed that Amelia had broken off her engagement with Sara like she'd broken off her relationship with me—with no clear reason or explanation. I'd also assumed that she'd sued Sara out of some kind of petty revenge. Even Meghan and Aunt Kate had seemed to think there was more to the story, but I couldn't see it.

"What happened between them?" I finally asked. "Between Sara and Amelia? What's the real story?"

She shook her head. "I'll answer all of your questions in a minute. I just need to be sure of something first." She paused, eyeing me warily. "I think I know the answer to this, Chloé, so please don't get too upset, but I have to ask, okay? I can't trust you until I know for sure, until I hear you say it."

"What do you want to know?"

She fixed me with a level stare. "Did you steal money from Amelia's company?"

The question was so unexpected and so ridiculous, I actually couldn't help but laugh. "What? Are you serious?"

She nodded.

"Of course I didn't. Why on earth would I do that?"

The last bit of tension eased out of Emma, and she collapsed into herself, covering her eyes with her hands. She started crying, and I got up and moved over onto the couch with her, pulling her into my arms. After a while, she moved back, wiping her eyes.

"I knew it," she whispered. "I knew Amelia was wrong."

"She thought I was stealing from her?" I couldn't help but feel disappointed, but on the other hand, it explained a lot about what had happened. Some of the uncertainty I'd felt about the breakup was starting to clear.

Emma nodded. "A few weeks ago, right after the birthday gala, one of Amelia's accountants reported a significant withdrawal from one of the company's accounts."

"How much money?"

"About five million dollars."

"Holy shit."

Emma nodded. "The money was impossible to trace. Amelia hired an IT security consultant to figure it out, and then things got worse. The consultant discovered that the money had been originally moved from one of the computers at the office. Apparently the thief, whoever it was, didn't even bother to try to hide the initial transaction. The money was sent to an offshore account and then rerouted thousands of times after that and disappeared, and, because there was no way to prove that it wasn't Amelia herself who moved the money, she's been forced to write it off as a complete loss."

I shook my head, disgusted. "That's terrible. Why didn't Amelia tell me about this? Where was I this whole time?"

Emma shrugged. "I don't know."

"And Amelia thought it was me? That I did it? That I stole the money?"

"Not at first. She started a covert investigation of everyone at the warehouse on the day the money was moved. She told me later she didn't even ask the investigators to look into you. Not then, anyway."

"But that's what she thinks now? That I stole it?"

Emma nodded.

My rage was instant and red-hot. "How could she believe that? Why would she? She knows I don't give a damn about money."

Emma shook her head. "She thinks that's all been a ruse, Chloé. She's convinced herself that you've been lying to her since the beginning, and that you were only after her money all along."

"But it's ridiculous!"

"You know that. And I know that now, too. I mean, I think I always knew that, but Amelia is totally convinced."

"Does she have any proof?"

She shook her head. "She only has proof by default. Everyone at the office has been cleared. No one else could have done it but you."

"But it wasn't me!"

She nodded. "Again, I believe you. But that doesn't help matters right now."

"But why wouldn't she just ask me? Why assume it was me?"

Emma sighed. "Well, that's the other part of this situation, and for that, we have to go back two years." She met my eyes. "Did you know she and Sara were engaged?"

My stomach dropped with dread again. Though it had been a week since I first heard the news, I still wasn't used to the idea of it. I nodded.

Emma relaxed a little. "That's good. I didn't want to be the one to break it to you. She swore me to secrecy when the two of you were first dating."

"Why?"

She shook her head. "I have my suspicions, but you'd have to ask her about that to know for sure. Anyway, I promised I wouldn't tell. Billy told me he almost let it slip at the birthday gala, and I about killed him."

I remembered his troubled expression when we'd talked about Sara. I'd wanted to ask him more about her, but we'd both been distracted soon after. How different things might have been if I'd known about the engagement sooner.

"My parents weren't happy about the engagement," Emma went

on. "They thought Sara was a money-grubbing gold digger, and they were right. I didn't much like her either, but Amelia seemed happy, so I went along with it. I tried to be supportive. Amelia wasn't really talking to anyone in the family but me at the time. No one liked Sara, but I hid it better. And you know about her family—they disowned her when she came out. That much of her story was true, anyway. So she and Amelia were going to have a small wedding and not invite any parents or friends or anybody, and then things fell apart."

"What happened? Why did they break it off?"

"For a whole bunch of reasons, all at once. First, some money went missing from the accounts at work."

My heart started pounding, and I suddenly knew where this was all going.

"It was Sara?" I asked.

Emma nodded. "And it wasn't just money. She'd also been going behind Amelia's back and selling some of the artwork on her own. She wasn't paying the artists or the company, either—just pocketing it all. She rerouted several sales through a shell company she created in New York. She was flying up there all the time, but she told Amelia she was interviewing for some kind of big job. When she told Amelia that she planned to move there for work, the whole thing collapsed, all at once. Amelia discovered the theft of the money and the artwork. She broke up with Sara, and then she sued her."

I could barely believe the depth of Sara's betrayal. The story did, however, explain a lot.

"Why didn't Amelia call the police? Have her arrested for fraud?"

Emma shook her head and grinned wryly. "She didn't want to ruin her life. She wanted the money back, but I guess she wanted to help Sara out, too. She did love her, after all, even if it was over by then. Anyway, that's why they settled out of court."

"Jesus," I said. It was all clear to me now. I'd been doing almost precisely the same thing as Sara. I'd found a new job right when the money had gone missing from the accounts at work. Amelia had become a little distant, but she still seemed to want to believe better in me than Sara. Then, when she found out I'd been talking to Sara, her suspicions got the better of her. She thought I'd done the same thing.

I looked at Emma. "I have to prove it wasn't me."

She shook her head. "I don't know how you could. She had some of the best people in the field looking for that money, and they can't find who did it or trace where it went."

"But if I had done it, would I still be here? In this little apartment?" Emma shrugged. "I don't know what's going on in Amelia's head. The more I think about it, the stupider it seems. But no one can convince her otherwise. She's sure it was you."

We sat in silence for a little while, ruminating on the dilemma. Emma was staring straight ahead, her eyes dark and somber. I touched her hand, and she jumped a little, clearly overwrought from fatigue and worry.

"Emma? How is she? I mean, besides thinking I'm a monster. Is she okay?"

Emma's eyes welled with tears, and she looked away from me, a hand going to her mouth to stifle a sob.

"She's bad, Chloé. Really bad. I've never seen her like this before. Even after Sara, she wasn't like this."

"What's wrong? What's she doing?"

"She's not sleeping, she's not eating. She won't talk to anyone. All she does is work. She looks awful. On top of everything with you, she's terrified she's going to lose the business unless she figures out a way to pay off the loss. She's thinking of cashing in her inheritance for part of it, but we've all been trying to talk her into letting it go—giving up the company, selling out, and doing something different." She shook her head. "She won't listen to anyone."

"So unless we find the money, she'll continue to think it's me, and she's going to lose her inheritance?"

Emma nodded.

I shook my head. "That's terrible. She shouldn't give up her money. We have to find out who stole it."

Emma nodded, but she didn't look very hopeful. We were quiet together for a while longer, and then I heard Emma chuckle. I looked over at her and was surprised to see her smiling.

"What? What's funny?"

She was still grinning. "I didn't tell you the rest of the news."

"What is it?"

"My parents are getting a divorce."

"What? Really?"

She nodded. "After forty years, Ted Winters has had enough.

We've all been expecting it, in a way, though of course we were still surprised. But they haven't been happy together in eons—not as long as I can remember, really, and maybe not even then. He hates all her stupid parties and her coldness, and she hates how nice and generous he is with everyone. He told me a couple of weeks ago that he'd caught himself drinking just to get through an evening alone with her, and he knew he had to end it, right then and there. He put down his glass of scotch, marched into the living room, and told her he wanted a divorce."

"Wow. That's incredible."

Emma grinned. "He's been staying at my place while they get the process started. So between my sister falling apart and my mother's screaming phone calls to my dad on the hour, every hour, I feel like I'm living in a nuthouse."

I leaned forward and gave her a hug. "Christ, Emma, that's a lot to take on. Are you okay?"

"Do I look okay to you?"

I laughed. "No. You look like shit."

"Gee, thanks."

"You could stay here tonight. I mean, if you want a break."

Her eyes lit up. "Really? Do you mean it?"

"Of course! In fact, stay as long as you want."

"Oh man, Chloé, even one night would be a godsend. Thank you."

"Sure. Let me go get you some pj's."

I stood up and she grabbed my wrist. "Chloé? I'm sorry. I mean, I'm sorry I ever doubted you, and I'm sorry my sister is treating you so badly."

I frowned and shook my head. "Thanks for saying that, Emma, but there's nothing to apologize for. I don't like it, but I can finally see where she's coming from. And you're right—all of this would have been cleared up with a simple conversation. Neither one of us trusted the other one—that's the problem."

"You're a good person, Chloé. I wish my sister was smart enough to remember that."

I couldn't help but wish that, too, but as I made my way up the stairs, I also couldn't help but feel angry with myself and with Amelia. We'd done this to ourselves, and it was going to be next to impossible for us to dig our way out of the fallout. Now that I knew the truth, however, for the first time I was starting to think that I could try to win her back. I couldn't let things rest the way they were now. More than simply wanting to clear my name, I did once love her, and I still loved her.

I went to my dresser to search for an extra set of pj's, but my eyes rested on the little black box I'd hidden in my dresser drawer. It had ridden around in my purse for a while until I took it out, sick of thinking about it every time I looked at it. I held the box in my hand for a long moment, nerving myself to open it. Finally, I took a long, deep breath through my nose, let it out, and cracked open the little case.

The ring held a large, dark, cobalt sapphire surrounded by smaller diamonds, all three stones in a princess cut. The band was white gold, and when I slipped it onto my finger, it fit perfectly.

I didn't realize I was crying until I saw a teardrop splash onto the back of my left hand.

CHAPTER SIXTEEN

The next day was Saturday, but I was determined to act on the new information immediately rather than wait until Monday. I called my third cousin Derek, a police officer, and told him the story of the stolen money. I wanted his advice about where to begin and was sure I could trust him not to make anything official unless I asked him to act on it. When I finished, providing just enough details for him to grasp the dilemma without getting too far into the related drama, he whistled, long and low.

"Wow, that's a real pickle, Chloé. The cop in me, however, would tell you to look to the most obvious cause of all of this: the person who's done it before. You say this Sara woman—the one who attacked you—did this a couple of years ago?"

"Yes."

"Then it's not a stretch to think she's done it again."

This was exactly what I was thinking, and I was glad to hear he'd made that leap as well. "But how? She had to get into the warehouse to do anything. The first transaction happened there."

He was quiet for a moment. "Yes, but maybe it wasn't her, exactly. Someone would have seen her and recognized her, right? She used to work there, so she couldn't risk going herself. Maybe she sent someone to do it for her. Paid them or something."

"But the whole staff has been cleared. The investigators checked everyone."

"Well, there's no police record of the theft, Chloé, so I don't know how thorough they were. Why didn't Amelia call the police?"

The last time this had happened, Amelia had kept the truth from the police and the press as much as possible. There were likely several reasons for this, partly business and partly personal. No company wants to appear vulnerable to theft. It makes a bad impression, and Amelia probably wanted to give Sara a break one last time. I gave Derek a quick run-through of what I knew.

"Well, I'll tell you this, Chloé: without involving the police, she'll never get to the bottom of this. You can be the best PI in the business, but even then you still need to ask the police for help most of the time. I'm sure she has the dough to hire the best, but in this case, with that kind of money on the line, she really needs to get the law involved. Maybe even the feds."

I sighed. "Well, I can try. Maybe I can get her sister to talk to her and she'll see reason." I paused. "Would you be involved in the investigation? I mean, if her sister can talk her into it?"

"No. I'm afraid not. That sort of thing's not in my wheelhouse. But we do have a great money guy here in the department. He used to work for the FBI. I bet you anything he could find that money, or at least the person who stole it."

We spent a couple more minutes catching up on family news, and he promised to call me back if he heard anything about the case. I'd used the phone in my bedroom, and when I went downstairs, Emma was still asleep on the couch. She didn't stir a hair as I walked by. I set the water boiling for coffee and poked around in my kitchen looking for something to make for breakfast. I still had some of the homemade strawberry jam my aunt had brought the last time she visited and part of a day-old baguette. I cut the bread in half and toasted it, smeared on some jam, and then washed the rest of my grapes. I poured coffee concentrate into two wide mugs and then topped it off with water, milk, and sugar, making it sweet and creamy. By the time I carried all this out into the living room, Emma was up. She'd already folded her blanket and pillow, and when she turned toward me, she looked a million times better for her restful night.

She greeted me, and then she cursed when she glanced at her watch. "Oh, crap."

"What?"

"I slept too late. I was supposed to…" She threw me a quick, guilty look.

"Supposed to what?"

She hesitated, clearly nervous. "Amelia and I were going to meet up for breakfast this morning. She probably called me earlier, but I turned off my phone last night." She looked at the breakfast I'd made for her and shrugged. "Oh well. I'll call her later and apologize. I could use a morning off from her shit."

She began eating, but my appetite had dried up. The idea that Amelia was out there waiting for Emma made my heart hurt. Ever since we broke up, I tried not to think about what she was doing, not in a concrete way at any rate. It was bad enough to remember how we'd been together for small, seemingly insignificant moments in the past. I didn't like to picture her now, in the real world, living without me, moving on with her life, and making breakfast plans without me. I could envision her now, probably annoyed with Emma and out of sorts, sitting in her giant dining room by herself, waiting for Emma to call. The vision was so clear in my mind I could have reached out and touched her.

Emma finally noticed my stillness and paused, her toast hovering over her coffee. "Are you okay? You look funny somehow."

I shook my head. "I'm okay. Just felt someone walk over my grave."

I hadn't picked up my toast yet, but I was clutching my coffee, and I suddenly saw Emma's eyes go wide when she spotted the ring. "What the hell is that?" She gestured with her toast.

I'd kept the ring on all night, and it already felt natural on my hand. I stared down at it, my stomach dropping with the dread of everything it represented: loss, pain, broken bonds. I shouldn't be wearing it. I should have sent it back to Amelia long ago, but now, after everything I'd learned last night, I wanted to wear it. It represented pain and loss, but it also seemed to represent something else to me now: hope.

"It's a ring," I said, stupidly.

"I can see that, dummy. I mean…" She paused, her face draining of color. "Did Amelia give that to you?"

I'd left out that part of my story last night. I hadn't told my aunt or Meghan about it either, and I didn't want to tell Emma about it now. It was too painful. All I could do was nod, and my eyes welled up with tears. Emma set her breakfast down and got up, took my mug from me, set it down, and pulled me to my feet for a hug. When she stepped back, her eyes were teary too, but she was smiling.

"Why do you look so happy?" I asked.

"Because you're going to be my sister-in-law! I kept hoping it was going to happen. I knew from the moment I met you that the two of you were meant to be together. I've never seen her as happy as she is when she's with you."

I had to laugh. "But we've broken up, Emma. She didn't even propose."

She looked confused for a moment, then shook her head. "But she bought the ring for you, so she was planning to propose, right?"

After a moment, I nodded.

Emma smiled again. "So that's enough for me. Once we get this straightened out, you two will be engaged."

I couldn't help but feel a little thrill of excitement and warmth at the idea, but I quickly suppressed it. I had still had a lot of work to accomplish before Amelia and I could have another chance. Even if she realized I didn't take the money, she didn't trust me. She thought I'd done it. And, if I was honest with myself, I hadn't trusted her, either. Even beyond this current dilemma, we had some major obstacles to conquer before we could move on and consider something like an engagement.

Emma seemed to sense my reluctance and hugged me again. "Don't lose hope, Chloé. We're going to figure this out. I don't know if it was getting a good night's sleep or having a night away from my family, but I feel so much better this morning. I think we can do this together, if we try."

I told her about my discussion with my cousin, and when I was finished, she nodded. "I agree with you and with him. I've been trying to get her to go to the police since I found out about the money, but maybe I need to figure out a way to insist. I'll talk to her later today and make her call them. I promise."

"Are you going to tell her you talked to me?" My heart started pounding, though I didn't know why. Something about the prospect scared me, deeply.

"Do you want me to?"

I hesitated and then shook my head. "No. Not yet. She might turn against you if she thinks you're colluding with me."

She nodded. "That's what I think. I'll keep it hush-hush for now. Then, when we have some proof of your innocence, I'll let her in on the secret—tell her it was your idea. Maybe it will be enough to get you past this."

Emma went upstairs to take a shower, and I put her smelly clothes in with mine in my tiny, European-style washer-dryer. I started it when I heard the water upstairs stop running. She's a little shorter than I am, but we have a similar build, so I was about to go upstairs to find her some clothes to borrow when I heard someone knock. Confused, I moved the little curtain that covered the window on my front door and was horrified to see my aunt and Meghan waiting outside. They both waved and hallooed when they spotted me, and I had to open the door.

"Hey, girly!" Aunt Kate said, holding up a grocery bag and stepping inside. "We knew your kitchen was probably bone-dry, so we thought we'd bring some food. Then we thought we might help you eat some of it while we were at it."

Meghan followed her in, giving me a brief hug. "I knew you'd bail on me last night, but I was so glad you came for a little while. I couldn't believe it when I saw you there."

I was still stunned to see them and desperately trying to think of a reason to get them to leave.

Aunt Kate noticed my reluctance and nervousness, and she put her hand on my forehead. "Are you feeling okay? You look funny. Not sick exactly, but…"

"Guilty, maybe?" Meghan said.

Kate and I turned to her, and Meghan pointed at the two mugs and two plates on my coffee table. It was obvious that someone else was here, and as it was still fairly early in the morning, it was obvious that someone had stayed over. As if on cue, all three of us heard the bathroom door upstairs open, and Meghan's face turned a startling shade of dark red.

"I'm going to kill her," she said, and moved toward the stairs as if to do just that. She stopped moving when Emma appeared at the top of the stairs, clad in my bathrobe. She was drying her hair with a towel, so she didn't see my two guests.

"Hey, Chloé?" she called, her voice muffled by the towel. "Where did you put my clothes?" She stopped drying her hair and looked down at the tableau below her. All three of us were staring up at her, and she blanched.

Aunt Kate and Meghan turned toward me slowly, their eyes wide with disbelief. I was about to explain, but then I started to laugh. This was too ridiculous for words. From their expressions, it was obvious what they thought had happened, and the gap between their understanding and the reality of the situation seemed unbelievably funny. I continued to laugh for several seconds, during which my aunt's face changed from surprise to anger, which made me laugh even harder.

"I'm glad to know you think this is funny, young lady, but I fail to find the humor in this," Kate said. "I mean, she's certainly a pretty girl, but why on earth would you get involved with that family again?"

Now my giggles verged on hysterics. Kate and Meghan shared a concerned look, and I bent double, clutching my stomach. They both took a wary step away, as if I might suddenly lose it, and a moment later, I was on the floor, laughing so hard I was crying.

An awkward conversation followed my hysterical laughter, even more awkward because Emma was in my bathrobe the whole time we talked. Once the initial situation was cleared up, I worked very hard to convince my aunt and Meghan to listen to her. They both distrusted her, and I had to coax and beg them to be open to hearing the truth. As Emma told them the story of Amelia's past, I slipped the ring off my finger and hid it in my pocket. It wouldn't do to make things more complicated right now. I would carry it with me until I could wear it openly, and until then, it would have to stay a secret between me and Emma.

As Emma talked, I watched Aunt Kate and Meghan's faces. Kate was the first one to crack. Her anger dropped away, replaced with guilt and pain. The entire time I'd been with Amelia, she'd judged the poor woman based on an incomplete understanding of what had happened between her and Sara. Now that she was learning the truth, she could see the injustice of her attitude.

Meghan was a harder nut to crack. Even after Emma finished her story, she remained stony-faced, looking at Emma with seeming disgust.

Meghan shook her head. "Look, I can sort of see why your sister might think Chloé stole the money—I mean, yes, the coincidence is hard to ignore—but why didn't she just ask her? Why assume?"

Emma shrugged. "I don't know. If I had to guess, though, I think she's so hurt she isn't seeing straight."

Meghan gestured at me. "But to accuse Chloé, her supposed

girlfriend, of embezzlement? With no proof? I mean, what does that say about her?" She looked at me. "Are you okay with that? And why did she lie about Sara to begin with? Why not just tell you about her?"

I shook my head. "I don't know. I have to believe she has her reasons about Sara, and for lying. But no, I don't like that she thinks I stole the money. It's awful, really."

Meghan look satisfied, but she still wasn't happy. "But you want to prove your innocence? Why? So you can get her back? She doesn't deserve you, Chloé."

Aunt Kate broke in. "I want to apologize for how I treated Amelia, Chloé, and you, too, Emma. I'd tell her the same thing if she were here. But I have to agree with Meghan, at least in part. I don't know whether she deserves you, Chloé. My own prejudice blinded me, I think, to who she really is. But Meghan is right—she doesn't trust you, and she lied to you. You can't build a relationship without trust, honey. It just doesn't work that way."

I nodded. "I agree. If Amelia and I can get past this misunderstanding, we're going to have our work cut out for us. We clearly have a lot of problems to work through. And maybe it won't work out—maybe there's been too much damage already. If that's the case, we can break up and I can move on. But I can't let what happened with the money be the end of things." I shook my head. "She has to know the truth."

Meghan's face contorted with disappointment and sorrow, but she eventually sighed and looked resigned. "What do you want us to do?"

"Nothing," I replied. "Nothing at all. Just be willing to give her another chance. She's not alone in this mess—I didn't trust her, either. We're both culpable, both at fault. Just..." I gestured feebly. "Just think about it, okay? Think about how much I loved...love her. Maybe that could help you love her, too."

"She's worth it," Emma added. Everyone looked at her, and she darkened a little, seeming embarrassed. "I know it doesn't seem like that right now, and you might not believe me because she's my sister, but it's true. She's worth it."

Aunt Kate and Meghan shared a look and nodded before turning to me again. "I wasn't fair to her before," Kate said. "If you two can work this out, I promise to give her another chance."

Meghan heaved a big sigh. "Me, too."

I gave them both a long hug. For now, it was enough that they were willing to try. I could make some peace with that possibility. It might, after all, be a moot point. If I couldn't persuade Amelia to trust me again, they might never have another chance to mend the distance between them. Still, I wanted them to understand my love for her and love her for my sake, at least, if not for hers. I wanted us to be the family we should have been from the beginning.

Now I just had to figure out how to start.

CHAPTER SEVENTEEN

With April fast approaching, I devoted a lot of my time the following week to wedding planning and shopping with my aunt and Meghan. Aunt Kate meant to keep the wedding small, but the guest list, as expected, had ballooned to about eighty people—the bare minimum of friends and family she could invite without causing permanent hurt feelings. And of course, despite trying to keep it casual, we still had a lot of details to take care of in the final weeks. Kate wanted my opinion about the flowers, and on Saturday, we chose the food. After some debate, she'd decided that, rather than having her ceremony at the courthouse the day before the party, they would have the entire thing—ceremony and reception—at a small venue, the beautiful St. Ann Cottage in the French Quarter. What had initially been promised as a casual get-together had, indeed, turned into an actual wedding.

Luckily, Meghan seemed to thrive on the stress, and despite being the second fiddle, she'd already taken a lot of the maid-of-honor responsibilities off my shoulders over the last weeks as I recovered from the breakup. When we showed up on Saturday at the venue for our appointment, she seemed to know every staff member by name, and they knew her. I couldn't help but feel guilty that I'd fallen apart right when my aunt needed my help, but I was relieved to see that Meghan had taken care of just about everything. We spent the afternoon eating everything possible on the wedding menu and debating long into the evening on the choices of food, wine, and cocktails.

Two weeks out, almost everything for the wedding had been set into motion. My dress was fitted, the food and flowers were chosen and ordered, the cake was well on the way toward being designed, and the

RSVPs were almost completely in order. I'd also been assigned three tasks to complete before the wedding. I had a list of the remaining family members and friends to call and pester for their RSVPs, I had to create the seating arrangement, and, as I had the nicest handwriting, I had to write the table-assignment cards.

In between wedding-planning events, I spent my days painting. It was therapeutic, and I realized that I'd been craving it without being aware of what I wanted and needed. The canvas absorbed all of my pain, reflected all of my hopes and dreams, gave voice to everything inside me clamoring to get out. I wasn't aware of most of this as it was happening. At the end of a very long day working on my new piece, when I put down my brush and looked at the finished painting, only then did I see what had gone into it, what it represented. The painting was me, entirely, and it was the best thing I'd ever produced—even I could see that.

I had to cover the painting up with an oilcloth to get away from it. It was captivating me. The emotions were too raw, too obvious to ignore, painted on my canvas for all to see. I went downstairs to get dinner but was drawn back to the canvas, almost as if by force. Seeing my problems there on display, seeing the heartache, the love, and the anxiety in blazing colors mesmerized me. I stayed up late into the night marveling at what I'd done. This wasn't vanity—more like fascination. Nothing I'd ever painted was more real, more vital than this picture.

Lying in bed late that night, unable to wrench my mind away from it, something occurred to me. Recently, I'd been making small moves toward finding some work to get me through until the fall semester. I'd called a few galleries, looked at a few ads, but my search was halfhearted at best. I knew I should take a more serious path to line up some temporary work, but I was reluctant to take that next step. It would make all of this real, once and for all.

As I lay in bed the night after I finished my new painting, however, I finally realized exactly what I could do to get by for a while. The idea was so stupidly obvious, I couldn't imagine why I hadn't thought of it before. Somehow, despite my excitement, the idea lulled me to sleep, and when I woke the next morning, I was more rested than I'd been since the breakup. I was certain about what I needed to do and how to do it. I just had to start.

I called Teddy first the next morning. She'd given me her cell number, and when she answered, she seemed surprised to hear from me.

"I'd heard that you and Amelia..." She hesitated. "I mean that you were no longer working for the Winters Corporation."

"You heard correctly. At least for now. The thing is, I wanted to let you know that the artist you liked is selling her work. I'm representing her and wanted to give you the first pick."

"Really? That's great news." She paused. "But wait. Won't it make things a little awkward? I mean, we really love that piece, and we'd like to put it up in our restaurant permanently, but we're working with Amelia for the next year. Won't she be, I don't know, disappointed?"

I decided to bluff. "I guarantee she won't be disappointed. It won't affect your working relationship with her at all."

"Give me a sec." She called her wife Kit into the room, and I could hear Kit's excited reply. She returned to me a moment later. "When can we see the piece?"

"I can bring it over this afternoon, if you're free. And a portfolio of the rest of her work, if you're interested."

"Sounds great. We're closed to the public for a couple of hours in the afternoon. Come over at two and we'll meet you in the dining room."

We hung up, and I spent the next couple of hours getting the painting and a portfolio ready. Amelia had taken pictures of everything I'd ever painted, but I made a printout of only the work I'd done in the last five years, as most of my juvenilia was rather limited. I also took a picture of my newest piece and printed that as well before putting all of the work in a small leather binder.

I took a long, hot shower and spent a good amount of time on my hair and makeup. The results were surprising. For the first time in weeks, I almost looked like a normal human being. I was still a little too pale, and my clothes hung on my body, but at worst I looked like I was getting over a protracted illness, not like I was still sick.

A few minutes before two, I tied the wooden crate with my painting to a dolly and grabbed the portfolio, heading outside and down the block to Teddy's. It was too close to drive, and the weather was beautiful. We'd had a colder winter than I could remember in New

Orleans, so the sunshine and warmth felt like returning home again. The birds seemed to be ready for spring, too, shrieking their happiness at me as I passed beneath them in the trees.

The restaurant was closed when I got there, but Teddy saw me and opened the door, motioning me into a darkened interior. She closed and locked the door after me and then indicated a table in the center of the room. Kit joined us a moment later, coming from the back and wiping her hands on a clean white towel. They seemed excited. I gave them the portfolio and let them leaf through it, pleased that they seemed to enjoy just about every piece they saw. When they reached the last print, a photo of my newest painting, they both stopped exclaiming and simply stared at it in silence for a long time.

Kit looked up first. "Well, I definitely want to buy the one we've already seen, but this is a masterpiece."

Teddy nodded. "It's incredible. I don't know that I've ever seen anything so evocative, so raw."

"I want the piece you brought, the one we saw earlier, for the restaurant, but I want this one," Kit touched the photo, "for our house."

Teddy grinned at her. "That's exactly what I was thinking." She looked at me. "So now, of course, you're going to fleece us silly."

I laughed. "No, no. In fact, since I'm her only representative, you'll be getting a significant discount over a gallery." I took out a small piece of paper, wrote two figures on it, and slid it over to them. "Here's the price for each piece."

They both looked at the slip of paper, and I was relieved to see that, rather than horror, they smiled widely and then shared an excited look.

"What a relief." Kit touched her chest over her heart. "I was convinced they would cost millions of dollars."

I couldn't help but flush with pride and shook my head. "No. The artist wants to make sure she's putting her work out there for regular people to buy."

"Can I ask you a little about her?" Teddy asked. "I mean, what's her story? The last time we talked, you seemed to think she wouldn't sell. What changed?"

I hesitated because I had no easy answer. I'd always been extremely reluctant to show my work to anyone, in part because I had no confidence in it. As an undergraduate, I'd studied fine arts with a painting focus, but my insecurity had convinced me to move on to something more certain, something safer, and I'd switched to art history in graduate school. That didn't stop me from painting, however. I just did it thereafter for myself. When Amelia had slipped that photograph of my work into the locals' portfolio, I'd not only been angry but also terrified. Although it wasn't easy to see the initials I used to sign my paintings in photographs of my work, I'd still been scared they would figure it out if they looked too closely or too long. My artwork had become personal, private over the years. Showing it to people was like showing them a part of myself.

Last night, however, as I lay in bed thinking about my newest painting, I realized that was part of the point. By sharing my work, I *was* sharing myself, and if people wanted to see that, I was finally ready for it because the person I'd been, the person I was before Amelia, was gone.

I took a deep breath and let it out, firm once again in my decision. They were both looking at me, confused by my silence, and I had to smile. "I'm sorry." I shook my head. "I've been deceiving you a little. These are my paintings. I'm the artist."

They were both amusingly shocked and then incredibly pleased.

"Wow!" Kit said. "Chloé! You're so talented." She paused, and her pale face colored. "I mean, I believe that you're talented—"

I laughed. "I know what you meant. Thanks."

"Your work is amazing, Chloé, especially these new pieces. I've never even considered buying a painting for myself before this, and now I want them all. Why didn't you say before?"

"I wanted you to buy them on merit. I didn't want to persuade you through, I don't know, loyalty or nepotism or something."

Kit grabbed my hand, squeezing it. "I would have wanted to buy them anyway, Chloé. They're wonderful."

Teddy nodded. "I love them." She indicated the wooden crate. "I want you to hang that one up right now, before you leave, if you don't mind."

"When will the second one be ready?" Kit asked.

I paused. "It's still wet. I just finished it last night, actually. I would give it another two weeks before it's safe for delivery."

"Okay," Kit said, nodding. "That will give us some time to clear some wall space at our house. Are you ever going to have a show?"

I grinned. "Funny you should ask. That's what I'm planning to line up next. I'm talking with some galleries this afternoon."

Kit smiled broadly. "Really? You'll have to tell us all about it. We'll hang up a poster in here and hand out flyers, if you think it will help."

I laughed. "Of course, it will, Kit. You're one of the most popular restaurants in town. If I could get even a fraction of your customers to my show, I'd sell out in a week."

We spent the next twenty minutes hanging my painting, which I'd finished last December. It was the first thing I painted after I got back to New Orleans, and I'd spent most of last autumn working on it. My early anxieties about Amelia, my happiness about getting together with her, and my jubilation at being back in the city were all in that painting.

When it was hung, and we all stood back to look at it, I realized this was what I'd needed all along. I needed to let those feelings go. Even if Amelia and I got back together—which still seemed very unlikely—I wouldn't need a reminder of those early days of our courtship. That was over and done with. Hanging it here, for the world to see, put that part of my past to rest.

"It's incredible, Chloé. It really is," Kit said, her voice quiet and raw.

Teddy agreed. "I think it's the best painting in here."

"Thank you," I told them. "I'm so proud to have my work here, and I'm so glad you like it."

I arranged to call them when their second painting was ready for transport, and I walked back to my apartment with a light heart and a huge check in my pocket. In one hour, I'd managed to make enough money to live in my apartment for the next six months without working. Beyond the money, however, I felt unburdened for the first time in ages. Painting helped me release my emotions, but by hoarding my work like I had, I'd been keeping permanent reminders of my past heartaches around.

Selling my work felt like letting go.

CHAPTER EIGHTEEN

Beyond wedding activities, I spent the rest of the next week working with a local gallery to plan my first exhibition. I'd managed to find a nice venue for my work, but the timing was tight. I had just over three weeks to get my work together for my show, but I also had to deal with all the rest of the wedding planning and the wedding itself in just over a week. I stupidly started a new painting that would be the centerpiece of the show, but once I got rolling on it, I was afraid I couldn't finish it on time. Despite being nearly overwhelmed, I was enjoying both kinds of work—the planning and the painting—because they took my mind off my disastrous personal life. If I hadn't had the projects to distract me, I might have sunk back into bleak depression.

By the following Friday, I hadn't talked to Amelia for just over a month. The pain was still there, still biting, still nagging at me, but it wasn't crippling me like it had four weeks ago. Now, as long as I stayed busy, as long as I worked so hard and so long that I dropped into bed exhausted, I could sleep and get through the day without being overcome with dread and loneliness. It was slow progress, but it was progress. I was still in daily contact with my aunt and Meghan, in part because of Aunt Kate's wedding, and in part because they still wanted to check in with me. I didn't exactly mind, however, and both of them seemed to trust me a little more as each day passed. Neither of them mentioned Amelia, and I didn't talk about her, but she was there in the background of every conversation, like a ghost.

The day after Emma had told me and the others about the stolen money, she'd finally convinced Amelia to go to the police. In the two weeks since Emma stayed at my place, I'd heard from her exactly twice—once to tell me that the police were involved and then a week later to let me know they had made no progress. It was difficult not to call her every day for updates. Both times we talked, she told me that things were still a mess, and Amelia was still convinced I'd stolen the money. That, more than anything, was the worst part. I hated that Amelia had lied to me, that she'd covered up such a major part of her past, but I couldn't stop feeling a combination of indignation and sorrow over how easily she'd been misled. Our love meant nothing in the face of her money.

Amelia's wealth had always been a problem, and I'd sensed from the beginning that it would cause more problems down the line. We'd already disagreed about it in the past when she overspent on gifts or when she seemed like a spendthrift on things I could hardly comprehend.

The phone pulled me out of my reverie, and I set my paintbrush down to answer it. Between the wedding and my upcoming show at the gallery, I had so many people to keep in contact with right now, I had to keep the ringer on even when I was painting. I didn't recognize the number, but my phone told me it was from Key West. I'd been expecting this call.

"Hello? Is this Jonathan?" I asked.

"Yes, Chloé, it's me," he said. Jonathan is Jim's son, and he was staying with me for the entire week leading up to the wedding. Jim's other sons were arriving tomorrow, but they were staying at my aunt's. All three were coming early for some father-son/bachelor time in New Orleans before the big event. Jonathan and I had been emailing back and forth for a few days, but this was the first time we'd actually talked. His voice was a surprisingly deep baritone.

"I'm in Miami now," he went on, "and I just wanted to let you know everything is on time. I'll be there at four this afternoon."

"Good. One problem: I don't know what you look like. How will I know who you are?"

He paused. "I can put on my porkpie hat. It's red. And I'm wearing a black T-shirt, if that helps. How about you?"

I looked down at myself. I had on some of my painting togs—a ratty T-shirt and paint-splattered jean shorts. "I don't know what I'll be wearing. But I'll bring a little sign with your name, like a chauffeur."

"Sounds good. Looking forward to meeting you, Chloé."

"Me, too."

I hung up, smiling. Now that Kate's wedding was only a week away, I'd begun to get excited about it. I'd long put to rest the idea that she would be moving away soon. I was still sad about that, but now that I was getting used to the idea, it didn't seem quite as depressing as before. I could tell she was ready for a change, and she deserved any happiness she could find, even if it took her far away from me. And anyway, after she finished the school year, she and I would have an adjustment period as she and Jim came back and forth for a while.

I spent a little more time than was probably necessary getting ready to go to the airport. I used to ignore, perhaps on purpose, the figure I cut on a first impression. For a long time, I'd considered myself above such things. After working with Amelia, who was very concerned about looks and appearances, I was now in the habit of looking my best for someone new. The weather was finally starting to heat up, so I donned a light afternoon dress and did my hair and makeup, almost as if I were meeting with a rich client of Amelia's. I arrived early at the airport and parked, getting out so I could meet Jonathan by the baggage claim.

When I made my way into the over-air-conditioned lobby, however, I saw on the arrivals screen that the plane had been early. I hustled over to the correct luggage carousel and spotted Jonathan long before he saw me. He was staring at his phone, his little red porkpie hat set back on his head, looking a little lost. I paused, straightened my dress, and walked directly over to him.

"Jonathan?" I asked.

He looked up, and I was greeted by a pair of startling deep-brown eyes. He was tall and tan, and clearly muscular from outdoor work. Like his father, he was in the construction business, though I'd gathered from what Jim had told me that Jonathan worked more on the design end of things than his father did. He had that casual, shaved-yesterday look about him, with messy auburn curls poking out from beneath the hat. With the clean, handsome lines of his face and his trim physique, he looked like a supermodel on his day off.

"Chloé?" he asked. He looked me up and down so quickly I might have missed it.

I nodded, and then we both hesitated before giving each other a quick hug. Neither of us had experience with this kind of situation. Soon we would be what, stepsiblings? Stepcousins? For me, at our age, either designation seemed strange and a little silly.

"How was the flight?" I asked.

He launched into the story as we made our way out into the now-sweltering afternoon heat. He seemed unfazed by the temperature, and I remembered that Florida was likely hotter, if anything, than here. When we approached my car, I saw him pause, his mouth dropping comically open.

"Is this your car?" he asked.

"Yes. What about it?"

He left his suitcase standing in the parking lane and walked around my Mercedes, eating it up with his eyes. When he finished, he whistled. "Wow. This is the CLA Coupe? The German model?"

I shrugged. "I think so."

He looked at me with wide, disbelieving eyes. "You don't know what kind of car you drive?"

I laughed. "No, I guess not. It was..." I paused, thinking of how to phrase the explanation. The car had been a gift from Amelia, but it seemed ridiculous to tell him that. I'd assumed the car was expensive but had never looked into it before. I was too embarrassed to know the cost.

I decided to fib. "It's for work."

He looked relieved. "Whew. You had me scared there for a minute. I didn't think you were that rich."

We got on the highway and immediately became stuck in traffic. As we waited, I got him to talk about his work in the Keys. He lives in Key West, but his work takes him all over South Florida, even as far north as Miami. He's an architect by training but became involved in construction right out of school, and now does a little of both—designing and building.

"So what kind of work do you do?" he asked. "You get to tool around in a sixty-thousand-dollar car, so it must be pretty lucrative."

I didn't know how to answer him, in part because I didn't know how much Jim had told him about my recent past. I would be lying if I told him I still worked for Amelia, but on the other hand, I hadn't completed any final paperwork that said otherwise. Still, I decided the truth was better.

"I'm an artist, and I start work at the state university this fall," I told him.

"Damn. You must be a great artist. I know professors don't make enough for this kind of vehicle."

I didn't respond. It didn't feel right to lie to this man—my future stepbrother?—but lying by omission was better than giving him the whole story, at least for now.

We were still inching along the highway, far from our exit, but Jonathan seemed at ease. I tried to relax, wondering what else we could talk about, but he provided the next topic a moment later.

"So, you taking anyone to the wedding?"

I turned to look at him and saw that he was grinning widely, expectantly. I shook my head. "No."

"That's good—me neither. Maybe we can hang out, dance a little, that kind of thing. I hate going to weddings on my own, and my brothers' girlfriends are coming later this week."

We were stuck in one spot, so I was still looking at him, and his face suddenly flushed with color as I continued to meet his eyes. "Wait—I'm sorry," he sputtered. "That came out wrong. I didn't mean to make it sound like I was hitting on you."

I laughed. "It's okay. I know what you meant."

The car in front of us moved an inch or two, and we crept forward and stopped again. I could feel his eyes on me and looked over at him again. He appeared puzzled, as if trying to remember something. His expression cleared when he did.

"Oh, wait. That's right. I forgot," he said.

I was looking ahead now, as it appeared that the cars in front of us were finally starting to move again.

"Forgot what?" I asked.

"I forgot what my dad told me about you."

"Oh? What's that?"

"You're a lesbian, right?"

I had to slam on the brakes as the car in front of me screeched to a halt, and we were both squashed into our seat belts for a moment. I breathed heavily for a long time, trying to calm my racing heart.

"Jesus, that was close," he said.

We started inching forward again, and I kept my eyes rooted to the road in front of me, hands clenched on the steering wheel.

He cleared his throat. "So? Are you?"

We'd come to a stop again, and I looked over at him. I'd been trying to suppress my annoyance, but it was now too strong to push down. "You want to know if I'm a lesbian? Why? What the hell difference does it make?"

He looked surprised and then mortified, but I had to return my attention to the road. We drove for about twenty seconds before we had to stop again. Our creeping progress had given me time to calm down, and I glanced over at him.

"I'm sorry," I said. "I shouldn't have snapped at you like that."

"I just remembered my dad said you and your girlfriend were having problems. I'm sorry. I shouldn't have pushed you. It's none of my business."

I tried to give him a smile, but I was suddenly teary and looked away. It was just like Jim to be open about something like this, and I couldn't blame Jonathan for wondering about me. I was curious about him, too. However, I didn't know what I was anymore if I didn't have Amelia. When we'd first started dating, I'd considering calling myself bisexual, but the longer we were together, the more certain I'd become that I'd found my true self through her—that I was, in fact, a lesbian. The problem now was adapting to the life of a *single* lesbian. I'd never had to consider that status before.

I gave him a quick grin. "To answer your question, yes, I'm a lesbian. I like breasts, I like sex with women, I like long legs in dresses, I like the smell of a woman after a night of sex, and I like seeing a woman wake up and look at me like I'm the only thing in the world."

He guffawed. "Hey—you and me both, sister."

"So that's one thing we have in common," I told him, and we both laughed.

We were finally reaching the accident that had caused all of this traffic, and it looked horrific, even from several cars back. I could see smoke and several fire engines and emergency vehicles, all of which had blocked off two lanes of the interstate. I started to merge to the left, and as we inched by, I glanced over at the wreckage. A car had been destroyed. It had flipped onto its roof and smashed into the guard rail. Something had caught fire, and the car was a blackened shell of smoking metal. I was certain that anyone in there had been killed. I couldn't see any other wrecked cars, but it was hard to tell if another hadn't already been towed off. I finally wrenched my gaze away and looked ahead, and a moment later we were free of the jam. The rest of the trip went quickly, but I drove more slowly than usual, the sight of a possible death making me cautious.

We stopped by a sandwich shop for an easy dinner, Jonathan buying a literal mountain of food, excited to see different ingredients than he was used to. We pulled into my driveway, and I helped him carry his suitcase and the food inside. Given his height, I'd already decided to give him my bedroom rather than make him sleep on my little couch, and we argued about the arrangement when I told him. I was glad our earlier awkwardness had passed. He was easygoing and took my teasing about his height lightly.

"The bedroom will be more private," I told him for the fifth time. "Especially for a giant." I leaned down once again to grab his suitcase to take upstairs.

He took his suitcase from me and then moved it over toward the couch. "And I told you, I don't care about privacy. And I like sleeping with my knees in my face."

I giggled again, almost ready to concede the fight, and then my phone rang. I saw his face transform into satisfaction, as if he'd won, and I held up a finger. "To be continued."

I reached into my purse and took out my phone. I turned away from him when I saw who was calling: Emma. "Hello?"

She didn't respond. Instead, all I heard was a great deal of background noise and something that sounded like a sob.

"Emma? Are you there?"

There was more sobbing, and then I heard her take a deep breath. "Chloé?"

"Yes?"

"Th-there's been an accident." She sobbed again.

I knew immediately what had happened. In that moment, I think I realized that I'd known before she called—part of me had simply been waiting for this phone call. Something about that car on the highway had seemed familiar, but that wasn't quite the word. I hadn't recognized the car, but I'd been drawn to it, as if it mattered somehow, as if it and the driver were connected to me. My ears were ringing, and my legs were giving way. Dimly, I was aware of Jonathan lurching forward to grab me before I hit the ground and helping me over to the couch. The phone had dropped out of my hands onto the floor. Jonathan knelt in front of me and was saying something, but the ringing in my ears drowned out his voice. I saw him look around, desperately, and then he got up and went over to get the phone. I closed my eyes, leaning backward into the couch, the world spinning around me. I couldn't help remembering that burnt-out wreck. I'd known when I saw it that anyone in it must have been killed.

She was dead. My Amelia was dead.

"Chloé! Chloé! Goddamn it, answer me!"

Jonathan was in front of me when I opened my eyes, his face a mask of fright and worry. He looked relieved to see my eyes, but he still looked frightened, shocked.

He held the phone out to me. "The woman on the phone—Emma?—she wants to talk to you."

I took the phone from him with numb fingers, staring at it blankly for a long moment. I didn't want to hear what she had to say. If I heard it, I would fall apart—I knew I would. Steeling myself, I put it to my ear again. My voice was stuck in my throat, and it took me a long time to say anything.

"Emma?" I finally managed to say, my voice hoarse and broken.

"Chloé, you have to come down here. Please. I need you here."

I swallowed again, my throat tight with pain and grief. I couldn't make myself ask the question, and I didn't need to ask it. I already knew the answer.

"Where are you?" I managed.

"At LSU Hospital. Please hurry." She choked again on a sob. "I don't know if I can…please. Just get here as soon as you can."

She hung up without saying another word, and I sat there, phone still pressed to my ear.

Is this what going crazy feels like? I asked myself. Does it feel like the world is falling apart and you're sitting in the middle of it? Hot tears were falling down my face, almost burning my skin. I could no more stop them than I could stop breathing.

Jonathan must have realized that the phone call was over, as he came back and crouched in front of me again. He took my phone from my numb fingers and set it on the coffee table. "Chloé? What can I do? Do you need me to get someone? Call someone? Should I call Kate?"

"I have to get to the hospital," I told him. I tried to get up, but my legs wouldn't hold me. He caught me before I fell again and helped me sit down.

"You've had a shock, Chloé. You need to wait until you can walk again."

I looked up at his pale face, trying to think of what I could do to convince him. My heart, however, wasn't in it. I didn't want to go. I didn't want to see her body. If I did, I would break into a thousand pieces.

"Let me call your aunt. She'll know what to do."

"Don't!" I said, snatching his arm. He looked surprised, and I let it go, embarrassed. "Please, don't call her. I couldn't bear it. I need to get to the hospital, Jonathan, and I need to go alone."

"You're in no shape to walk, let alone drive. At least let me give you a lift."

I almost argued with him, but I knew he was probably right. I nodded, and he looked relieved.

"I'll get you some water," he said. "In the meantime, do some deep breathing. I don't want you passing out on the way."

Not long after, we were back in the car, Jonathan relying on his phone to get us there. I'd lost the ability to speak or give directions. I'd already died a little inside.

We found the emergency room in the usual chaos of a city hospital on a Friday afternoon. When we walked through the door, the sights and sounds of pain and panic immediately accosted us. I tore my eyes away from the carnage, looking around desperately for Emma. Jonathan was still helping me walk, one arm linked with mine. I clutched at him, my fingers white.

He helped me over to the front counter, and we had to wait for several moments as the woman behind it finished what appeared to be a very unpleasant phone call. She stared at me after she put the phone down, and I couldn't speak. Both she and Jonathan were looking at me now, but my voice was stuck in my throat. I swallowed several times, desperate, but every time I opened my mouth, nothing came out but a dry click.

"Chloé!" someone shouted.

I spun toward the voice and saw Emma. We ran at each other, and I launched myself into her arms, almost wailing. My legs felt weak again, and they buckled a moment later. I pulled her to the floor with me. Almost immediately, Jonathan was there, kneeling next to us. His hand was on my back, rubbing it, but my focus was on Emma in my arms. Her body was hitching against mine as she sobbed, and I could feel tears coursing down her cheeks. I drew back after a while to meet her eyes, surprised to find her smiling. It took me a long time to understand what she was saying. The ringing in my ears finally stopped enough for me to hear her.

"Chloé, she's going to be okay. Do you hear me? She's all right."

CHAPTER NINETEEN

I don't know how long I was out. Luckily, I didn't have far to fall or I might have hurt myself. Instead, I simply slumped over right there on the ground in the emergency waiting room. I'm sure I caused a scene, and I felt bad later for giving everyone more work to do, but at the time I couldn't help it. All I could think of when I opened my eyes were Emma's last words to me: she was okay. My Amelia was alive and she was okay.

I was on a bed surrounded by blue hospital curtains. I still wore my dress from earlier, but someone had removed my shoes. I'd been left alone, but when I sat up, I could see that they'd hooked up an IV in my hand while I was out. My head felt muddled and painful, and my heart was racing.

"Hello?" I called out. "Is anyone there?"

A moment later a nurse moved one of the curtains aside and came in. Her face was stern and blank.

"You're awake," she said. She came over and took my free hand, checking my pulse against her watch. After a moment she said, "Your heart rate is still very fast."

"Where are my friends? The ones I came in with? Can you go get them?"

She shook her head. "We're crowded back here already, as you can see. We don't need extra bodies."

"When can I get out of here?"

"The doctor will be with you shortly, and she'll let you know." She made a quick note on my chart before leaving and closed the curtain again behind her.

I lay back, trying to calm down, but it was impossible. The thought that Amelia was nearby somewhere didn't help at all. I decided to wait ten minutes before doing something, but I barely made it five. Finally, I swung my legs off the side of the bed and stood up. I waited a moment to see if there would be an alarm, but nothing happened. I grabbed the IV pole, wheeled it with me to the far curtain, and pulled it back to peer out. A series of curtained beds surrounded me, and several nurses and doctors were walking around looking harried. I watched and waited, peering in after the staff when they drew back curtains, but I didn't see Amelia. A doctor spotted me, and I quickly moved back to my bed before she came in. She appeared a moment later, and neither of us said anything about my nosiness.

She looked at my chart and my vitals and then took my pulse again. I could feel my heart racing, and I saw her frown.

"I just want out of here," I told her. "I was here for someone else. I'm upset, not sick."

She looked at me, trying to gauge my honesty, then nodded. "I know what happened. Quite the show you put on out there in the lobby."

"So can I leave?"

She shook her head. "Not yet. I want to see that heart rate down a little before I let you go. No need to have you pass out on us again. The IV is for fluids—you're dehydrated."

"But I need to know how my friend is doing. Can you tell me?"

"Not unless you're a family member," she said.

I cursed myself, having already given it away. "Well, can you please just let me go, then? I'm fine, really."

She looked at me levelly and then shrugged. "We have a shift change in about ten minutes, and I'll check on you one more time before I leave. If you can get your heart rate down by the time I get back, I'll sign you out. Otherwise I want you lying down for at least another hour until the next doctor can get to you."

She left, and I made myself lie almost prostrate, my head elevated a little because of the bed. I breathed deeply with my eyes closed to calm my racing heart, but every time I pictured Amelia, somewhere nearby and hurting, my heart rate sped up. I could feel it in my chest, a pounding so hard and strong it pulsed in my ears. I tried to focus on the rhythm, willing it to slow, but nothing worked. It hammered as if

I'd been running a race. My entire body thrummed with electricity and nerves.

I heard the curtain draw back and kept my eyes closed, hoping I could calm myself in the last couple of seconds. The doctor didn't say anything, and I opened my eyes a moment later, wondering what she was doing.

It wasn't a doctor. It was Amelia.

It took me a long moment to recognize her. Her cheeks were wan and pale, and her body overall looked diminished, sickly. Her eyes were sunken and raw-looking, and her hair, normally lustrous and full, hung in limp, damp, sweaty rings on the side of her face. She'd cut it since I'd last seen her, and it was much shorter than I was used to, but it wasn't the cut that made it look so terrible. Coupled with her sickly thin and pale face, her sweaty, knotted hair made her look downright ill.

One arm was in a sling, and she had a large, bloody bandage taped to her forehead and a smaller one across the bridge of her nose. She smelled strongly of something like a campfire, and her skin was smeared with soot. But she was walking and conscious. Again, I remembered the wreckage I'd seen on the side of the road, and I could hardly believe that, two hours later, she was standing here on her own two feet. Like me, she had an IV hooked into her hand, and unlike me, she wore a hospital gown.

"It is you," she said. Her voice was scratchy, hoarse.

I set up straighter and nodded.

"I thought I heard your voice," she said. She motioned to the side. "I'm in the cubby next to yours."

We continued to stare at each other, neither of us doing anything but looking. It had been so long since I'd seen her, and she looked so different from the old Amelia, that I was shy of her again. Yet even in her current condition, she was stunning, at least to me. My eyes ate her up as if they'd been hungry for her. Hot tears prickled the corners of my eyes, and I blinked quickly, not wanting to lose sight of her long enough to cry.

Finally, I heard her sigh. The sound of it was weary, pained, but her expression remained blank, closed off. She turned as if to go.

"Amelia!" I cried. She turned back to me, frowning. "Amelia, please don't go. Stay with me." I held out a hand. "Please. Don't leave me here alone."

Her face broke then, and she launched herself at me. I had just enough time to sit upright before she was in my arms. She had only one good arm to both of mine, but we clutched at each other tight and hard. I was too overwrought to cry. My eyes felt hot, burning, but they remained dry. I pulled her closer, wanting to lift her into bed with me, and she gasped in pain.

"Shit, I'm sorry," I said, letting her go.

She shook her head. "Don't apologize."

We clutched each other again, and this time the tears started falling. I could feel hers in my hair and streaking down my neck, but neither of us said anything or did anything. I attempted to favor her injured arm a little, giving it some extra room to avoid crushing it, but she squeezed me so hard with her good arm, I'm sure it hurt her anyway. I no longer cared.

Finally, she pulled back. On top of her pallor and thinness, her bloodshot, red-rimmed eyes did nothing for her appearance, but I don't know that I've ever seen anyone more beautiful. She was here, and that was all that mattered.

Sitting up that way was uncomfortable, and I finally lay back. She sat down more firmly on the edge of my bed, looking down at me. She wiped her face with her good hand, smearing the soot with her tears, then took my hand in hers. Her fingers were cold, clammy.

"Should you be out of bed?" I asked. "You were just in an accident."

She shook her head, clearly unfazed. "It doesn't matter. I just want to look at you." She paused, her face a mixture of joy and disbelief as she stared. After a moment, however, it crumpled again, and she lifted her good hand from mine to cover her eyes.

"My God, Chloé, I'm so sorry. You have no idea how sorry I am. I really fucked up."

I could hardly breathe. I didn't think we'd get into this here, but clearly she thought it was time to start. I touched her, and she let me take her hand in mine again. I didn't respond, and she continued to look down at me.

"I got the news today from the police."

"What news?" I managed to say.

"News I'm sure you were expecting. News everyone but me seemed to see coming long before they had proof." She swallowed back her tears before going on. "Sara stole the money. She was arrested this afternoon."

We were quiet for a long time as I absorbed what she'd said. While it felt good for the truth to finally be out in the open, it clearly didn't solve everything. Amelia had still betrayed me. She'd turned her back on me in the name of profits and dollars. Yes, she thought I'd stolen from her, but with no proof beyond coincidence, it didn't speak well for her.

She made herself look me in the eye, and I could tell that it was a struggle for her to look at me at all. "I'm sorry, Chloé. I don't expect you to forgive me. What I did was...unforgiveable. Really. It was."

She seemed to be attempting to convince herself, as if preparing herself for whatever blow would fall next. She looked so lost, so broken, my heart constricted in pity. I squeezed her hand.

"Do you know why I'm here?" I asked her.

She shook her head.

"I came here for you, Amelia. Emma called me and I came."

She looked confused, and I held up a hand to stop her from speaking.

"I-I convinced myself that you were dead." I couldn't help sobbing on this last word. Tears came spilling down my cheeks again. "When Emma told me that you were fine, that you were going to be okay, I couldn't handle it. I've never been happier, more relieved."

Her eyes were wide. "So earlier, when I heard you talking to the doctor, when you said you were here for your friend?"

"I came here for you, Amelia."

She was crying again, too, but she seemed unaware of her tears. "Do you think it could be true? Could we be friends now?"

I hesitated and then nodded. I wasn't sure if it was possible, but I cared enough for her to try.

My response brought a smile to her face for the first time since I'd seen her. The smile was uncertain, weak even, as if she hadn't smiled in a long time, but it was there nonetheless. I smiled back, and just when I opened my mouth to say something more, the curtain was drawn back and the doctor came in. She froze when she saw us, and both of us jumped with startled guilt.

The doctor frowned. "Miss Winters, you should be in bed. You don't even have your cast yet, and you've had a head injury."

Amelia saluted her and got to her feet. She looked back down at me. "When will I see you again?"

"I'll wait in the lobby with Emma. We'll take you home."

Her lip started wobbling again, and my own eyes welled up with tears in response. Finally, she nodded and turned, making her way around the doctor, who watched her with clear annoyance. Amelia threw me a quick wink before disappearing, and I couldn't help but smile.

❖

I was released a while later, and when I entered the lobby, Emma and Jonathan, both on their phones, immediately hung up and came over to me. Emma gave me a hard hug, and Jonathan looked relieved.

He held up his phone. "I was just talking to Kate. She knows the whole story now. I just convinced her not to come. I told her you were okay and needed to be alone."

I squeezed his hand. "Thanks, Jonathan. I appreciate it." I grinned. "I'm so sorry about all of this. Welcome to New Orleans. What a shit show."

He laughed. "It's no problem, really. I can always use a little excitement in my life. Who knew I'd end up in the hospital *before* the bachelor party?"

"You should go," I said. He tried to protest and I held up a hand. "No, really. Go back to my place. You have the keys now. I'm going to stay here and wait."

He looked relieved, but he was polite enough to ask, "Are you sure?"

"Yes. Please go. I probably won't be back tonight."

He nodded, his eyes suddenly grave. He came close and gave me a quick hug. After this disaster, it didn't seem awkward at all.

"Okay," he said. "I'll go. But if you need anything, don't hesitate to call. I can come get you if you need it."

He started walking away and I called out to him. "Hey, Jonathan?"

He turned. "Yes?"

"You might wanna take my car for a little spin while I'm gone. It could get lonely without me."

He laughed and almost dashed out the door in excitement.

I turned back to Emma, who was grinning at me. "Thanks for waiting with me, Chloé. I really appreciate it."

I hesitated. "I can't leave her here, Emma. I just can't." I told her about meeting Amelia in the back room and what we'd talked about.

She nodded. I saw a hint of elation in her eyes before she looked away. The two of us made our way over to some chairs farthest from the screaming, bloody mob as we could get.

When we sat down, Emma explained why the rest of her family wasn't here. Her mother was on a charity mission in Mississippi, and her father, Bobby, Dean, Ingrid, and the kids were all on a spring-break trip together in Orlando. She'd also called Michael, her only other close relative in town, but she still hadn't gotten in touch with him. She'd been left to handle this whole thing on her own, and I could tell it was weighing on her badly. She looked almost as bad as the other people in the emergency room—pale and haunted.

It was a very long wait. We saw the gamut of sick and injured people as we sat there, each of us throwing the other horrified or amused glances as the cases dictated. I realized as we waited that I hadn't been in an emergency room in a long time. I'd broken my collarbone as a teenager while roller skating, but I didn't remember much of that experience. The only other time I'd been in an emergency room, I was waiting to hear news about my parents after their car accident. The thought made me shudder, and I clutched Emma's arm. I knew the news wouldn't be like that time—my parents had died, almost immediately—but being here didn't help me feel much better. Hospitals meant death, pain, and heartache, rarely joy.

Several hours later, a doctor came out to tell us that Amelia was recovering nicely, and that, after he'd seen the X-rays of her skull, he'd decided to release her instead of giving her a room overnight. Her concussion was mild, and the other injuries had now been treated. She would be fine if she slept with her head elevated for a few nights.

The time between when he told us this news and when she was finally wheeled out of the back was a long one, though. When I saw her, my nerves were so frazzled and frayed from waiting and seeing and hearing the sights and sounds of the chaos around us, I could barely stand it. Again, I hardly recognized her. She looked small, reduced somehow. The chair seemed to dwarf her body. She still wore a hospital gown, her clothes having been cut off her, and I realized then that one of us should have gone to get her something to wear while we waited. We hadn't thought of it.

She looked surprised to see me, and I couldn't tell if her surprise was pleasurable or not. I'd told her I would wait, but she clearly hadn't expected me to keep my word. A staff member wheeled her all the way to Emma's SUV, and Emma and I trailed after them the entire time, all of us silent. When we finally reached the car, Emma helped her up and into the backseat before giving me the keys. My hands were shaking, but I could see that Emma was in bad shape herself. I drove us back to Amelia's place as quickly and as safely as I could, Emma in the backseat with Amelia.

Amelia was capable of walking to the door of her house, and the two of us followed her in. Beyond greetings, none of us had spoken a single word since we'd been reunited, and when we all sat down in the living room together, that silence expanded into something incredibly awkward and uncomfortable. I sat in an armchair, and Emma and Amelia were on the love seat together, clasping hands. Amelia wouldn't meet our eyes, and Emma was staring at her with concern. I looked back and forth between the two of them for a long time, wondering what I should say or do. I couldn't tell if they wanted me to be here, but I also didn't want to go home. Tonight wasn't the night to get into any of the shit that had come before this, but I couldn't make myself leave. Seeing Amelia again—just seeing her—fulfilled a part of me that had been empty and hollow for the last month. I couldn't get enough of her. I knew I was basically staring, but I couldn't help myself. I wanted to look and look and look.

After what seemed like an eternity, Amelia finally sighed—the first sound I'd heard her make since the hospital. She looked up at me, very quickly, her eyes darting away, and then at Emma. "I'm really tired. I'd like to go to bed now."

"Of course!" Emma said, lurching to her feet. "Let me help you."

Stupidly, I followed them upstairs to the hallway outside of Amelia's bedroom. Emma helped Amelia sit down on the bed and started rooting around in her wardrobe. I stood in the doorway, looking in at them, still struck dumb. I still couldn't tear my eyes away from Amelia's face. It was obvious she was looking at anything but me. I didn't know how to take this, whether she didn't want to see me or was afraid to for some reason, but her evasion didn't exactly bother me. She knew I was here whether she looked at me or not.

I turned my eyes away when Emma handed her some pj's, and then I walked down the hall to one of the guest rooms. The room was well appointed, with gorgeous antique furniture and beautiful modern art. The dresser held several new-looking sets of pajamas, and I poked around until I found an appropriate size. I changed quickly and then stood there, staring into space. I wasn't sure what I was doing here. Had Amelia asked me, I would have left immediately, but as she hadn't, I wanted to stay here until I knew she was all right.

Emma came into my room a few minutes later. I was sitting on the edge of my bed as if waiting for her. She gave me a wan smile and then flopped down into the gorgeous Queen Anne chair in the corner of the room. She put a shaky hand over her eyes and then removed it.

"Jesus. She's a wreck."

I nodded.

"She's been making herself scarce for the last few weeks, so I hadn't seen her up close in a while. She's lost a ton of weight."

We were quiet, absorbing the implications of this change. Finally, she met my eyes and then sat forward, resting her weight on her elbows. "What's the plan, Chloé?"

I shook my head. "I don't know, Emma. I really don't."

She stared at me for a long time, as if testing my words. After a while, she nodded. "Okay. But you came to the hospital and you're here—that's a good sign. That means you still care for her."

"Of course I still care for her, Emma. I never stopped. But the things that have happened between us—all of it—she and I can't just sweep them under the rug. I don't know how we can get past this."

She got to her feet and came closer to me, resting a hand on my shoulder. "You might not be able to, Chloé, but I think both of you need some closure. You look like hell yourself. Make some peace with her, at least."

"I will. I want to."

She nodded. "Okay. I guess that's all I can ask." She paused, and I saw the weariness she'd been holding at bay seep into her face. She yawned. "I need some sleep. Wake me if you hear anything from her room, okay? I'll be in the other guest room next door."

She left, and I turned off the light and flopped onto the bed, too tired to crawl under the blankets. I was asleep in moments.

❖

When she came to my room, it was still dark. My eyes snapped open as if in alarm, and I sat up straight on the bed, instantly and fully awake. Despite the darkness, I could see her silhouette in the doorway. She'd stopped at my abrupt movement, and the two of us remained immobile for a long while, staring at each other. Finally, I scooted up on the bed and flipped the bedcover open. I then patted the empty spot next to me.

She didn't hesitate. In seconds, she was in the bed and in my arms, her head on my shoulder. She felt fragile and insubstantial, her bony shoulder blades and ribs poking out underneath a thin layer of feverish skin. The cast on her arm was heavy. It rubbed across my stomach painfully, but that was the last thing I cared about at that moment. Instead, I let her nestle closer, her lips near my neck. My body was warm from the weight of her, and my nose filled with her scent.

She was sickly thin, she was broken from her accident, but she was still my Amelia. I squeezed her once as if grasping for life, and then we both fell promptly asleep.

CHAPTER TWENTY

Emma woke us the next morning by accident. She came into my room to talk to me and then yelped in surprise when she saw Amelia in bed with me. We both sat up quickly, and I was amused to see that both sisters' faces turn the same rosy hue.

Emma's eyebrows were up, and she backed out of the room slowly. "I'll just, uh, head home then, ladies. Looks like the two of you have some catching up to do."

I made a weak protest, and Emma raised her hands. "It's okay. Don't worry about me. I'll call you later, Amelia." She almost bolted from the room.

Amelia scooted away from me a little in bed. She was looking at her hands. I stared at the side of her face for a while, but she refused to meet my eyes. Finally, I had to physically turn her face to get her to look at me. She was still cagey, her eyes flickering away from mine, so I moved my face around until she looked at me completely.

Once she did, I nodded, satisfied. "Okay then. There you are."

Her eyes filled with tears and she glanced away again. I moved closer to her on the bed and put an arm around her shoulders, hugging her. I let her cry, quietly, for a long while, until her body went still beneath my arm. Certain she was okay for the moment, I got up and out of bed and went to the bathroom. I washed my face and grabbed one of the guest bathrobes for some extra warmth. When I came back, she was standing at the window, looking out into her garden.

She turned toward me, her face lighting up with something like real happiness for the first time since I'd seen her again. She still looked terrible, but I've never witnessed anything as lovely as that smile. I smiled back, and if anything, she brightened further. We walked toward each other, and I took her free hand in mine.

"I missed you," I said simply.

She nodded, and her troubled, haunted expression returned. She looked away. I squeezed her hand to get her attention again. "Hey," I said. "Stop that. We're going to talk now, okay? And after we talk, we can make some decisions."

It took her a long moment to nod, and I realized then that she was afraid. She obviously didn't know if this would be the first or last conversation of the rest of our lives. I was thinking the same thing, but with this fragile Amelia, I needed to take charge and force the issue. She was still too shattered to make decisions.

She excused herself to the bathroom, and I went downstairs, grateful to find an empty kitchen. I'd been terrified to find her cook or another servant, but it appeared that Emma had sent everyone home to give us some privacy. I made some coffee and found a pitcher of freshly squeezed OJ in the fridge. Some French bread lay on the counter, and I cut it in half and put it in the toaster oven. Amelia came in just as I was taking it out, and we sat down on the little stools across from each other at the island in the center of the kitchen. It was the least formal room in Amelia's house and had long been my favorite. Amelia knew this, and we often ate in here when I stayed over. I watched in satisfaction as she buttered a large piece of bread, and we both sat quietly while she ate and drank a cup of coffee.

All the while, I watched her, still hungry for the sight of her. In the morning light, away from the ugly fluorescents of the hospital, she looked ghostly as opposed to green, but she still looked awful. She'd taken the smallest bandage off her nose, and the injury had blossomed into two black eyes and a jagged cut across the bridge of her nose. The cut was sealed with a tiny row of stiches. The bandage on her forehead was much larger, and it was stained a little pink from the blood pooling beneath it. She'd put her broken arm back in the sling, and it was clear from the way she was moving that she was being careful to avoid pain. She was wrapped tightly in a bathrobe, and she still hadn't washed her face. It seemed to have taken a lot out of her just to put her sling on, as she looked like she hurt all over.

"Did they give you any pain meds?" I asked. "Now would be the time to take them—with food."

She nodded and then shook her head. "I have some, but I'll wait a little while yet. I had to take this same stuff when I had my wisdom teeth out, and it always makes me sleepy." She looked at me hopefully. "Do you think I could have a drink instead?"

I laughed. "That's a terrible idea, Amelia."

She nodded, clearly disappointed. "I know. I just…"

"Need some liquid courage?"

She grinned and then winced, her free hand going to the bridge of her nose. "Ow. It hurts when I smile."

"I bet. How did you hit your face? Were you wearing your seat belt?"

She nodded. "Something hit me and broke the glasses on my nose."

My throat constricted. "You could have been killed."

She lifted her eyebrows and shook her head. "I don't know how I wasn't. My car was completely wrecked. It caught on fire. German engineering saved me, I suppose."

"What happened? Do you remember why you had the accident?" I'd been curious about this last night but hadn't asked her or Emma.

She squinted as if trying to remember and then shook her head. "Not exactly. I was at the airport to pick up a shipment for work. I remember getting the phone call with news about Sara from the police, and I remember getting in the car." She looked at me. "I was upset. I know that."

I felt sick. She'd wrecked her car because of Sara and what she must have realized about me.

Amelia clearly realized what I was thinking. She used her free hand to squeeze mine. "Don't blame yourself. I shouldn't have been driving when I was that upset—that was stupid."

We were quiet for a while, absorbing this news. I wanted desperately to start talking, but I also didn't want to say a word. I was enjoying this moment of complete understanding, this quiet pause before the storm. Sitting here, in her clean, white kitchen, surrounded by memories of other mornings here, I was almost home again. Not because I was here in this house—I'd never liked it—but because I was here with her. Amelia was home, no matter where we were.

My eyes filled with tears, and I had to look away and blink rapidly to prevent them from falling. Crying would not be useful right now.

When I looked back at Amelia, her face looked pained and remorseful, her eyes lowered and her mouth quivering. Her hand was still in mine, and she rubbed the back of it with her thumb.

I heard her take a deep breath, as if readying herself, and she finally spoke. "I hate what I did to you."

I hesitated and then nodded.

She couldn't meet my eyes. She stared out the window above the sink for a while before going on. "I could blame Sara. She's the reason I lost a lot of trust in the world. But that's not fair to you or to her." She looked at me again. "I should have known, Chloé. You would never do something like that."

I nodded again. It wasn't that I had nothing to say. I could have started telling her about my pain, my disappointment, my humiliation, but now wasn't the time. I wanted her to talk, to explain things, and making her feel guiltier wouldn't facilitate conversation.

She sighed and looked away again. "A little over two years ago, when I found out that Sara had stolen money from my company, I almost lost my mind. When my accountant showed me the proof, I still didn't believe him. It took someone outside of the company to finally prove it to me. I just couldn't believe she'd done it."

"Did you love her?"

She winced and then nodded. "Very much."

A knife of pain sliced across my heart. I must have reacted physically to her words, as she looked at me sharply and then frowned.

"I should have told you about us, Chloé."

"Why didn't you?"

She paused. "For lots of reasons, at first."

"Like what?"

"During the lawsuit, we both agreed to a nondisclosure agreement. Neither of us was allowed to talk to the press or the public about what had happened with the money, and we were forbidden to talk about the other person in public. We also agreed to avoid each other, which was easy enough, as I could hardly look at her, and she was living in New York by then, anyway."

She shook her head and threw me an embarrassed glance. "I know all of that that sounds like a stupid excuse for not telling you, but by the time you and I met, I was just kind of used to not talking about her. I'd made myself stop thinking about her as much as possible, and I'd half-convinced myself I'd gotten past what she'd done to me, so there was no use dwelling on it."

She took my hand in hers again, the exchange so natural and unpracticed I barely thought to object. We often held hands when it was just the two of us, and despite being separated for a month, we weren't used to acting differently around each other.

She sighed. "So that's my first excuse—the lawsuit. Of course, she broke her end of the bargain long ago, when she started sending messages and threats to my girlfriends and to me. I could have gone to the press then and told them the truth about her, but I didn't. I was stupid. I wanted to protect her from herself. Now I know I should have told all long ago." She paused and frowned. "I got no end of grief from that lawsuit. A lot of people thought I'd sued some penniless, innocent girl."

Aunt Kate and Meghan had believed just that. I squeezed her hand to encourage her to keep talking. She smiled at me, and then, as if realizing what she was doing, she withdrew her hand from mine.

She looked up at me, her eyes dark and sad. "All of that is pretty feeble, Chloé. I know that. I've been thinking about it a lot since we broke up. Even before I knew you hadn't stolen the money, I was wondering why I hadn't told you." She met my eyes. "Actually, I think I was ashamed."

"Of what?"

She shrugged. "Of my relationship with her failing. Of being a dupe." She paused. "She took everything from me, Chloé. My trust, my heart, my money."

"But it wasn't your fault, Amelia."

She looked at me sharply. "But wasn't it? I clearly didn't give her enough. She needed more than I could provide. Otherwise, why would she steal from me?"

I shook my head. "It doesn't matter what her motivations were, Amelia. She had no right to do what she did to you or to your company."

Amelia looked uncertain for a moment, and then her eyes hardened again. "But she wouldn't have done it if it hadn't been for me. I failed her."

I held my hand open and waited. Amelia was suddenly shy and hesitant. She looked at me several times before slipping her hand in mine. I clasped it in both of mine.

"Listen to me, Amelia: it wasn't your fault. Sara is delusional. She's unbalanced. I've seen it myself. The things she says are believable, because sometimes she seems as sane as you or me, but she's not. She stole money from you because she wanted it, not because you didn't give her enough of your love or your money. You didn't break her. She was already broken."

Amelia sighed. "I wish I could believe that, Chloé, but I don't. Not entirely." She looked up at me. "Just before I found out that she'd stolen from me the first time, we had a fight. A big one. She wanted me to sell my business and my place and move with her to New York. I'd been thinking of opening a second office there, but I didn't want to move there full-time. I was cruel to her—cold. Not long after that, some of the money went missing."

"Again, Amelia, it's still not your fault. It wasn't her decision whether you moved or not—that was yours. Could you have handled the decision better? Maybe. But stealing from you because of her hurt feelings wasn't justified. It was petty and vengeful."

She still looked uncertain. She was staring at the butter dish in the middle of the island as if weighing my words against her memory. Finally, she shook her head and looked at me. "Anyway, it doesn't matter now."

"Of course it does!"

"No, Chloé, it doesn't. Whether I'm right or you're right, Sara still managed to get her revenge. I mean, for God's sake, look at us. We're in this situation almost entirely because of her."

I paused for a second and then laughed. "Christ, you're right. My God. We need to stop talking about her." I shook my head, disgusted. "I'll just say one more time, for the record, that I'm sorry—I'm sorry for listening to her. And to Daphne Waters."

Amelia made a dismissive motion with her hand. "Please. I'm the only person that needs to apologize here. And fuck Daphne."

"I can't believe I fell for it when she called me out of the blue like that."

Amelia sighed. "I did the same thing—don't blame yourself."

"Still, I should have known better. And I shouldn't have let her talk me into waiting to tell you. I should have told you about the meeting with Sara right away." I frowned, anger bringing heat to my face. "Do you think she knew what would happen?"

Amelia shrugged. "I wouldn't put it past her. Daphne loves to stir up drama. She's a miserable old bag. She knows all those gorgeous men only hang around her because of her money, so she can't stand it when other people are genuinely happy. After what happened last November, when Sara attacked you, she must have known I'd be upset that you and Sara talked behind my back. I wouldn't be surprised if she'd planned the whole thing. And we fell right into her trap." She shook her head. "I hope I never have to see her or Sara again."

We were quiet for a while. I couldn't look at her for very long without feeling my stomach twist into knots. I kept my eyes on my hands just to have something to look at and twisted my coffee cup nervously. There was so much we needed to say, to talk about, and it was all so painful. The urge to leave and flee this conversation was strong. Finally, just to get my good-bye over with, I looked up and met her eyes. Amelia was staring at me. Her expression was pained and repentant, but she also seemed unable to look away. This time I held her gaze. Being able to look at her felt a little like being back at the surface after diving a little too deep. You breathe heavily, trying to catch your breath, your lungs tingling with pain, but the main thing you feel is relief—relief to be back where you're supposed to be, head above the water.

Finally, I had to speak. "Look, Amelia, I've had a few weeks to get used to things. I found out about your engagement and the lawsuit, I found out about the money stolen from Winters Corporation. Even before that, I knew this breakup wasn't about us, not entirely anyway. I've had some time to get over it." I paused. "I understand, in theory, why you didn't trust me. I don't agree, obviously, but I can see things from your perspective. It must have looked like Sara, Part Two."

Amelia grinned slightly. "Little did I know it was *literally* Sara, Part Two." She shook her head, appearing disgusted. "It all seems so obvious now, Chloé. I don't know how I ever thought it was you." She looked at me and then away, clearly embarrassed. "For a few days there—right after? I thought you and Sara had been having an affair. How stupid is that?"

I made a face. "More than stupid. She's not even my type."

Amelia laughed and then winced again, putting her hand up to her nose. She jerked in pain from moving too quickly, and I had to smile at how utterly pathetic she was. I rose to my feet and walked around the island to her side. I gave her a delicate hug and she looked up at me, her eyes hopeful. Just about every impulse in me yearned to kiss her right then, but a small, cautious part of me overcame the urge. I turned my eyes away and grabbed her plate, and I sensed rather than saw her deflate. I spent the next couple of minutes cleaning, not looking at her, but I could feel her watching me.

After the dishes were drying in the stand by the sink, I finally made myself look at her again. Her eyes were sad and her shoulders were drooping. She seemed to be taking her last fill of me.

"I blew it, Chloé, didn't I?"

I didn't respond immediately. I didn't know how. I searched my heart, I searched my soul, and the only thing I found there was pain. Yes, I wanted what we'd had—desperately, in fact. My whole spirit yearned for her. And now, for the first time since she'd broken up with me, it seemed like I could have her, if I wanted her. But I was also afraid of her love now. Having those feelings between us again would mean opening myself up to the possibility of more pain, more heartache. I wasn't sure if I could take any more.

I weighed my response carefully. "Is it enough that I don't know yet, Amelia? Because I don't. I wish I could give you a straight answer, but I can't. I need more time."

She paled, her bruised eyes standing out in even firmer contrast on her wan face. She looked as if I'd given her bad news.

Finally, she nodded. "I understand." Her voice was hoarse and subdued.

The sight brought tears to my eyes, and I excused myself to go get changed. I was starting to become desperate to leave. I didn't want to look at her anymore. If I kept looking at those sad, bleak eyes, my resolve to stay strong would crack.

She called to me when I was in the doorway to the kitchen, about to leave. "Chloé?"

I turned and raised my eyebrows, waiting.

She licked her lips, silent for a long moment, and I could see that she was fighting back tears. She took a deep breath and seemed to force herself to go on. "What happened to the ring? I went back there, a couple of days later, to look for it, but I didn't find it. I was just wondering…" She shook her head and laughed at herself. "I'm sorry. It's a stupid question. It doesn't matter."

I continued to stare at her, and while I did, something shattered inside me. The resentment, the fear, it all evaporated in a heartbeat. The answer to all of this had been here all along—I simply hadn't acknowledged that it was in the room with us already.

I continued to keep eye contact with her and then started unbuttoning my pajama top. The air-conditioning in her house was always set much cooler than I liked, so it wasn't unusual for me to bundle up like this when I stayed over, but I'd also been hiding something from her and from me. Her eyes went wide, but I stopped two buttons down. I paused, searching my heart again for the answer to my own question, but I knew it already. I'd known for weeks. I reached into the shirt and pulled out the thin gold chain I'd been wearing since I showed Emma the ring. The ring dangled from the bottom of the chain. I held it up for Amelia to see. It had been resting next to my heart, hidden, all this time.

Amelia immediately burst into tears, burying her face in her free arm on the island counter. I watched for a moment and then went to her, putting my arm around her back. She continued to shake and cry for another moment and then sat up. She was in my arms a moment later, the two of us hugging each other so hard, she fell off her stool. We laughed after she almost fell to the floor, and I steadied her on her feet. She was still crying, but she reached up to wipe the tears off her face, smiling widely. She hugged me again, and when she pulled back, our eyes met. I saw her pause, waiting to see how I would react, and then we both moved forward.

After our first, it was the best kiss I'd ever received. Unlike the first, this one was untainted by uncertainty or fear. The kiss was forgiveness, it was starting over, it was moving on. When we drew apart and our eyes met again, things had already begun. In the coming weeks, we would have to talk about what had happened—all of this would still be there, but now I knew there would be coming weeks for both of us, together.

We continued to look at each other. Neither of us needed to say anything—it was there in the room with us already. Her face, which had been troubled and closed and hurt since I saw her yesterday, was open again, her brow clear. Her body, which had been tight and small, as if warding off a constant threat, looked relaxed and solid again. She stood straighter, taller, a bit of her confidence returning to her face. She met my eyes evenly.

"We should get cleaned up," I told her.

She wrinkled her nose. "I know—I can smell myself."

I took a step toward her, lowering my eyelids. "You might need some help since you have a cast."

She grinned. "I might at that. I don't know how I'll do everything with one arm. The doctor suggested I take baths for now, until the cast comes off."

I took another step closer. "I might know someone who can help you. But she's kind of a tyrant."

She was smiling widely now, clearly in on the joke. "Oh, is she now?"

"She'll only help you if you let her do all the work. It's better that way."

"Oh?"

I nodded and then took her hand, leading her upstairs to the large master suite. Her bathroom had a huge, Jacuzzi-style tub, and I lowered the stopper and turned the water on before dumping in some bubble bath. I turned back to her, and she was watching me, her eyes shy and scared-looking in her pale face.

"You can't get in the water wearing a bathrobe," I told her.

She nodded, seeming a little reluctant, and started struggling to shirk off her clothes. I saw her wince again and went immediately to help. I unhooked the sling, slid off her robe, and then paused before moving my hands to unbutton her pajama top. She froze. Then our eyes met, and I saw her confidence flicker back to life. She nodded, a slight smile drawing up one corner of her mouth. I began unbuttoning her top, my hands shaking slightly. I went slowly, looking at her face, not at what I was doing, making sure she wanted me to. She continued to meet my eyes, her cheeks flushing slightly. I reached the final button and then helped her shrug her top off her shoulders and pull it over her cast.

We continued to gaze at each other for a long time, and then, no longer able to help it, I looked down at her body. What I saw made me feel both heartbroken and glad. I rarely saw her naked body, even before all of this, but she was agonizingly thin and was marred and singed all over. Her ribs were bruised on one side and taped, and she had another dark-blue, almost hand-sized mark on her chest just below her collarbone, apparently from the seat belt. She had several little burns, but, given the fact that her entire car had gone up in flames, they seemed fairly minimal. I grabbed her shoulders, leaned forward, and then kissed the largest bruise over her heart. As I did, her body twitched under my hands. When we moved apart, her eyes were wide with surprise and pleasure.

"Now the pants," I said, pointing at them. We both looked down, and as she bent to take them off, I put out a hand to stop her. "Allow me." She let me yank them over her narrow hips, and then she stepped out of them almost primly.

She was completely naked now, and for once, I still had my clothes on. We'd been in the reverse situation so many times that it was momentarily disorienting, but the current moment wasn't about sex—it was about trust. I wanted Amelia to trust me, and I needed to show her that she could.

Ever since I'd heard the news about her engagement to Sara, a lot of things had become clear to me about our previous sex life. When we'd first talked about her problem, Amelia had told me she no longer liked being touched, but she didn't know exactly why. Now that the truth about Sara had been revealed, I think I knew, at least in part, why she was so reluctant to let her guard down. Sara had warped her sense of confidence, both in herself and in others. I needed to show her that she could have faith that I would never hurt her.

I turned off the water and then returned to her, leading her over to the tub. She stepped in, gingerly, using me for balance. The last time we'd been in this bathroom together, she'd watched me take a bath, her eyes hungry and impatient, the whole thing a prelude to sex. This time, I was the one watching, and all I wanted to do was show her gentleness.

I wrapped her cast tightly in a towel and made her lean back into the water, her arms on the outside of the tub. She looked uneasy for a moment, and then she relaxed, closing her eyes. I soaked a rag in the hot water and started gently scrubbing the exposed skin on her chest and neck. I could see her wincing against my ministrations, but there was nothing for it. She had blood, soot, and grime all over her. I moved slowly, carefully, making her stand up so I could reach her lower body. I touched parts of her she'd never allowed me near before, but I went slowly, still looking up at her face periodically to make sure she was comfortable with what I was doing.

Finally, I helped her back into the water, and she seemed almost completely worn out. She'd been okay with everything I'd done, but it was testing her defenses nonetheless. I continued to clean as she kept her eyes closed. I was especially careful with her face, using a little sponge with mild soap to remove the worst of the caked-on blood. The bandage on her forehead needed changing, and I used the water to help lift off the tape in order to lessen the pain. The cut underneath was jagged and long, but thin. Like her nose, it had been stitched shut. Who knew what kind of scars she would be left with when she healed. It didn't matter. Even with the angry-looking wounds on her face, she was still beautiful.

"We should wash your hair in the sink," I finally told her.

She opened her eyes and blinked stupidly for a moment, clearly just one step from falling asleep. I smiled then, proud that she'd let herself relax that deeply. I helped her stand again, and as the tub drained, I toweled off her entire body, patting every inch of her dry. She was grinning slightly now, that earlier nervousness almost entirely gone. I helped her step out of the tub, and we walked to the sink together. She bent over, and I used a nearby glass to soak her hair and then started lathering it. It took a while to rinse and even longer to towel it dry.

"I've never seen your hair this short," I said after I set the towel on her shoulders.

She ran her fingers through her damp waves. "I've never had it this short. I regret cutting it, if that makes you feel any better."

I laughed. "I didn't say I didn't like it."

"But it's terrible, right?"

Her hair was still damp, but I looked at it for a long time, scrutinizing it. I'd only seen her new style dirty and careworn, but, now clean, it looked better. She had thick, wavy hair, and she usually kept it long enough to hit the middle or lower portion of her back. Her new cut was perhaps four or five inches long on top, parted over one side, the sides a bit shorter. Styled, the haircut might look quite dashing, but it was definitely very different from the way it had been before.

"Actually, I think it suits you," I said.

She looked surprised. "Really?"

I nodded. "I mean, I want to see it dry and styled to give my final opinion, but even like this, it looks good. And it must be nice to have all that hair off your head."

She rolled her eyes. "You wouldn't believe how nice it is."

"Well, you should keep it like this, then, if it feels better. It's silly to have long hair in this climate anyway."

She smiled. "Well, if you like it, then I do, too."

The two of us worked together to apply a new bandage to her forehead, and I fished out some painkillers from the bottle for her. Back in the bedroom, I pulled back the covers and motioned for her to get in. Last night, she hadn't gotten into her own bed. Like me, she'd either fallen asleep on top of the blankets, or she'd been waiting here, awake, until she came into my room. We didn't bother getting her into pj's again, as it was clearly a painful and unnecessary step. She slid into bed naked, and I drew the covers to her chin and tucked her in. She laughed, enjoying the attention, and I bent down to kiss her forehead. When I stood up again, I saw tears in her eyes, and she looked more content than she did yesterday.

I was about to open my mouth when my phone rang. I'd put it in the pocket of my bathrobe. We both looked down at my ringing pocket, and I glanced up. She nodded, and I took a couple of steps away from her to answer it.

"Hello?"

"Hey, sugar. This is Aunt Kate."

"Hey, Kate."

"I'm just checking in with you. I came over here to your place to see how you are, but Jonathan tells me you haven't been back yet."

I hesitated. "I'm still at Amelia's."

There was a long silence. She obviously already knew where I was, but hearing it from me still seemed to throw her. "How is she? Is she okay?"

I looked over at Amelia and smiled. Even cleaned up, she still looked objectively terrible, but I'd hardly seen anything more beautiful in my entire life.

"She's okay, Kate. I just got her settled for a nap."

"Will you be over later? For dinner?"

I had, of course, forgotten all about dinner. Jim's other sons were flying in today, and all of us, including Meghan, were supposed to meet and eat together this afternoon. My aunt wanted Meghan and me to get to know the sons a little since we were all members of the wedding party.

"Of course, Kate. I'll be there."

I was watching Amelia, and I saw her face fall. She clearly didn't want me to leave.

Aunt Kate was quiet for a while. "Meghan's Zach will be here, too," she said. "If you want, you could bring Amelia. I mean, if she's up for it…"

I smiled at Amelia, and, apparently upon seeing something hopeful in my eyes, she smiled back.

"I'll ask her. Thanks, Kate."

"I just want you to be happy, sweetheart."

Her words made my eyes wet with thankful tears. "Thanks, Kate. I mean it." I paused and swallowed. "I'll see you later."

We hung up, and I gave Amelia a quick hug before telling her about Kate's invitation. She wasn't in any shape to go and wouldn't be later, even with some rest, but I wanted her to know that she'd been invited.

"She doesn't hate me?" she asked.

I shook my head and then explained what Kate and Meghan had thought and then what they'd learned about her from Emma. Amelia didn't look at all surprised when I finished my story.

"A lot of people thought Sara was the victim back then," she said quietly.

I sat down on the bed and took her hand in mine. "Well, now that all of this new information about her will come out in the papers, maybe the record will be set straight."

Amelia nodded but still looked troubled. I leaned down again and kissed her lightly on her forehead again. When I sat back up, her expression had brightened perceptibly.

"Stop worrying about it," I told her. "Try to relax, and get some sleep. You just had a major accident."

"Will you still be here when I wake up?"

"I should be. Dinner isn't until two. I'll wake you up if I have to leave, okay?"

She nodded, and a moment later her eyes drooped closed.

CHAPTER TWENTY-ONE

To say Amelia and I were connected at the hip the week leading up to the wedding is overstating it a little, but we did spend nearly all day, every day together. I had some wedding activities to attend part of every day, but otherwise I was over at her house keeping her company and helping out. However, after that first night, I went to my place at night. We didn't talk about why I did this, and Amelia didn't seem to mind or expect anything different. It was simply a natural thing, for now, to avoid any awkwardness that might arise should I sleep over. Whether I stayed in her room or in a guest room, we weren't ready to spend the night together. It was too intimate for us for now. We also kept our distance from each other physically when we were together. We kissed cheeks hello and hugged good-bye, but that was it, for the most part. We both seemed to need to keep it that way for the time being.

I ran into several of her family members at her place that week, most of whom seemed overjoyed to see me again. Luckily for me, the impending divorce was making Amelia's mother's presence extremely awkward for everyone, so she visited only once that week. Her mother was less than cordial to me during her visit, but as it was very brief, I didn't feel the need to leave while she was there. I just hid in the library. In the past, she'd been the hardest to win over, and even before Amelia and I broke up we hadn't exactly been what one would call friendly. I was, however, beginning to realize that the only thing I could hope was that her mother could, with time, be civil. She was maybe one degree above lukewarm with most members of her own family. I decided I could live with this type of behavior if Amelia could, especially as I wouldn't be seeing her at every family function anymore. Amelia's brother Dean and his wife Ingrid were only slightly warmer with me than her mother was, but the rest of her family treated me like one of their own. Not one of them seemed to resent the breakup. I almost cried when I saw Amelia's dad for the first time. He came straight to me and gave me a bone-crunching hug. Emma and Amelia's other brothers, Bobby and Michael, were just as excited that I was back. All was clearly on the way to being forgiven.

Amelia and I talked a lot that week. Very few of our conversations were easy ones, but we made ourselves get through them with no small amount of tears, hurt feelings, and awkwardness. Now that she'd decided on full honesty, the floodgates were open, and I learned more about her in our conversations that week than I had in the months we'd been together before our breakup. As I'd always suspected, she'd dated or slept with almost all of her previous assistants at work. Amelia herself had been seduced when she just out of college by the woman she trained under when she was learning the business—an older woman we'd run into once in a lingerie store months ago. As the words spilled out of her, I was in stages shocked, appalled, horrified, and finally bemused with her past. More than anything, her frantic search for lovers bespoke a sad kind of desperation on her part—a desperation she clearly hadn't filled with empty sex and meaningless relationships. The fact that she'd stayed with me, had fallen for me, out of all of those people made me feel a little proud now, as silly as that is.

Sara's involvement with the theft and her subsequent arrest hit the newspapers the same day Amelia decided to drop a bombshell on the art world. I got to her place early that morning to make her breakfast. I'd brought in the newspaper as I came inside, and as I waited for the coffee to finish brewing, I opened it to a full-page spread about Sara's arrest in the crime section and then another full-page spread about Amelia's news in the arts-and-leisure section. Amelia had decided to sell her business, Winters Corporation. She'd told me her plans last night, but I hadn't realized how quickly the sale would be announced. I refolded the paper and took it and the tray with her breakfast up to her room. She was still sleeping when I walked in, and I set the tray down on a little table before gently shaking her awake.

She blinked stupidly for a moment and then grinned up at me, stretching widely before flinching. Her bruises and stitches were healing but still painful. Gingerly, she scooted up in bed, and I moved some pillows around behind her so she could sit up straight.

She watched me bring her tray over, beaming when I set it down over her lap. "I can't even get my cook to bring me breakfast in bed, Chloé, and I pay her. I don't know what I did to deserve you."

"Don't worry—I'll make you pay for it later," I said and winked at her.

I picked up the newspaper and showed her the article on Sara. She read it slowly, her eyes hard and angry. When she was finished, she set it down on the bed next to her, shaking her head. "I don't know why, but this reporter clearly knows more details than I do. I wonder why none of my lawyers called me with this information. According to this, Sara hired an intern at work to install a money-hoarding virus. That's how she got in. The intern was arrested last night on conspiracy charges."

"Good." I paused. "Does all of this mean you'll get the money back?"

She nodded. "Eventually, anyway. My lawyers are working on the recovery. Some of it has been spent, but now the insurance company will have to pay the company back for all of it, as far as I know. But it might take a while. It's not my money per se anyway—it was the business's money, really. It will be absorbed with the sale, I guess, when I get it back."

I grabbed the arts section of the newspaper and handed it to her, and her brow furrowed with annoyance. "This wasn't supposed to be announced until next week."

I sat down on the edge of the bed next to her. "I had no idea Winters Corporation was selling out so quickly. When you told me what you were planning, I thought you meant at the end of the year or something, not now."

She nodded. "It's time. No, more than that, it's long past time." She took my hand. "Even before the accident, I was thinking about it, and now that I have you..." She blushed. "I mean, now that we're friends again, I'm determined to let it go."

We hadn't yet had a conversation that defined what we were to each other now. Anyone watching us that didn't know better would think we were close friends, but nothing more. Except for the first bath after her accident, we remained chaste and clothed around each other. We kissed cheeks and touched arms and hands, but nothing more than

I would do with my aunt or Meghan, for example. We weren't ready for more than that, and we were both okay with waiting to decide. Still, it made for awkward conversations. What were we now? Friends? We loved each other—that was clear and undeniable. But our relationship was too complicated to label as friendship.

She let her hand rest in mine. "I think I was using work as a place to hide all of these years. I didn't use to mind the hours or the work. It kept me busy, I was good at it, and I made a lot of money. But ever since you and I got together last fall, it's started to seem like a burden. Even before the accident, I was exhausted and burning out quick. It takes up too much of my time—time I'd rather spend having a life with my family and with…other people that matter."

I smiled and squeezed her hand. "How long will it take to wrap up business?"

She shrugged. "I'll start liquidating next week. And of course nothing will be final until the stolen money is recovered. A few projects will continue even after the final sale—the installation at Teddy's, for one, but I can sort out those kinds of details with the company's buyers. I also want to help place as many of my employees as possible in new jobs before we wrap up." She seemed thoughtful. "Still, if I'm lucky, I can be done by the end of the fiscal quarter in June."

"So soon?"

She nodded.

"Have you given any more thought to what you want to do next?"

She smiled. "Yes. I want to work for Art for the People—that charity I raised money for at the gala. You know, the one that provides art training and supplies for kids and teens?"

I let go of her hand and leaned down to hug her. "That's wonderful. What a good idea. You'll be great at it."

"It's a nonprofit, so I won't make very much money—if any—but I don't care."

She flicked her eyes up to mine and glanced away. "Actually, I've also been thinking of downsizing. I want to sell this house and move somewhere smaller."

"But Amelia, why would you do that? You love this house, and it's part of your family history." If she sold it, it might pass out of family hands forever.

She shrugged. "Actually, I'm starting to hate it. It's old, so it takes a mountain of upkeep, and I rattle around in here like a ball bearing in a box. My cousin Gertrude has shown some interest in it before, so I might be able to keep it in the family." She looked at me. "I could take the sale of this place and invest it, and perhaps use some of the dividends for Art for the People."

"But where would you move?"

Her fingers rubbed the back of my hand. "That all depends. It won't sell immediately. It takes a while to move a house like this, even when someone's interested. I was thinking of putting it up for sale in May or June, and then hopefully I can sell it by the end of the summer."

I knew now what she was getting at and why she was being so cagey. Since we had decided to give each other a second chance, we both knew that we might someday become more intimate again. If that happened, we might decide to move in together. All of these were *might*s, though, and the *might-not*s hovering around us still weighed on them. It was too early to tell. But if we did take that next step, the end of this summer might be just about the time we would decide to take the next step. We were both thinking this without saying it, and I was tense with suppressed anxiety. We would have to make a decision about our current status sooner or later, but I wasn't ready for that conversation.

Seeking to avoid just that, I sat back down in the armchair and let her eat. While she did, I read the two articles in the newspaper more closely, stunned again to think that the mighty Winters Corporation would close its doors for good in the near future. It was an institution— something as much a part of the art world as the artists themselves. The art community would certainly suffer.

I glanced up at Amelia. She was reading a different section of the paper while she munched on her toast. She had the usual little wrinkle between her eyes, the one she always had when she read, and I couldn't help but stare at her, my heart heavy and tight in my chest. I still couldn't get enough of the sight of her. Even now, with her mussy, bed-head hair and her bandages and bruises, she was the most beautiful woman in the world.

Chapter Twenty-two

The morning of the wedding was the first markedly hot day we'd had this year. New Orleans has what most locals think of as one and a half seasons: a short winter and a long summer. Generally by March, or even late February, the city is already heating up, and the heat builds over what is technically spring and lasts until late October before cooling off slightly. Our winter had been longer than usual this year, and while we'd had very warm afternoons for the last two weeks, when I walked outside of my apartment the morning of the wedding, it felt hot for the first time. I paused, squinting against the sun, and then struggled to maneuver my dress and my bag of wedding essentials into one hand as I rooted around in my purse for my sunglasses. Jonathan emerged a moment later, locking the door behind us. I'd essentially loaned him my car for the week in return for shuttling me around, and he loved every minute of it.

We both had several bags of things to take with us to the wedding venue, and I realized about three blocks from my place that we'd forgotten something. By the time we left again, we were running a little late, so Jonathan drove like a madman through the French Quarter. I closed my eyes most of the way.

Aunt Kate and Jim's ceremony was scheduled to start at two, but the rest of the wedding party was supposed to arrive as early as possible to take care of all of the last-minute tasks and situate the guests before the bride and groom showed up. While I'd been out of it and recovering from the breakup, Meghan had taken on the bulk of preparation work. Really, with all her work, she should have been the maid of honor, but when I'd suggested that we switch roles, she and Aunt Kate had been flabbergasted, so I backed off.

That morning I had to meet several of the vendors and direct them where and how to set up. Jim's other sons, Jim Jr. and Jack, had been here all week like Jonathan, and they arrived at the venue soon after us. Jonathan and I chatted with them a bit before we all returned to work. I already liked Jonathan very much, and he and his older brothers were almost carbon copies. All three men worked in some facet of the construction business, and all three were tall and striking. Jim Jr. and Jack were both attached right now, but my aunt was working her hardest to decide which female cousins she should steer Jonathan's way today. I'd humored her in her plans, as she seemed to get a kick out of the idea that he might find one of them attractive, marry her, and move to New Orleans.

Guests started to trickle in a little after one, and I had my hands full keeping them occupied and getting them to their places. Bucking tradition, Jim and Aunt Kate had decided to arrive together, so as the official start time drew closer, all of us were simply waiting for them to show up.

As time passed, I grew more and more anxious for Amelia's arrival. This would be her first time out of the house since her accident, and it would be the first time she'd seen my friends and family since before we broke up. She arrived just after one thirty, looking better than she had all week. Her black eyes still looked painful and alarming, but overall, her color was much better, and she seemed to be filling out a little again. Since the cut on her forehead had stopped seeping, she'd also been able to replace the bandage there with a much smaller one, mostly for appearances at this point. She still looked banged up and injured, but now it didn't necessarily seem as if she should be resting in a hospital bed somewhere, either. She'd decided to wear a suit today, and it hugged her slight curves beautifully. Even smacked around and dinged up, she looked wonderful.

We raced to each other and hugged, and I think my fierceness surprised her a little since she drew back a moment later.

"I'm sorry," I said. "Just nervous." I gestured around me. "About the wedding, about having you here. You know—everything."

She laughed. "You and me both, Chloé. I know you said your aunt didn't mind having me here, but I can't help but think that she hates me after what I did to you."

"She'll get over it, Amelia. Anyway, she feels bad about how she treated you before. You can use that against her."

She laughed, and I led her into the courtyard where the chairs for the ceremony had been set up. Several guests were milling around sipping champagne or lemonade, and I paused, not quite sure where to put her. Jim's sons solved this dilemma a moment later by coming over to greet us. Jim Jr. and Jack's girlfriends had arrived, and we all introduced ourselves. I could see all of these strangers appraising Amelia and was satisfied to ascertain that everyone was simply interested in getting to know her—none had any preconceived notions about her. Unlike just about everyone else coming to this wedding, these five people, in addition to being younger than almost everyone here, were just about the only outsiders attending today. Jim's brother and his brother's wife were here, too, but otherwise the entire guest list consisted of my aunt's friends and family. This didn't bother Jim or his family in the slightest, but it did make things a bit awkward for them. Amelia, like them, was an outsider, and it made sense to leave her with them. Jim Jr. and Jack's girlfriends invited her to sit with them during the ceremony, which was a weight off my shoulders.

Meghan came over a few minutes later to get my help, and she and Amelia greeted each other with a nod. Meghan was too distracted to say anything to her, and again, I was relieved to find things running so smoothly. I quickly hugged Amelia before following Meghan off to the side, where she tasked me with helping some of the older guests to their seats. Technically Jim's sons were the ushers as well as the groomsmen, but as there were so many people to help at this point, it didn't really matter who did what.

Finally, Meghan and I were called back inside the cottage—the bride and groom had arrived. We passed Jim as we walked through the rooms, and he gave us a quick hug and directed us to my aunt. We found her in the wedding suite, and when she turned toward us, I couldn't help but get a little teary. She was wearing a long, billowy ivory dress in a folksy, bohemian style. She had a crown made of natural flowers and a simple wildflower bouquet. Her face was more made up than I'd almost ever seen it before, but it suited her. All three of us hugged and had to blink back tears for a couple of minutes in order to calm down. Eventually Jonathan appeared in the doorway, and we gave him a thumbs-up, ready to start. The music began a moment later, and we waited for our cue to begin.

The ceremony was brief and sweet. Jim and Kate had written their own vows, and they made just about everyone cry. I glanced over at Amelia just once and saw that she was becoming emotional, too. I had to look away quickly, trying to keep my calm as much as possible. As the bride and groom kissed, the machines we'd rented began to billow bubbles into the crowd, and everyone cooed and clapped in appreciation. Jim and Kate raced through the crowd back to their special suite, and the rest of us were directed over to the table with the seat assignments for the reception. Having made the table assignments myself, I knew where I was sitting, so I went directly to Amelia, launching myself into her arms, and we squeezed each other long and hard. I didn't need to explain why I was so happy to be in her arms, or why I needed her in mine—she knew. We hadn't talked about the ring she'd given me, or what it might mean, but I was still wearing it on a chain around my neck. The chain was long enough that no one could tell what hung at the end of it. It was our secret for now. Whether the ring would end up on my finger remained to be seen, but wearing it this way was a step in that direction. When we looked at each other, I could tell we were thinking the same thing: if we decided to take the next step, to get back together for real, it might be our turn at the altar someday.

While Jim and Aunt Kate would have their own special table, the rest of the wedding party and our partners would be sitting together. As we waited to be invited into the reception room, the nine of us stood around chatting. Meghan and Zach stood as far away from me and Amelia as possible. I was disappointed, but I also didn't expect anything more from her for now. I knew she felt badly about how she'd treated Amelia in the past, but she hadn't forgiven her for breaking up with me yet, and with reason. Still, if Meghan couldn't get past what had happened, we would have problems down the line. But this also wasn't the place to get into it.

We were all finally directed inside, and a few minutes later the bride and groom were announced. Our table clapped the loudest and the longest, all of us on our feet. Meghan whistled, causing several people to look over at us and laugh.

Kate had forbidden speeches, so dinner passed fairly quickly. While we ate, the courtyard where we'd had the ceremony was cleared of chairs, and the dance floor was laid down. Jim and Kate both loved to dance—had met in a swing class, actually—and they wanted to make as much time for it as possible. They had a band and a DJ that would take turns through the afternoon and evening. A proper Creole wedding lasts all day and night, after all, and for Kate and Jim, that meant boogying until your legs fall off. Amelia and I took the floor most of the slow songs, her arm and bruises preventing anything more lively. I went out a couple of times early on with Meghan and Kate, and Amelia watched us, grinning, from the sidelines.

Kate was, of course, extremely busy and distracted, but she'd made an effort to ask Amelia about her injuries and thank her for coming. Kate seemed almost natural with her, and I could only hope that the remains of her reserve would disappear the longer Amelia and I stayed friends. Even now, they were well on the way toward mending bridges.

Early in the evening I excused myself to the restroom, and when I came back, I couldn't find Amelia. I looked around for a few minutes and finally spotted her speaking with Meghan. They'd hidden at the far end of the reception room. Just about everyone was outside in the courtyard now, so they had the place almost entirely to themselves. Both of them looked grave and serious as they spoke. I decided not to interrupt, understanding that they needed to talk, but I stood in the doorway just in case. Eventually, I was relieved to see Meghan give Amelia a quick hug before she turned to leave. Meghan threw me a wink as she passed me, and I watched her rejoin Zach before going over to Amelia.

"Everything okay?" I asked her.

She nodded, looking thoughtful. "Better than okay. She apologized to me for how she'd behaved before."

My shock must have shown on my face, as Amelia laughed. "I apologized to her too, Chloé. I should have pushed a little harder to be pleasant with her before. She means a lot to you, and I want all of us to be friends."

"Did you talk about the rest of it? I mean about this last month?"

She shook her head. "No, it's not the time or place. But we're getting together next week to do just that. Just the two of us. We both want to clear the air a little, and I think we should do it alone. I invited her out for lunch."

I gave her a long hug. "Thanks, Amelia."

"For what?"

"For trying. I know it would be easy just to brush her off. She can be a pain in the ass, and she holds a mean grudge."

She looked at me evenly. "That might be true, but she's your best friend. It matters to me that she like me, or, if not like, at least doesn't hate me. We're both a part of your life, Chloé, and we both want to make it work as well as possible."

My pleasure was overwhelming and I couldn't hold back. I grabbed her and squeezed her much harder than I should have. She gasped in pain, so I drew back a little, and then she pulled me into her again. A moment later we eased up to look at each other, our faces inches apart. I saw the question in her eyes and met it by moving forward. Her lips met mine, and her tongue flickered into my mouth. I instantly heated up. I touched her tongue with mine, and we were soon lost in the kiss. I was instantly on fire for her, my excitement immediate and strong. My nipples hardened and my legs weakened as her tongue continued to explore mine. I'd rarely been as turned on.

After a long time, we both yanked apart, gasping for breath. I took a couple of careful steps away from her, almost afraid of what we might do if we kept going. My hands and legs were shaking, and I was light-headed and weak with desire. I was tempted to take her, right here, twenty feet away from a party of family and longtime friends.

We grinned at each other, and then we were laughing, the laughter exploding out of both of us on a wave of anxious excitement. The laughter killed most of the mood, and we joined hands before walking back to the courtyard together.

We managed to keep things fairly chaste the rest of the night—holding hands, kissing briefly and infrequently. However, that moment we'd nearly lost control seemed to haunt us. I would catch her looking at me, eyes dark and hungry, and I'm sure she caught me doing the same.

She left the wedding fairly early, her injuries wearing on her, and as we stood outside on the sidewalk waiting for her driver to show up, we kept a wary distance, only kissing the briefest of good-byes before she climbed in and disappeared.

I didn't know if the kissing meant we were a couple again. It seemed to, of course, since friends don't kiss like that, but we would need to talk about it and make it official. If we decided we were together, I still didn't know when we'd be ready to make love again. But one thing was now very certain: when we were ready, we would tear each other apart.

CHAPTER TWENTY-THREE

Happily, Amelia was overjoyed when I told her about my art show. I'd been afraid she would feel betrayed, since I was using a gallery unassociated with her company, but it wasn't an issue. In fact, she seemed to think it was a good idea to keep my art separate from her business, to avoid any taint of favoritism. She did, however, use some of her influence for promotions, and the gallery owner told me in the days leading up to the show that he'd received more inquiries about it than for anything he'd ever held there. Teddy and Kit had called and let me know that they'd been pushing the show too, telling nearly everyone that came to the restaurant how great I was and showing off the painting they'd already bought. All of this served to make me both more excited and more nervous about the show than I already was. I wanted it to be a success, of course, but it was terrifying to think that a lot of people might be there, too, all of whom would be looking at my work and talking about me.

On the morning of the opening, Amelia showed up at my place early, and I realized as I opened the door for her that it was the first time since I'd known her that she'd taken a day off except for a vacation or holiday. In the week and a half since the wedding, things had progressed quickly with the liquidation of the Winters Corporation. Most of the inventory had been shifted to other dealers, and with that almost entirely taken care of, Amelia was spending a good deal of her time talking to gallery owners and museums around New Orleans, the state of Louisiana, and other parts of the South, trying to secure new positions for her employees. Luckily for them, experience working for

Amelia Winters was like a gold star on their resumes. Most of the art-restoration specialists had already found positions, and several people from her sales team had also been placed. It was Amelia's hope to have everything wrapped up by mid-to-late May, a full month ahead of the schedule she'd originally set for herself. Despite the long hours she was still pulling, I had never seen her so carefree and lighthearted. It was clear from her buoyancy that she was making the right decision.

The opening night of my show was scheduled to begin at eight that evening, but Amelia was over early that morning for moral support. She knew how jittery I'd been. She handed me a large bouquet of white roses and gave me a quick kiss. I ushered her inside, still nervous to have her in my place. She'd been over briefly once or twice since the accident, but this would be the first time she would stay more than a few minutes. Also, my apartment was a snake pit of chaos, with promotional flyers everywhere and serious evidence of my lack of homemaking skills. Plates and coffee cups littered nearly every surface in the living room, and a distinct odor was emanating from my kitchen that I hadn't had time to address. Amelia took one look around and started laughing.

Seeing my face, she tried to stifle her glee, but she had to struggle to stop. "I'm sorry, honey. It's just that no one looking at you would think you were such a slob."

"I can't help it! I just haven't had time to clean up. Between the wedding, setting up at the gallery, and finishing my new painting, I've been swamped."

She tried to make her expression serious and failed, grinning at me. "So how is the new painting going?"

I sighed. I knew now that I shouldn't have promised to create a new piece in three weeks. While my previous painting had come together quickly, I hadn't had the extended, uninterrupted time I did last time to work on my new one. The new piece was, however, going to be the centerpiece of the show, so I had to complete it by tonight.

Seeing my hesitation, she gave me a hug. "Listen—why don't you go work on it, and I'll clean up a little around here. Does anything else need to be done today? I'm all yours."

I handed her my cell phone. "If you could field my calls, you'll do more than enough. Every time I start working on something, someone interrupts me. If I could have two hours to myself, I might be able to figure out what I need to do."

She took my phone from me, saluted, and then winked. "I'll expect payment in full tonight."

I couldn't help but blush. Having attended many, many art-show openings, I knew mine would likely last until well past midnight. Two days ago, without thinking about the implications, I'd invited Amelia to spend the night after the show. My invitation had come from a concern for her well-being—I didn't want her to have to drive home that late. She was recovering but still weak and easily tired. Her company uses a luxury-car service she could have called instead, but I hadn't thought of it at the time. The second the invitation was out of my mouth, however, I realized what it might mean to her. She'd agreed instantly, and the sexual tension between us had ratcheted up considerably since.

It wasn't that I didn't want to sleep with her—just the opposite. Lately I could hardly bear it when we separated every night. My desire and frustration was a growling, hungry animal in the pit of my stomach. Since the wedding, we'd kissed again once or twice a day, but we were both still very shy and hesitant with each other. Moreover, we hadn't yet had the talk about what we were now. We seemed more like a couple than we had before the wedding, but we certainly weren't back to where we'd been before the breakup. So yes, I wanted her, desperately, but I wasn't sure we were ready to start sleeping together again.

I was about to say something along these lines when the doorbell rang. Sighing, I turned to the door, surprised to find my Aunt Kate on the other side. She was holding a basket full of muffins and a small bouquet of wildflowers. Her smile faded slightly when she spotted Amelia, but only for a moment. She handed the flowers to me and came inside.

"I just thought I'd stop in to see if you needed anything, Chloé." She glanced around the room. "And it looks like you could use some help."

I closed the door, my frustration getting the better of me. "What difference does it make what my place looks like? I'll clean tomorrow."

They stared at me with the same confused and hurt expression, and I felt instantly terrible. "I'm sorry. I didn't mean to snap at you. I'm just nervous. Aunt Kate, Amelia came over to help, too. She's going to be answering my phone and cleaning. Maybe you two can work together."

They looked at each other, clearly a little anxious at the prospect of extended time alone, but I decided to force the issue. I was sick of pussyfooting around the two of them—they'd have to figure it out on their own.

"Okay then," I said. "I'm heading upstairs to paint."

I closed the door to my studio and almost sagged with relief. I could only just manage the strain. When I'd decided to throw a show, I'd thought it would be an exercise in forcing myself to be more open about my work, but I'd grown to regret it. Now that the show was finally here, and people would be looking at and judging my work—and by extension, me—I was sick with nerves. This was another reason I was struggling with my new painting. Usually I painted in complete seclusion. Although I usually showed my work to close friends and family members, before this it had never faced the scrutiny of strangers. Now I was painting with a much larger audience in mind, and my creativity was suffering.

I took a deep breath and approached my easel. I'd thrown a drop cloth over it two days ago, sick of the sight of it, and hadn't looked at it since. Carefully, almost as if I were afraid of it, I drew back the cloth and looked at it fully for the first time in a long time. What I saw was a pleasant surprise.

I usually paint landscapes and street scenes, rarely people, and when I do have human figures, they're minimized and unrecognizable. The Impressionists are my direct influences, but my color palette has always been more vibrant and louder than their muted tones. I'm interested in the physical spaces around me at the time of my painting. While I was in Paris, all of my work consisted of French scenes and landscapes, and now that I was back in New Orleans, the same was true.

My current piece depicted a dilapidated house I'd always loved in the Marigny. It was about four blocks from my current apartment, and I used to walk by it all the time. The house had been abandoned during Katrina, and now it sat silently sagging and rotting amidst the colorful Victorians and Painted Ladies on either side of it. It wasn't a large house. Unlike some of the neighbors, it had one story with a full front porch. Judging from the outside, it had perhaps two or three bedrooms, but even when it was in good shape, I'd never actually been inside.

I remembered the house from when I was younger, before Katrina, as a showpiece for the whole neighborhood. As a kid and young adult, I passed it nearly every day on the bus to school or college and always wondered what it would be like to live there. When I saw it for the first time after Katrina, my heart actually hurt for it. A large tree had fallen on the roof, and for whatever reason, the owners simply abandoned it and never came back. Looking at it after the storm was like seeing the wreck of an old friend. Almost ten years later it was even worse than it'd been. I often walked by wondering why it hadn't been torn down.

In my new painting, one half of the house was falling apart, reflecting its current condition. That half of the piece was dark, with lots of blues, grays, and dark greens, like the house was today. The other half of the painting showed the house as it once was, with sunny skies and bright, stunning yellows and reds. Two days ago when I was working on it, the whole thing had begun to seem contrived and derivative, but now, looking at it closely, I was proud of the way it had turned out. I realized in an instant what it needed to be complete and started immediately.

Several hours later, I was initialing the corner of the painting when I heard a tentative knock at my studio door. I set my brush down, satisfied, and called out. "Yes? Come on in."

Aunt Kate opened the door slowly and poked her head in. Having lived with me growing up and, more recently, for a couple of months last autumn, she knew that I often became upset when someone interrupted me in my studio. I smiled at her to reassure her, and she came into the room with more confidence, holding a cup of coffee. I took it from her gratefully. A moment later, I saw her eyes fix on the painting behind me. Like with so much of my work before it, she would be the first person to see the painting.

She stared at it for a long time as if mesmerized, unblinking and unmoving. I sipped at my coffee nervously, waiting for her verdict, but she stared at it in silence for what felt like an eon. Finally, she turned to me with tears in her eyes.

"I used to walk by that house all the time," she said. "It was always my favorite before the storm."

My shoulders relaxed with relief, and I nodded. "Me, too. I can't help but love it still."

She nodded and looked back at it, still teary. "It's wonderful, Chloé. It's like looking at time itself—destruction and rebirth in an endless cycle. Anyone that lives around here will recognize it immediately, and those that don't will love it anyway."

I heard another tentative knock on the door, which was still partway closed, and Amelia appeared in the doorway a moment later. "I heard you talking in here, so I thought it was probably safe."

Like my aunt, her eyes were drawn to the painting, and she froze. Her eyebrows went up to her hairline, and she walked over to the painting, bending down to peer at it closely. A moment later, she looked back at me with an expression of startled surprise.

"You know this house?" she asked, pointing at it.

"Well, yes," I said. "It's always been one of my favorites."

Amelia burst out laughing, and Aunt Kate and I shared a confused glance. Seeing our expressions, Amelia laughed even harder, and it took her a few moments to calm down. She was wiping at her eyes, clearly still amused.

"Why are you laughing?" I couldn't prevent my petulant tone. I hadn't expected her to love my painting, but I didn't like her laughing at it.

She realized her error and shook her head quickly. "I'm not laughing at you or your painting, Chloé. In fact, I love it." She came closer and pulled me into her arms, giving me a solid kiss on my cheek before letting me go. "I'm simply laughing at the coincidence."

"What coincidence?"

She looked at me levelly for a moment and then shrugged. "It was going to be a surprise, but I think I just gave it away."

"Gave what away?"

"When was the last time you looked at the house in your painting?"

I couldn't remember. While I'd grown up passing it nearly every day, and had looked at it several times since I got back to New Orleans last fall, it wasn't on my regular route to anything now. I had painted from memory.

I shook my head. "I don't know. A couple of months? Maybe more?"

Amelia looked at Kate. "You know this house, too, I take it?"

Kate nodded.

"But you haven't seen it in a while either, right?"

Kate hesitated and then shook her head. "No. I guess not. It's not on my way here, so I don't know when I saw it last."

I could see Amelia's glee, but I wasn't sure what it meant. "Why are you asking, Amelia? Do you know something about it?"

She nodded. "It might be better to show you. Come with me."

Aunt Kate and I shared a confused look but wordlessly agreed to go along with her. I took off my smock, and the two of us followed Amelia outside, down the street, and around the corner. We walked for about three blocks in silence, Amelia ahead of us.

About a block from the house I'd painted, she paused and turned back to us. "As you might know, it's very difficult to buy a house in the Marigny. The neighborhood has only a few open rentals most of the time and even fewer places for sale. Anything available to buy tends to be small—half of a shotgun—or really big."

I'd had a little experience with this reality when I was looking for a rental a few months ago, so I nodded.

"As you also know, my dad's in real estate, and he's had his eye out for a smaller, single-family home in this area for years now. The market here is so lucrative, he actually hasn't had any luck. Every house he's tried to buy has been poached from under him. Then, a couple of months ago, he finally saw something for sale, but when he showed up for the open house, I'm sure by now you understand what he saw."

My heart was in my throat now. I knew exactly what he'd seen— I'd been painting it all day. "He found a rotting pile of boards overgrown with vines."

She grinned. "He decided to go ahead and buy it, thinking that, at the very least, he could build a new house on the same lot."

She turned and started walking again, and I was suddenly scared to see what had happened. While I knew the best thing for the neighborhood, and for the house really, was for the rotting hulk to be torn down, it also made me very sad. It was like losing an old friend. Swallowing my hurt, I followed her, wishing I could close my eyes.

As we drew nearer, however, I was surprised to see that the house was still standing. A large scaffolding stretched around the entire thing, and piles and piles of rotten wood and roofing lay all around it, but the frame of the house was, overall, still intact. I stood rooted to the sidewalk, staring with disbelief. Finally, I looked over at Amelia to find her smiling at me.

"I can't believe it," I told her. "I thought it would have to be bulldozed."

"I didn't believe it either. When my dad told me he bought this house, I knew exactly which one he was talking about. You and I walked by it a few times last fall, and I remember thinking it would have to be demolished. After the sale, my dad had it inspected, and much to everyone's surprise, many of its major structural elements could be salvaged. He threw a neighborhood meeting about it. It would take longer to fix it than to tear it down and rebuild, but everyone who attended the meeting, like him, voted to restore instead of rebuild. He decided to return the house to its pre-Katrina condition."

I had tears in my eyes, and when I looked at Kate, she too seemed a little choked up. Despite the decade that had passed, Katrina was an open wound in most New Orleanians' hearts. All of us had lost something in the storm, and many people had never recovered from it. While the city had bounced back to vibrancy in many ways since, that resurgence had come at the cost of some of its history and culture. Restoring this house was like bringing back a little piece of the past.

I took Amelia's hand. "It's wonderful, Amelia. It really is. I'm so glad he decided to buy it and even happier that it could be salvaged. It's always been one of my favorite houses."

She smiled widely. "Well, that's good, because I just bought it from him a couple of days ago."

I stared at her, my mouth open, gaping and gasping for words. "What?" I finally managed.

She laughed. "You heard me. I was going to show it to you later this summer, when the renovations are finished, but I guess it's better this way. You might have seen it before then and grown curious."

I looked back at the house, tears spilling down my cheeks. "But that means—"

"I bought it for you, Chloé. For us."

I jumped into her arms then, squeezing her tight, her cast be damned. She hugged me back, just as fiercely, and hot tears continued to spill down my cheeks. She kissed the side of my head, and I pulled back a little to kiss her mouth. When we stepped apart, my aunt was smiling and crying, her hand over her mouth. Kate grabbed Amelia by her free arm and yanked her into a hug, and I laughed in delight.

CHAPTER TWENTY-FOUR

I had the gallery come pick up the new piece, giving them special directions on how to handle a wet painting. Even if it sold tonight, it would hang in the gallery for the duration of the show until the end of the month, which would give it time to settle and dry enough to go home with someone. I wasn't sure anyone would buy it—it was a little more experimental than my other work, but I was proud of it anyway. I'd keep it in my own living room if no one else wanted it.

A couple of hours before the show, Amelia surprised me with another treat: instead of doing my own hair and makeup, her stylists—Jean-Paul, Lizbeth, and Margaret—were coming over to help me. In the months since my first makeover, I'd gone to see Jean-Paul every month for upkeep on my haircut and had my hair styled and makeup done by the women for a couple of major events. I hadn't seen any of them since a few weeks before our breakup, so after they came through my front door, they barraged me with friendly criticism and horror over my split ends and bushy eyebrows. The three of them led me into the kitchen to work on me, and by the time they were done, I was transformed. I went upstairs to change while they styled my aunt and Amelia, and by the time the three of us were ready, we looked like we belonged on the cover of a magazine. I invited the three stylists to the show, and they were more than happy with the invitation. They set off ahead of us.

As the gallery was on the closer end of Royal Street in the Quarter, I'd wanted to walk, but Amelia insisted on using her usual car-service driver, George. I hadn't seen him since before the breakup either, and he was all smiles when the three of us walked outside. He kissed my aunt's hand and squeezed mine as we piled into the back of the Rolls-Royce, where we found a split of champagne waiting for us.

"For nerves," Amelia said, opening it. "Just a half glass for all of us. No need to get sloppy."

We clinked glasses, and the bubbles felt wonderful traipsing across my tongue. I closed my eyes to roll the flavor around my mouth, and when I opened them, Amelia was looking at me with clear yearning. I blushed under her gaze and looked over at my aunt. She was blushing and looking out the window, having witnessed our exchange. I was curious to know what she and Amelia had talked about all day while I was painting, but the result was clear: she and Amelia were easier with each other than I'd ever seen them. Not only were they chatting with ease, but I'd also caught Kate looking at Amelia several times with something like fondness. As we were almost at the gallery, I decided my questions could wait until later.

The car pulled over and George got out to help us. He opened the door and extended a hand for each of us in turn, Amelia insisting that I exit last for show. The crowd began clapping when they saw me, and I was shocked to see how many people were here already. Generally an opening night for an art show for an unknown artists attracted perhaps fifty people over the course of an evening, but that many or perhaps more were here already, waiting for the doors to open. Jim stood next to Meghan and Zach, and several of my cousins were in the crowd as well. Teddy and Kit were standing nearby, next to a group of women around their age. My future dean was huddled in a group of some of my art-history colleagues from the college. Most of Amelia's family was here—her dad, her brothers, Emma, and Billy. I was about to walk over and greet each of them in turn, but I heard a yodeling squeal behind me and was only just able to turn toward it before I was enveloped in a tight embrace. It took me a moment to recognize that it was Lana. Jess, her fiancée, was just behind her, looking happy but embarrassed to have the whole crowd staring at us.

I was so touched to see Lana, I could hardly speak. "What are you doing here? I thought you couldn't make it."

She had tears in her eyes too, and she smiled widely. "A certain someone called me this morning and offered the use of her private jet.

She said she could get me and Jess here and home again in a single evening. How could I refuse?"

I turned to find Amelia looking happy and satisfied with her surprise and gave her a hug before kissing her soundly. The crowd erupted around us in cheers and applause, and as we stepped away from each other, both of us colored from the attention. She took my hand in hers, and we turned toward the gallery, ready to begin the night.

❖

The show succeeded beyond my wildest expectations. Not only did it sell out within a couple of hours, but the people who saw my work raved about it. My future colleagues at the university were especially pleased and impressed, my dean going so far as to compare me to a well-known contemporary painter whose work hung in just about every modern-art museum in the world. He was clearly overstating things a little to flatter me, but he and the others did genuinely seem to like my work, much, I think, to their surprise. My friends and family were pleased twofold—both by the art and by the attention it was receiving. I saw my aunt and Meghan in happy tears several times throughout the evening. I think they were as excited by the whole thing as I was.

Several local arts magazines and newspapers interviewed me, and many of them suggested that I could expect enthusiastic reviews. I was also invited for a consultation with the Ogden Museum here in New Orleans. They were doing a special exhibit next year on female artists of the South and were interested in hanging one of my pieces.

To say the evening was a dream come true is understating it by a monumental amount. I'd never been so happy and so proud of anything in my life.

None of this would have happened without Amelia. She'd clearly pulled some strings to get all of these people in the room with me at the same time, and her confidence in my work was perhaps the most moving part of the whole evening. I would never have believed in myself enough to attempt a show on my own without her influence. She'd long thought my work was worth sharing with the world, and her genuine insistence on doing so had in part convinced me to try.

When we made it back to my place, long after midnight and

long after a barrage of good wishes and good-byes from friends and strangers, I was still dazzled by my success, lost in thoughts of future shows I wanted to run. I closed the door behind us and turned to find her looking at me with a strange expression.

I looked down at myself. "What is it? Did I spill something on this dress?"

She took a step closer and held out her free hand for mine. "It's strange."

"What is?"

"I always knew you were talented, from the moment I first saw your paintings. But until tonight, I was afraid no one else would ever be allowed to see your work, in public, I mean. Yet they did, and they loved it as much as I did."

I laughed. "Does that surprise you?"

She shook her head and stepped closer, close enough to kiss. "Not at all. I was just realizing that you recognize your own talent now, too. You believe in it."

I mulled over her comment for a long moment. While several of the people that had been at my show were friends and family, most of the ones who attended the show over the course of the night had been strangers. Everyone, whether they knew me or not, seemed to love my work.

I met her eyes and nodded. "You're right. I believe now."

Her face lit up from inside. From her reaction, you would have thought I'd told her the best news in the world. Her joy was infectious, and the warmth of it spread through me. I was relieved at my success, to have the show over with, to have sold out, but this feeling—making her happy—was the best part.

We kissed then, delicately at first. It was an exploratory kiss, both of us testing the waters. We'd kissed with more and more frequency since the wedding, but we hadn't let it get to us the way it had then—we were still cautious. This kiss, delicate though it was, had a smoldering fire behind it, on both sides. I drew her into my arms, letting the heat rise a little, putting some strength behind it. She kissed back with the same fierceness, and a new tension settled between us. After I broke away from her lips, I met her eyes, looking for the answer to my question, and saw the same one in hers. I nodded and she grinned, happily. I stepped away from her and held out my hand for her free one, but when

I turned away from her to go toward the stairs, she stopped. I looked back at her, confused.

She motioned with her cast. "I don't know how this is going to work with this thing." She looked so despondent, I almost laughed.

"We'll manage."

She nodded, still looking uncertain, and I turned again. She followed me, and I wanted to race up the stairs. I made myself go slowly, letting the tension and anxiety build as we climbed. I detected a slight tremble in her fingertips.

The bedroom was pitch-black. It sits at the back of the house, overlooking a small yard, and the trees out there block the streetlights. I flicked the switch, which lit three small lamps, and then I turned off the two brighter ones. Amelia was still standing in the doorway, still looking a little uncertain, so I began to undress. Despite the dim light, I saw her eyes light up with pleasure, and as I took off each piece, I stepped closer to her. By the time I'd removed my bra, I stood just in front of her, clad only in my underwear. I held out a hand, and she took it eagerly before following me over to the bed. We sat down on the edge, and I let her simply look at me for a while. Finally, as if she could no longer help herself, she touched one of my breasts.

I couldn't help but moan and close my eyes. Ever since the wedding—and even before that—I'd yearned for her touch with the sort of desire I had to ignore if I wanted to get anything done. Alone after we'd parted every day, I had to touch myself just so I could get to sleep at night. But it was like a sip of water in the desert—never enough. It took the edge off, but my body was still hungry—famished, even.

I opened my eyes and looked at her, and her expression was one of dazzled joy. She seemed to hardly believe that we were here together again, after all this time. The expression brought tears to my eyes, and I pushed her back onto the bed, kissing her as if to make up for all the kisses we'd missed out on while we were apart. We were already flushed with heat and longing, and the passion simply built the longer we kissed. Eventually I wrenched my mouth away from hers and kissed her throat, and she tilted her head back to give me room. I sucked at the delicate skin over her pulse, and it quickened under my lips. She moaned, and the sound nearly drove me wild. Suddenly, as if she couldn't take it anymore, she was sitting up and moving on top of me, and our positions reversed. I writhed underneath her as her lips touched my throat, and I ached for her with every breath. She continued to kiss me but was having difficulty keeping herself stable with only one arm. I used this handicap to my advantage, pushing her back and pinning her beneath me once more. She let out a little surprised yelp, and I grinned at her.

"I've got you right where I want you, Amelia. You'll stay there until I tell you to move."

She grinned and nodded. "Understood, Doctor."

I started kissing her again and let my hands begin to explore, first on the outside of her shirt, and then, as if daring her to stop me, I slid one underneath. As my fingers hit the hot skin on her stomach and chest, she hissed against my mouth, and her whole body arched up to meet my hand. I slid it up to her breast and squeezed, hard, and she cried out in surprised pleasure. The sound sent fire racing through my veins, and my kisses became rougher, harder on her mouth and neck.

Then suddenly, as if she couldn't stand it anymore, Amelia pulled on the arm underneath her shirt. Thinking I'd gone too far, I immediately stopped and slid it outside again, and then she grabbed my hand and put it between her legs. She was wearing a skirt, which, during the furious activity of the last few minutes, had been hitched up over her hips. My hand met her underwear, and for a moment I was so startled I didn't do anything. She writhed under me, clearly desperate. Instead of doing what she wanted right away, I kept it there, completely still, though I put a little pressure behind it by leaning into her. She thrust against me, up and down, pushing against my palm, and I held it there for her a moment longer before taking it away. Her eyes opened wide, the expression on her face something like anger.

When she spoke, a hint of warning sounded in her voice. "Chloé…"

I grinned at her. "Do you want something?"

I was playing a dangerous game. For the first time in our relationship, she was asking me to do exactly what I'd wanted to do to her since we first became lovers. A part of me worried that if I hesitated, she would have second thoughts. Another part of me, however, the part I decided to heed, could feel her desperate desire. She wanted me to touch her, and touch her I would. But in my own time.

"Y-yes." Her voice was hoarse and she stuttered a little.

Her eyes, dark blue, were pools of anguished yearning, and the power I suddenly felt sent something hot and wicked thrumming through my veins. Now I understood why she always made me wait. Torturing her like this was delicious.

"What do you want, Amelia?"

She swallowed, clearly at a loss. She didn't know what she wanted—that was obvious. She did know, however, where she wanted it, and she put her hand on top of mine. Then she was pushing both of our hands down into the space between her legs.

"Touch me," she said. "Please. Please, Chloé. I-I want you to touch me. Here."

It was enough—I was done teasing her. Even had she not begged me to, I would have started soon enough, but hearing her plea sent a kind of wild madness racing through me. I sat up and ripped off her underwear, exposing her for the first time since we'd been together.

While I'd seen her completely naked in passing once or twice, this was the first time she'd let me look. I sat marveling at her for a long, quiet moment. She was beautiful. Like the dark hair on her head, the curls were dark, almost black. She kept the area trimmed but, like me, didn't believe in shaving. Her trimmed pussy looked so appealing, I could have cried.

I finally wrenched my eyes away and gazed up at her, and she was staring at me with something like dread. I put all of my feelings into the smile I gave her.

"It's the most beautiful thing I've ever seen," I told her.

Her face lost her previous expression, and in an instant she was beaming at me, clearly relieved. I climbed on top of her for a kiss, her cast pinned between us. Her shirt was unbuttoned almost fully, and I took a moment to remove it before I returned to her lips. Her cast rubbed my stomach and chest, and I tried to keep as much weight off it as I could. I left my hands on her sides for a long moment and then set one of them on her thigh. She began writhing underneath me again, and a little rumble of frustration came from her throat. I smiled against her mouth and finally moved my hand between her legs.

Her hot wetness was a revelation. Based on explorations of my own body, I'd always expected that touching her would feel something like touching myself. It wasn't. In fact, she felt so different, it was a brand-new, thrilling experience. What made it especially pleasurable, however, was watching her react to my touch. Her entire body wriggled under me, not just her legs. She became stiff and rigid one moment, and then she was writhing against me with incredible strength. Her face expressed a mixture of pleasure and torment, her body clearly in a state of extreme need. Her eyes were pinched shut, and she was biting her lower lip, but every time she bucked her hips, a low groan emanated from her throat. It was the most erotic thing I'd ever heard.

I ran my hand up and down her slit, briefly touching it before skipping over her clit and moving back down toward her hole. She was incredibly wet, and getting wetter, and her entire body, including her sex, was scorching hot. It was as if her desire, bottled up for so long, was erupting out of her in one go. I toyed with her a while longer, and then, as if she couldn't stand it anymore, she put her hand on the back of mine again, pushing at it as I passed over her hole. I looked up and met her eyes.

"You want me inside you?"

She nodded, obviously incapable of words.

I gave her what she wanted, and her head whipped back in pleasure, exposing her long, pale throat. I kissed it and bit down a little, and she reared up underneath me, crying out. The tension in her body told me that she was going to come and soon, and I was tempted to drag this moment out a little longer. She must have sensed my hesitation, as she looked at me again, her eyes almost angry.

"Don't you *dare* stop."

I grinned and stopped, and she looked so startled and upset, I chuckled. "Just wait a little longer, Amelia. The longer you wait, the better it will be."

"Please, Chloé," she whispered. "I can't."

"That's what I always say to you, so I'll tell you what you always tell me: you can wait. You will. You have no other choice—I'm the one in control here, not you."

Almost as if my words had set her off, her orgasm built up inside her. A tremor shook my fingers, and her eyes started to glaze over. Knowing her climax was inevitable, I began to move my hand again, and it was all over. She threw her head back, and her body arched into her orgasm as it crashed down on her.

At first she was silent—she didn't even breathe. A moment later, however, she was screaming, the sound rising and falling as she writhed against my hand. The strength behind her struggles was significant, and it took a lot of work to keep my hand where she clearly wanted it to stay. Her orgasm went on a long while before she finally collapsed onto her back, moving my hand away from her once the sensation became too intense.

I shifted to her side and lay down next to her, resting my head on her free shoulder. A long while later, she lifted her arm, and I snuggled into her, my face resting on her chest. We said nothing, did nothing, for a long, silent pause. Finally, as if sensing what she was doing, I looked up and saw her crying.

"Are you okay, Amelia?"

She nodded. "More than okay, Chloé. I've never felt better."

I smiled, so pleased that tears rose in my eyes, too. "I'm so glad, Amelia. I love you so much. I want you to be happy."

She nodded, still choked up, and I settled back down onto her shoulder.

We stayed that way long into the night until we both finally dozed off.

EPILOGUE

The caterers were late, the wine hadn't arrived, and our guests were due any minute for the housewarming party we were throwing. We'd been in our new house exactly two weeks and were finally unpacked. Renovations had taken all summer and most of the autumn, but that had ended up being a good thing, as we were both so busy. Between wrapping up my art show, staging and selling Amelia's house, getting Amelia's new branch of Art for the People up and running downtown, and starting my new job, we hadn't had time to move before then anyway. The extra months had also allowed us to spend time together as a new couple before living together, which was a very good thing. We moved into the house exactly a year to the day after we'd gotten together the first time. It seemed like a good omen.

We were strictly designers on the renovations, and I'd found the experience quite interesting. Amelia had a little familiarity with house renovations, as she'd worked with her dad in high school and early college doing just that, but it was all new to me. We wanted to keep the house as authentic to its original time period as possible, which meant going all over the state to look for antique tile, wood, and fixtures. We agreed on two contemporary updates: central heating and air-conditioning and a new kitchen, but the rest of the house was as close as we could get to the original as possible.

We had the outside painted in the bright reds and yellows I remembered from before, and Amelia's gardeners completely renovated the yard. They transplanted some of her rose bushes from her old place, and I think that tiny nod to her past life was enough to help her ease into the more modest home. Amelia had made enough money during her years running Winters Corporation to live comfortably in her Garden District mansion the rest of her life, but she'd wanted to make the change for me—for us, really. She knew I would never be comfortable in her old house, and our new place meant that we could meet somewhere in the middle. It was a larger house than any I'd grown up in, but it wasn't ostentatious. The first day we walked through the front door, each of us carrying a box, we already felt like we belonged here.

Everyone and everything arrived all at once, of course. The caterers from Teddy's came in directly behind Aunt Kate and Jim, and Meghan and Zach walked in with the wine sellers. To avoid the awkwardness it would cause, Amelia's mother had agreed to come over later in the week for a smaller, one-on-one dinner with us. The rest of Amelia's family, however, was shortly in attendance. Emma and her now-fiancé Billy showed up a few minutes after Aunt Kate, and by the time Amelia's dad, brothers, nieces, and nephews showed up, chaos reigned. At one point, while the children played a lively game of tag around the new furniture, and while Aunt Kate and Amelia's dad had a loud debate about college football, I looked over at Amelia and saw her elation. We'd had dinners and cookouts with everyone fairly often over the summer, and it appeared that our efforts had paid off. Despite marked differences, our families were finally comfortable with each other. Instead of two separate entities, they already seemed like one.

This was, of course, exactly why we finally felt comfortable enough to share our news with them. We'd already had our private conversation about it two days ago, but we'd waited to make an announcement until everyone was here together. Amelia let the chaos continue a while longer, and then she knocked a knife against her champagne glass. Emma was passing out glasses of bubbly to all the adults, and Amelia's brother Bobby had poured some sparkling juice for the kids. Once everyone was holding a glass, they turned to us, waiting expectantly. Amelia and I clasped hands, and I let her begin.

"Welcome, everyone, to our new home."

The room echoed with cheers and shouts, and Amelia let them go on for a while before continuing.

"As you know, this year has been one of big changes for both Chloé and me, and no more than in the last few months. Now that the two of us have moved in and are starting new jobs, we both decided that we wanted to take the next step in our lives together."

The room was silent for a moment, everyone waiting, and I hesitated as long as I could to build up tension.

Finally, I held up my left hand to show off the ring. "We're getting married!"

The room erupted into a cacophonous melody of joy and jubilation, and I was instantly pulled into a series of hugs and kisses from our closest friends and family members. By the time I finally made it around the room to my aunt, she was crying freely, her face stuck in a permanent smile. Her hug was fierce, and when we drew apart, she didn't seem to want to let go. She clasped my shoulders and stood there, gazing into my eyes. She didn't say anything and neither did I. We didn't need to. She knew how happy I was, and she shared my happiness.

Amelia joined us a moment later, and Kate gave her a similar hug. When she let Amelia go, Amelia turned toward me, and I saw little tears sparkling the ends of her eyelashes. She and I took a couple of steps away from Kate to the front of the room, our hands clasped, unable to stop touching.

I could never get enough of looking at Amelia. It didn't matter who or what was in the room. She was always the loveliest thing there. Even after all these months, months we'd spent almost sutured together every moment of the day, I could barely stand to look at anything or anyone else. She was my heart, my love, and my happiness, and she would be until the day I died.

When we kissed a moment later, I barely registered the cheers and cries of happiness from our friends and family. There in her arms, I was in the only place I wanted to be.

I was home.

About the Author

Charlotte Greene grew up in the American West in a loving family that supported her earliest creative endeavors. She began writing as a teenager and has never stopped. She now holds a doctorate in English, and she teaches a wide variety of courses in literature and women's studies at a regional university in the South. When she's not teaching or writing her next novel, she enjoys playing video games, traveling, and brewing hard cider. Charlotte is a longtime lover and one-time resident of the City of New Orleans. While she no longer lives in NOLA, she visits as often as possible.

Books Available From Bold Strokes Books

Canvas for Love by Charlotte Greene. When ghosts from Amelia's past threaten to undermine their relationship, Chloé must navigate the greatest romance of her life without losing sight of who she is. (978-1-62639-944-0)

Heart Stop by Radclyffe. Two women, one with a damaged body, the other a damaged spirit, challenge each other to dare to live again. (978-1-62639-899-3)

Repercussions by Jessica L. Webb. Someone planted information in Edie Black's brain and now they want it back, but with the protection of shy former soldier Skye Kenny, Edie has a chance at life and love. (978-1-62639-925-9)

Spark by Catherine Friend. Jamie's life is turned upside down when her consciousness travels back to 1560 and lands in the body of one of Queen Elizabeth I's ladies-in-waiting…or has she totally lost her grip on reality? (978-1-62639-930-3)

Taking Sides by Kathleen Knowles. When passion and politics collide, can love survive? (978-1-62639-876-4)

Thorns of the Past by Gun Brooke. Former cop Darcy Flynn's heart broke when her career on the force ended in disgrace, but perhaps saving Sabrina Hawk's life will mend it in more ways than one. (978-1-62639-857-3)

You Make Me Tremble by Karis Walsh. Seismologist Casey Radnor comes to the San Juan Islands to study an earthquake but finds her heart shaken by passion when she meets animal rescuer Iris Mallery. (978-1-62639-901-3)

Complications by MJ Williamz. Two women battle for the heart of one. (978-1-62639-769-9)

Crossing the Wide Forever by Missouri Vaun. As Cody Walsh and Lillie Ellis face the perils of the untamed West, they discover that love's uncharted frontier isn't for the weak in spirit or the faint of heart. (978-1-62639-851-1)

Fake It till You Make It by M. Ullrich. Lies will lead to trouble, but can they lead to love? (978-1-62639-923-5)

Girls Next Door, edited by Sandy Lowe and Stacia Seaman. Best-selling romance authors tell it from the heart—sexy, romantic stories of falling for the girls next door. (978-1-62639-916-7)

Pursuit by Jackie D. The pursuit of the most dangerous terrorist in America will crack the lines of friendship and love, and not everyone will make it out from under the weight of duty and service. (978-1-62639-903-7)

The Practitioner by Ronica Black. Sometimes love comes calling whether you're ready for it or not. (978-1-62639-948-8)

Unlikely Match by Fiona Riley. When an ambitious PR exec and her super-rich coding geek-girl client fall in love, they learn that giving something up may be the only way to have everything. (978-1-62639-891-7)

Where Love Leads by Erin McKenzie. A high school counselor and the mom of her new student bond in support of the troubled girl, never expecting deeper feelings to emerge, testing the boundaries of their relationship. (978-1-62639-991-4)

Forsaken Trust by Meredith Doench. When four women are murdered, Agent Luce Hansen must regain trust in her most valuable investigative tool—herself—to catch the killer. (978-1-62639-737-8)

Letter of the Law by Carsen Taite. Will federal prosecutor Bianca Cruz take a chance at love with horse breeder Jade Vargas, whose dark family ties threaten everything Bianca has worked to protect—including her child? (978-1-62639-750-7)

New Life by Jan Gayle. Trigena and Karrie are having a baby, but the stress of becoming a mother and the impact on their relationship might be too much for Trigena. (978-1-62639-878-8)

Royal Rebel by Jenny Frame. Charity director Lennox King sees through the party-girl image Princess Roza has cultivated, but will Lennox's past indiscretions and Roza's responsibilities make their love impossible? (978-1-62639-893-1)

Unbroken by Donna K. Ford. When Kayla and Jackie, two women with every reason to reject Happily Ever After, fall in love, will they have the courage to overcome their pasts and rewrite their stories? (978-1-62639-921-1)

Where the Light Glows by Dena Blake. Mel Thomas doesn't realize just how unhappy she is in her marriage until she meets Izzy Calabrese. Will she have the courage to overcome her insecurities and follow her heart? (978-1-62639-958-7)

Her Best Friend's Sister by Meghan O'Brien. For fifteen years, Claire Barker has nursed a massive crush on her best friend's older sister. What happens when all her wildest fantasies come true? (978-1-62639-861-0)

Escape in Time by Robyn Nyx. Working in the past is hell on your future. (978-1-62639-855-9)

Forget-Me-Not by Kris Bryant. Is love worth walking away from the only life you've ever dreamed of? (978-1-62639-865-8)

Highland Fling by Anna Larner. On vacation in the Scottish Highlands, Eve Eddison falls for the enigmatic forestry officer Moira Burns despite Eve's best friend's campaign to convince her that Moira will break her heart. (978-1-62639-853-5)

Phoenix Rising by Rebecca Harwell. As Storm's Quarry faces invasion from a powerful neighbor, a mysterious newcomer with powers equal to Nadya's challenges everything she believes about herself and her future. (978-1-62639-913-6)

Soul Survivor by I. Beacham. Sam and Joey have given up on hope, but when fate brings them together it gives them a chance to change each other's life and make dreams come true. (978-1-62639-882-5)

Strawberry Summer by Melissa Brayden. When Margaret Beringer's first love Courtney Carrington returns to their small town, she must grapple with their troubled past and fight the temptation for a very delicious future. (978-1-62639-867-2)

The Girl on the Edge of Summer by J.M. Redmann. Micky Knight accepts two cases, but neither is the easy investigation it appears. The past is never past—and young girls lead complicated, even dangerous lives. (978-1-62639-687-6)

Unknown Horizons by CJ Birch. The moment Lieutenant Alison Ash steps aboard the *Persephone*, she knows her life will never be the same. (978-1-62639-938-9)

The Sniper's Kiss by Justine Saracen. The power of a kiss: it can swell your heart with splendor, declare abject submission, and sometimes blow your brains out. (978-1-62639-839-9)

Divided Nation, United Hearts by Yolanda Wallace. In a nation torn in two by a most uncivil war, can love conquer the divide? (978-1-62639-847-4)

Fury's Bridge by Brey Willows. What if your life depended on someone who didn't believe in your existence? (978-1-62639-841-2)

Lightning Strikes by Cass Sellars. When Parker Duncan and Sydney Hyatt's one-night stand turns to more, both women must fight demons past and present to cling to the relationship neither of them thought she wanted. (978-1-62639-956-3)

Love in Disaster by Charlotte Greene. A professor and a celebrity chef are drawn together by chance, but can their attraction survive a natural disaster? (978-1-62639-885-6)

Secret Hearts by Radclyffe. Can two women from different worlds find common ground while fighting their secret desires? (978-1-62639-932-7)

Sins of Our Fathers by A. Rose Mathieu. Solving gruesome murder cases is only one of Elizabeth Campbell's challenges; another is her growing attraction to the female detective who is hell-bent on keeping her client in prison. (978-1-62639-873-3)

Troop 18 by Jessica L. Webb. Charged with uncovering the destructive secret that a troop of RCMP cadets has been hiding, Andy must put aside her worries about Kate and uncover the conspiracy before it's too late. (978-1-62639-934-1)